DEVILS
ISLAND

ALSO BY MIDGE RAYMOND AND JOHN YUNKER

BY MIDGE RAYMOND

My Last Continent: A Novel

Forgetting English: Stories

BY JOHN YUNKER

The Tourist Trail: A Novel

Where Oceans Hide Their Dead: A Novel

DEVILS ISLAND

A NOVEL

MIDGE RAYMOND
AND JOHN YUNKER

OCEANVIEW PUBLISHING
SARASOTA, FLORIDA

ISBN 978-1-60809-614-5

Published in the United States of America by Oceanview Publishing

Sarasota, Florida

www.oceanviewpub.com

10 9 8 7 6 5 4 3 2 1

To our families

I know my course. The spirit that I have seen
May be a devil; and the devil hath power
T' assume a pleasing shape; yea, and perhaps
Out of my weakness and my melancholy,
As he is very potent with such spirits,
Abuses me to damn me. I'll have grounds
More relative than this. The play's the thing
Wherein I'll catch the conscience of the King.

—*Hamlet*, Act II, Scene 2

EXCERPTED FROM
ONE PLANET TRAVEL GUIDE

DESTINATION: TASMANIA, AUSTRALIA

Tasmanian devils (*Sarcophilus harrisii*) can smell a dead body from half a mile away. Normally solitary creatures, they will gather to swarm it, greedily and ferociously, playing tug-of-war with the carcass, all the while emitting spine-tingling screeches and growls, sounds that terrorized the European settlers, who named the animals *devils*.

The size of a small dog, with black fur, reddish ears, and teeth that can crush bones, the Tasmanian devil is the world's largest carnivorous marsupial, reaching up to twenty-six pounds.

Devils are opportunistic nocturnal hunters, subsisting on a strong sense of smell and whatever prey (dead or alive) they find, even digging into the ground for the corpses of buried domestic animals, from dogs to horses. They can run up to sixteen miles per hour, and have been known to climb trees and forge rivers.

The devils can devour a large animal like a kangaroo within hours—muscle, organs, fat, bones, even fur—leaving nothing. For their size, they have the most powerful bite of any living carnivore, with jaws that can open up to 80 degrees. They can eat nearly half of their body weight in thirty minutes.

Once existing in vast numbers across Australia, the devils are now found only in Tasmania, in danger of extinction due to a facial tumor disease that has spread across the island state, decreasing the devils' population by up to 90 percent. In 2012 and 2013, a small group of healthy devils were released on Marbury Island, a few miles off the coast of Tasmania, though not without controversy. The devils have thrived on Marbury, almost dangerously so. They will fight for food and for mates. They have been known to steal the eggs of Cape Barren geese and other local birds, the belongings of the island's human visitors, and anything resembling food. The island is known locally as Devils Island.

ACT I

CHAPTER 1

BROOKE

As spray from the wake begins to feel more like rain than a gentle mist, Brooke inches away from the bow until she is under the boat's plastic canopy and standing shoulder to shoulder with Bryan, the blond-haired Australian guide. She looks over at Jane and sees her friend holding onto a metal post, swaying with the movement of the boat, her hand a few inches from that of one of the Australian guests: Malcolm, Brooke remembers. She's been trying to memorize everyone's names since they will be spending the next four days together, hiking and camping the length of Marbury Island. There are eight of them crowded together on this tiny former fishing boat, skirting across the bay toward the island, forty minutes off the southern Tasmanian coast, and now Brooke glances around until she sees Charlotte, Malcolm's wife, who for some reason is on the opposite side of their little boat.

As Brooke watches the small marina at Triabunna disappear behind them, she can't help wondering whether William has tried to get in touch. Though she'd moved out of their apartment a month ago, she texted him last week to let him know she was leaving the country. Why she did this, she isn't sure; they hadn't been in touch since she'd moved out. But perhaps it was a way of making it seem real. She still hasn't told anyone they're separated—not her parents, not her colleagues, not Jane. Maybe she's feeling guilty about her abrupt departure from their marriage. It had been more sudden than even she had imagined.

She didn't hear back from him, of course. Finally, just before takeoff in Seattle, she put her phone in airplane mode and forced herself not to check her email. She might as well get used to it, and not just because she's been warned that cell service is close to nonexistent on the island. It's over.

She catches Jane's eye, and Jane winks at her, pulling her from her dark thoughts. Jane leans forward and calls out over the rush of the water, "Feeling okay? You look a little seasick. Remember Lake of the Ozarks?"

Brooke winces as she thinks back to that infamous Sigma Chi "beach party" that Jane had gotten them invited to back in college. The fraternity had rented a houseboat, a DJ, and a school bus to transport partiers from campus, and Brooke drank so much on the way that if it weren't for the blurry photographs she saw later, she wouldn't have any memory at all of that night. And in a way, she wishes she didn't, since she still hasn't lived it down—the dancing on tables, the skinny dipping, and, inevitably, the bottomless puking off the upper deck as Jane held back her hair.

"It wasn't the waves that made me sick," Brooke says. "It was the mai tais."

"Or the Jell-O shots."

"Ugh." Brooke feels her stomach churn. "Thanks for reminding me."

Now Jane's eyes turn toward Bryan, which doesn't surprise Brooke. She herself had noticed Bryan's curly hair grazing his broad shoulders, his strong, suntanned biceps and forearms. But Jane has always had a way with men that Brooke has not, and it doesn't surprise her that Jane has never married. It's not in her nature to limit herself to just one man.

Brooke turns toward the sounds of chatter behind her. The two Australian couples—in addition to Malcolm and Charlotte, there's Margaret and Ian—have gathered in a semicircle around the other guide, Kerry, who is talking about the history of Marbury Island, once home to convicts sent from England and now uninhabited save for wallabies, echidnas, wombats, kangaroos, and, of course, the endangered Tasmanian devils. All creatures Brooke has only seen in books and online, and as exotic to her as the accents of their guides, a constant reminder that she's more than seven thousand miles from home.

While Bryan can't be more than twenty-five, Brooke estimates Kerry to be in her mid-thirties. Her long, strawberry-blonde hair is pulled back in a rope-like bun atop her head, and freckles scatter her suntanned face. Both Australian couples are older than Brooke and Jane by at least a decade, probably in their early forties, but they look far more fit than Brooke feels. They are friendly and pleasant, but when they met she noticed something a little odd about them—or maybe it was just Charlotte and Malcolm. Charlotte looked as if she didn't want to be here at all, and Malcolm looked like a deer in headlights as he shook their hands. Maybe they'd had an argument on their flight from Sydney—or maybe they, like herself, are simply wondering what the next four days of extreme proximity with total strangers will be like.

Brooke has never taken a trip like this before—she hasn't done much traveling at all, in fact, in the decade since college graduation, when the reality of real-world life set in: work, dating and then marriage, moving across the country for her husband's job, taking a string of part-time jobs as she decided what to do with her new life.

Jane, on the other hand, was living the life they'd both dreamed of back in school. They'd been drama majors, and after graduating they moved together to New York, where they shared a narrow railroad flat in Queens, waiting tables and auditioning for small and infrequent parts in off-off-Broadway productions. Then, at the beginning of their third year in the city, Brooke took a full-time job in marketing at a tech company, longing for steady income and healthcare benefits (and a respite from the rejections that never seemed to bother Jane). And that's where she met William, while Jane kept auditioning and found a small measure of success: a leading role in an off-Broadway play, a few good reviews, a television commercial. By the end of that year, William got a new job and Brooke moved with him to Seattle, where they got married. That was the last time she saw Jane, at the wedding five years ago.

She and Jane hadn't talked much after that, mostly because of what happened at the reception, and Brooke knew Jane moved to LA only thanks to Facebook, which eventually became their sole method of communication. In fact, that was how Jane extended the invitation to Tasmania, via Facebook message, with a link to the Marbury Island Track. *Pack your bags, sweetheart, and book a flight to Hobart. I'm treating you to the trip of a lifetime. A luxurious, all-expenses-paid hike across one of the most beautiful islands in the world. And sorry, but Billy Boy is not invited.*

Well, that wouldn't be a problem.

Despite the invitation coming out of the blue, despite the now-precarious nature of their longtime friendship, Brooke felt as though the timing was perfect. When she'd opened Facebook and seen Jane's message, she'd been alone in the apartment she was subletting, finishing a third glass of wine and trying to tell herself that, by being on Facebook, she wasn't really drinking alone. She was also wondering whether to change her relationship status, but she couldn't find an appropriate category. She wasn't actually "single"—not yet, anyway—and the closest thing to "separated" was, "It's complicated." If only, she thought as she poured herself another glass, there were a few more options, along the lines of, "I wanted to try counseling," or "We married too young," or "He wasn't what I expected."

Or, she thought as she took another long drink, "What the hell have I done?"

It took only a few moments to accept Jane's offer. A chance to catch up, to learn details about Jane's glamorous new life, to escape the mess her own life had become—why not? As for the questions of why Australia and why now, Brooke couldn't begin to answer, but perhaps it was Jane's way, however belated, of apologizing for ruining her wedding. From the Facebook updates, it seemed Jane had steady work, was making good money, and maybe she was finally ready to make things right again.

Earlier that morning, at the airport in Hobart, where she was waiting at the curb for the Marbury Island Track Co. van that was scheduled to pick them up, Brooke was fighting off the daze of exhaustion from the fifteen-hour flight to Sydney, followed by a three-hour layover and a two-hour flight to Hobart, and she didn't recognize Jane when she saw a woman in a large sun hat walking toward her, waving. Then Jane pulled off the hat, releasing a wave of bright red hair, and called out, "Though she be but little, she is fierce!"—and in that moment Brooke felt twenty years old again, hearing the words as if they were back onstage together in *A Midsummer Night's Dream*, playing Helena and Hermia. And even through the fog of jet lag, her own line came back to her, as if the last decade hadn't passed: "'Little' again!" she called back. "Nothing but 'low' and 'little'!"

It had been a joke of theirs from the moment their roles were cast, as Jane was nearly half a foot taller than Brooke, lean and striking, and Brooke, while at five-foot-four was not exactly tiny, always looked small by comparison, especially since they were inseparable.

And, if she was honest, she felt insignificant compared to Jane in more ways than her height. But when she hugs Jane at the airport, it feels as though nothing had changed, as if the past five years had disappeared.

If only they actually had.

Brooke reaches into her backpack for her water bottle, but what she's really checking for is the bottle of pills, her security blanket. She's tried to continue taking them on schedule, despite the time change and the jet lag, but she still feels a lingering anxiety that she wishes hadn't followed her here.

She hears a voice in her ear and turns, finding Bryan's face right next to hers. "Look," he says, and Brooke follows his eyes over the white-capped waves.

"What?"

"Keep looking," he says.

Just then she sees a fin slice through the waves, and a shiver shoots up her spine. "Shark?"

"No, dolphins. Five of them."

Suddenly the dolphins are right next to the side of the boat, swimming alongside it, porpoising out of the water, one after the other, playing in the waves.

Brooke hears the rapid-fire clicking of a camera and turns to see that Ian has pulled out a camera with a monstrous lens, barely able to stand upright as he balances the weight of his camera with the pitching of the boat. "Ian, they're far too close for you to get pictures with that thing," says his wife, Margaret. "Here, use my phone."

He ignores her and continues to shoot, though Brooke can tell by the way the camera sways that the photos aren't going to turn out. Stubborn, this Ian. He reminds her of William.

The boat makes a sudden lurch, and Brooke feels her body tilting until Bryan's arm steadies her, pulling her upright. "Thanks," Brooke says. "That was close."

"No worries." His eyes match the coral blue of the water, and, like the sea, they seem to change shades depending on the location of the sun.

Brooke had felt an immediate spark upon meeting Bryan, and she hopes it's not obvious as she remains close to him, as if she is worried about falling again, when in fact she feels a sizzle of electricity by being near him. She hadn't really thought, until now, of just how long it's been since she's had sex, and as she watches the muscles in Bryan's arm flex against the movement of the boat as he grips the metal post, she tries to remember the sleeping arrangements. Tents, she recalls vaguely, and she and Jane will be sharing.

Then she inwardly shakes her head. Ridiculous, to think of this journey as the time and place to have a fling. She's here with

Jane, to renew their friendship, to make up for years of lost time. But she's pretty sure sex will be part of the trip, at least in conversation—it's sure to be among the first topics they broach; it always has been. Brooke is rather dreading this part, since Jane doesn't know that she and William have separated. That they hadn't had sex in nearly six months before she finally left. Perhaps it would have been easier to tell her sooner if Jane hadn't predicted—publicly, during her drunken so-called wedding toast—that their marriage wouldn't last five years. And Brooke can't bear to admit that Jane had been so completely right.

"We're almost there," Bryan says, pointing up ahead.

Brooke turns to face the island. The white-sand beach stretches for a mile in either direction of the middle section toward which they're headed, and the curve of sand is bordered by a mix of trees and bushes, with hills rising beyond, in the distance. There are no buildings, there is no dock—there are no signs of civilization, other than their approaching vessel.

"Marbury Island is a national park now," Kerry told them earlier. "First the Aboriginal people lived here, then the convicts, followed by a few pioneers and eclectic, get-rich-quick types. There's only one semi-permanent resident on Marbury—a park ranger who lives part-time in Saltwick. We'll meet him when we get there, on our final day."

Now, as the boat begins to slow down, Kerry calls out, "This will be a wet landing, guys. Take off your shoes, roll up your trousers, and get ready to form an assembly line to ferry our packs to the beach."

Brooke is about to lean down to untie her hiking boots when she sees motion onshore, a blur of movement in her peripheral vision. She looks back at Bryan, who is preoccupied with readying the backpacks, and asks to borrow the binoculars attached to a strap across his chest.

When he hands them over, she tries to find the spot where she saw the movement, which from a distance looked like someone parting tree branches to watch the boat approach the shore. But now, she can't see a thing as she scans the vegetation along the beach. Each wave dislodges her view the minute she tries to focus.

Then, there it is—a body, a human body, a head and back disappearing as the tree branches snap back into their normal position as he retreats. At least, she thinks it's a he; she didn't get much of a glimpse but could see short, dark hair beneath a wide-brimmed hat.

She turns to Bryan. "Is there someone waiting for us?"

"Where?"

"On the beach," she says. "Or was. He just went into the bushes."

Bryan shakes his head. "Must've been a wallaby," he says. "There's no one on this part of the island but us. We're a good twenty kilometers from Saltwick."

She feels a flicker of annoyance. "I know what I saw."

He takes the binoculars back and puts them to his eyes. A moment later, he hands them back to her and points. She follows his finger, looking through the glasses, until she sees a pair of large brown marsupials, their short front paws hanging in front of their chests, eyes wide as they gaze right back at her through the ferns.

Wallabies, just as he said.

She lowers the lenses and hands them back to him. "I guess you're right," she says. "Must be the jet lag."

"You'll get a good night's sleep tonight," he says. "I guarantee it."

He turns away, and she bends down to take off her shoes. When she straightens up again, she keeps her eyes on that spot onshore. The wallabies have disappeared, as quickly as the person she saw. Despite what Bryan said, she is still convinced she saw a human, not a wallaby. Her only question is, if not part of their group, what would someone be doing out here, in the absolute middle of nowhere?

CHAPTER 2

KERRY

Whatever you do, she tells herself, don't yawn.

As Dan, the boat's pilot, angles the vessel toward the flattest part of sand on the beach, Kerry stands at the edge, tempted to dive into the cool, greenish-blue water—not so much to escape the eager and expectant travelers firing questions at her bone-weary brain, but because she thinks it's the only way she will stay awake for the rest of the day.

Don't let them know you haven't slept in two days, that you spent all night at the Royal Hobart Hospital waiting to hear if Meg would survive. Don't let them know that, after the doctors said she would be okay, you felt your hands begin to shake all over again as you realized that you would be leading the next group to Marbury Island all by yourself. Above all, don't let them know it's your first go as the lead guide, that you still have not committed the track to memory.

As the boat lurches, Kerry grabs hold of the rail and looks back at Dan.

"Sorry," he calls out. "Bit of a sandspit there. I'm going to have one more go. She'll be right."

The boat moves forward again, then the deep rumble of the engines in reverse fills the air. A relief—it's impossible to talk over the noise.

She's a bit surprised that she hadn't been sacked straightaway, after what happened the day before. Meg had let her lead the group into Saltwick while she went on ahead to open up the house and prepare happy hour and drinks—the far less glamorous part of being a guide—and Kerry had been happy for the opportunity to take a leisurely hike, to talk about the island and its inhabitants.

If only she hadn't overlooked the limestone rock that indicated where she was supposed to turn. She'd been so busy chatting with a guest she'd walked right past it—in fact, she'd probably taken great care to step over it, she thinks now—she may as well have picked it up and moved it out of the way, for all the good that landmark was to her. So, instead of leading the group straight into town, where beer and wine and snacks awaited them after their final day of hiking, along with warm showers and electricity and other comforts of civilization on their last night before departing Marbury, she led them in circles for the next hour.

It wasn't until she finally consulted her compass and the map that she got them back on track, and by then Meg had come looking for them, finding them shuffling through masses of knee-high ferns and flax, only about four meters off the proper trail.

Meg ingeniously had brought a pack filled with chocolate, cookies, and thermoses of coffee and tea, and they took an impromptu tea break along a row of fallen eucalyptus trees. This is the type of expertise Kerry lacks—knowing that you're not only a naturalist, you're a hotel manager, a waiter, a maid, a concierge. She has a lot to learn about this job, and she whispered her thanks to Meg as they sat down among the guests, who were happy now, relieved to be back in good, competent hands.

What none of them knew was that lurking somewhere under those fallen trees was a tiger snake.

Tiger snakes are not aggressive—they would rather avoid anything to do with humans—but if you are careless and they are underfoot, they become as dangerous as land mines. Tiger-snake bites kill about a dozen Aussies a year and, while the bites aren't always fatal, if left untreated, they usually are. Meg had reassured them all on day one that there was only about a 30 percent chance of encountering one of the island's four venomous snakes, and even if they did see one, it would be little more than a fleeting glimpse as it slithered out of their way.

A Kiwi named Annie, seated on the tree, was the first to see the snake. She let out a scream that would have woken the Tassie devils, and as Meg rushed to her side, the snake slid under the very fern that Meg just happened to be stepping through.

Kerry heard Meg curse under her breath, and when she looked up at Kerry, the blood in her face was frozen white. Kerry knew the bite itself wasn't painful but that the aftermath would be—the headache, the vomiting, the whole-body pain—unless they got her to a hospital. Quickly.

This time, Kerry had one chance to get her directions right, and she didn't trust herself. Using the company-issued phone, she called the park ranger, putting Meg on the phone to lead him to where they were while Kerry dug through the first-aid kit and applied a compression bandage, then a splint.

Now, as the boat rams into the sand, Kerry feels the same lurching in her stomach as she did the day before as the snake incident unfolded. The fact that they were so close to Saltwick, that they had several able-bodied travelers to help carry Meg and avoid spreading the venom, that the ambulance was waiting in Triabunna, that Meg was fine—none of it made up for the fact that this wouldn't have happened if Kerry hadn't gotten them all lost, taken them off the well-worn trails into the bush.

She can't dwell on it now. Dan has cut the engine, and it's time to get everyone ashore.

"Ready, guys?" she calls out. They are all stuffed into the bow, where she'd sent them to enable Dan to get as far up onto the sand as he could. "Now I need you all up here, to keep us anchored so we can unload all our gear."

With her shoelaces tying her hiking boots together, she loops the laces around her neck, feeling her shoes hit her in the back as she jumps out of the boat, the water crisp and cold against her feet.

She looks for Bryan, but he's still in the bow, chatting with one of the American women.

"Bryan," she says.

"Yeah?"

"We need to unload the boat."

"Oh, yeah. Right."

She wonders if he's even removed his shoes yet, but when he leaps out of the boat, she sees he's wearing thongs.

"Thongs?" she says, nodding toward his sandals. "You're wearing thongs?"

He nods. "Made sense for a wet landing."

"You'd better have hiking shoes."

"I'm pretty sure I packed them, yeah."

If anyone had to be bitten by a tiger snake, why Meg and not someone like Bryan?

By "unloading the boat," Bryan apparently thought she meant the guests instead of the packs and supplies. He lifts one of the Americans from the side of the boat and carries her all the way to the dry sand, like a honeymooner crossing the threshold. Then he goes back to the boat for the tall one. Bloody pantsman. At least he'll keep those two entertained so she can focus on the others.

She begins to help the four Australians out of the boat, careful to keep them from falling into the water and starting their adventure with a splash. The air is warm enough for shorts and T-shirts, but the water, churned up from Antarctica, is far less inviting than it looks. Fortunately, they're all nimble, and one of the women, Margaret, makes a point of not accepting her outstretched hand.

Once everyone disembarks, Kerry takes backpacks one by one from Dan and hands them over to Bryan, who ferries them a few more steps to shore. Her pack and Bryan's are the heaviest, stuffed not only with their own clothing but four days' worth of fresh food and other supplies; the camp is well stocked, but they have to cart in the perishables. When Dan hands her a third heavy pack, the last one, she takes it to shore herself. "Is this one of ours?" she says to Bryan, not recognizing it.

"Oh, that's mine," says one of the Americans—Jane, the redhead. She comes over and takes it from Kerry, heaving it over her shoulder. "Sorry," she says apologetically. "I'm not a very efficient packer."

Kerry's not surprised—this one looks particularly high-maintenance—but she smiles at her and refrains from telling her she hopes she's got some pain reliever in that monster pack because her back will be killing her by this time tomorrow.

On the beach, the group is scattered about, wiping off the water and sand from their feet. Kerry glances around, observing them; Meg told her that the ones who are first to have their shoes back on will be the least trouble to manage. She notices that the shorter American is the first one to stand up.

"Are we boring you?" the man named Malcolm asks.

Kerry turns to look at him. "Sorry?"

"You just yawned."

"Oh, that's not you," she says. "I just had a long night, that's all."

"Oh?" Malcolm gives her an inquisitive look, and his wife, Charlotte, who is sitting next to him, rolls her eyes. "Do not listen to him, Kerry," she says. "My husband likes to create drama where none exists."

"Well, I am a director, aren't I?" Malcolm grins. His wife, shoes on, stands up and brushes the sand from her backside, rolling her eyes yet again. Then, in an annoying show of self-importance, Malcolm takes out his mobile and squints at it, looking for a signal.

"I recommend putting your mobiles in airplane mode," Kerry says, looking from Malcolm to the rest of the group. "There's no signal out here, and no way to recharge your batteries, so if you use your mobile as a camera, you'll need to save the battery."

Malcolm scrolls through something on his phone before putting it away, without acknowledging Kerry. She's not surprised. She'd recognized Malcolm from the celebrity television show he judges—one of those Who Wants to Be a Model?–type shows that nobody admits watching yet miraculously leads in ratings. Her partner, Paul, had watched it during his time off, when all he wanted to do was lie on the couch, and she often joined him.

That was back when she had a couch, back when she had a partner.

Kerry looks at the other couple, Ian and Margaret. They are all old friends, Malcolm had said when they first did the introductions, something about him and Ian going to school together. But she senses a distance between them, an invisible something, like a magnetic field in the air subtly keeping them apart. Ian especially seems more interested in birds than his fellow humans. As on the boat, his eyes are glued to the horizon, and he holds his telescopic camera ready. That thing alone must weigh half as much as her pack, or Jane's.

Just then he turns toward her. "Are we going to see the forty-spotted?"

"I certainly hope so, but I make no promises."

The forty-spotted pardalote is the rarest bird in Australia, a draw for a large percentage of guests. Kerry still hasn't seen it and doubts she'll be able to spot it, but she's not about to let that out of her already overstuffed bag of secrets.

She also hopes it never comes up that this is only her second time out on this track. It's not that she doesn't know what she's doing—she's been a naturalist for the past decade—but knowing a landscape and its animals isn't the same as being able to guide people through it with any sort of skill or grace.

Six guests. She can do this, she assures herself. The Australian couples know each other, so that makes it easier. The two American women know each other, too, though she doesn't know how. She only hopes they are not as loud as the Americans on the last trip, a family of four, with two teenagers, one who was so terrified at the possibility of running into a snake that they had to split into two groups because she was walking so slowly. And then, on the last day, to see their guide get bitten—well, if that had been an irrational fear in the making, it had to be a full-blown phobia by now.

And then there's Bryan, whom she's starting to think of as another guest rather than a fellow guide. At first she was relieved that he'd been able to fill in for Meg last-minute—he was usually the company's part-time van driver, but she reckoned anyone would be more experienced than she was. She was wrong.

He was nice enough to look at, but the way he was flirting with the short American reminded Kerry of the smarmy blokes at uni, and on the way over, she was tempted to shove him overboard.

Maybe she'd feel less bitter about it if she hadn't just broken up with her partner of five years.

But despite it all, she knew she'd done the right thing. Things between them had changed overnight—usually that was just a metaphor, but her life literally had turned completely upside down only three months ago. Even now, she wouldn't have it any other way. She couldn't take more of what she'd had to face every day. The cancer. The death. The disfigurement. It was too much.

She took this job as the cure, the way to heal herself from the dead and dying that was not just all around her but seeping into her very soul. She needed hope; she needed to see the devils as they once were, as they should be now—as they may one day be, all over the country, once again. While everyone else calls this place Devils Island, naturalists know it as Noah's Ark. There is no disease here. No contagion. Here, finally, this species is rebounding. And maybe she will, too.

She turns around when she hears one of the Americans making a fuss about something. It's the shorter one, Brooke, pointing toward the sand and gesturing to Bryan.

"I knew it," she says. "Look. Footprints."

Kerry has just laced up her own boots, and she walks over.

"I knew I saw someone here," Brooke is saying.

Kerry looks down at the sand. "These prints are from the last group."

"Then where are the other sets?" Bryan asks.

Kerry feels the urge to slap him. By now, he should be walking to camp to start getting everything set up for the guests.

"The other prints were probably washed away by the tide. The water rarely gets this far up. Surely you can see that, Bryan."

"Are you positive?" Brooke asks. "I was so sure I saw someone. When we were on the boat."

"You probably saw a wallaby," Kerry tells her.

"That's what I said!" Bryan says.

Brooke opens her mouth again, as if to argue the point—Americans always have to be right about everything, don't they?—and Kerry cuts her off by saying to the whole group, "Right, everyone, let's go over the schedule. I'm going to go on ahead, and Bryan here will lead you up the beach and over to the spot where you'll have your lunch. Then, you'll take a nice long walk across another beach that will bring you to camp."

Bryan looks as surprised as she is at her last-minute change in plan. But she has just now decided that she can't bear another moment of human company. As tedious as it is to set up camp, she needs to be alone.

As the guests don their packs, she picks up the large canvas bag filled with lunch boxes and hands it to Bryan. "You know the way," she says. "Stop for lunch, show them the birds and the trees, don't rush. I need at least two hours."

She turns before he can say anything, sticking out her knee to balance her pack there before hoisting it onto her shoulders. Then she starts up the beach, stepping over the footprints that Brooke had pointed out, which disappear into the bush. Looking at where they end, Kerry doesn't see a trail, just a wall of dense foliage.

Then she remembers something that Mark, the park ranger, had said when he called her that morning. "If you need anything, just give me a shout," he said.

"I could use an extra guide." She'd just met Bryan.

Mark laughed. "Afraid I can't help you there. But you know I'm only an hour away by ute."

The dirt-and-sand road that runs from north to south is barely accessible by utility vehicle, especially given how rutted and swampy it is in places, but his willingness to be there for her gives her some comfort. Meg had told her in the hospital, *He's mad for you, can't you tell?*—but then, Meg had been on a lot of drugs, and Kerry thinks it's more likely Mark only feels sorry for her— there she'd been, out on her first trip as a guide, and she'd totally carked it.

"Oh, and there's one other thing," Mark said just before they hung up.

"What's that?"

"Not to worry you," he said, "but we're told to be on the look- out for poachers."

"Poachers? Of what?"

"Parrot eggs. They climb into the trees to snag 'em, then smug- gle them into Indonesia. I've never seen any signs of poaching on Marbury, but apparently they're coming over from the mainland now."

Kerry was glad to be talking over the phone, so he couldn't see her involuntary shudder. "Are they dangerous?"

"Doubt it. They just don't want to be caught. Don't worry about it. Meg never did."

Now, Kerry pauses mid-step to return her eyes to the footprints. The water was indeed high enough two days ago to wipe all signs of humanity away—including these. She knows this because of the storm she and Meg mucked their way through with their guests fifteen kilometers north of here, forcing them off the beach due to the high waters.

So whose footprints are these? She forces the question out of her head and begins walking again. She has more pressing challenges ahead, like making sure the entire trip doesn't go balls up before they make it to Saltwick.

CHAPTER 3

BROOKE

She looks up at Bryan, who's standing on the top of a sand berm, his arms raised as if he were speaking to a legion of followers instead of just the six of them. "Welcome to Marbury Island. Over the centuries, home to natives, convicts, explorers, entrepreneurs, misfits, runaways—and, now, us."

Brooke finds herself smiling along with the others, a bubble of giddiness rising at the idea of hiking across a remote island in a part of the world she couldn't even find on a map three weeks ago. Even though she can't completely forget her disaster of a life back home, being here, right now, she feels refreshingly unfamiliar to herself, as if she could look into a mirror and see radiant eyes, a face that is easy and relaxed and something like happy. As if she's been granted an opportunity to start over, which makes her feel what she hasn't felt in a long time: optimistic.

Bryan continues. "Right now we're standing on Twelve-Mile Beach, part of a narrow isthmus that connects the south and north sections of the island."

Ian turns his head in both directions. "Sorry, Bryan," he says. "I can't be the only one to notice that this beach isn't twelve miles long."

"The number refers to the distance from here to Saltwick in the north, where we'll ultimately be hiking. Some of you will be doing quite a few more Ks, of course. Those who hike to Haunted Bay this afternoon, and of course those who elect to summit Mount Marbury in two days' time."

"Not me," Charlotte says, her small, fine-boned features lighting up as she laughs. She's wearing mascara and lip gloss, Brooke notices, and this, along with her slight frame and milky skin, imply she's not nearly as outdoorsy as the friends she's traveling with.

"It's not too much of a slog, but if there's really a storm coming, there won't be much of a view."

"The storm won't prevent us taking the hike, will it?" Margaret says. In contrast with Charlotte, her skin looks as if it's seen plenty of sun and wind, her expression eager and a little serious. "I know it's only a thousand meters, but that's the reason I'm here."

"*Only* a thousand meters?" Brooke says, turning to Jane. "What's that—three thousand feet or something?"

"I'm a mountaineer," Margaret says, and it looks to Brooke as if she actually stands a bit taller as she speaks. "I summited Everest five years ago. Ian's here for his birds, and I said, 'Well, I'm keen if there's a chance to stretch my legs a bit.' I'm counting on gaining a little elevation."

"You know how you can tell someone's climbed Mount Everest?" Jane asks.

"How?"

"They tell you they've climbed Mount Everest. Over, and over, and over—"

Brooke watches Margaret turn an icy stare toward Jane, and when Brooke looks at Jane, she sees a fleeting smile, brief as a wisp of smoke over her lips, as Jane looks away. An uneasy feeling washes over Brooke, a rogue wave pulsing through; she has always been both fascinated and alarmed by Jane's daring. Even with—perhaps especially with—total strangers, Jane can't seem to resist finding a person's emotional buttons and punching them, and Brooke has always held her breath, at once riveted and anxious, never knowing how someone might react. For Jane, of course, that seems to be the fun of it.

"Who knows?" Bryan interrupts cheerfully. "There's a chance we'll climb Marbury. Tassie weather will always leave you guessing. In the meantime, while it's still decent out, let's shoulder our packs and get moving."

Brooke lifts her pack onto one shoulder, nearly toppling over with the weight of it, and she wonders if she should have left a few more things behind. Despite the detailed packing list Jane had forwarded along, Brooke knows she packed more than she needed; she can tell by the way the others hoist on their packs with far less effort than it takes her to get hers onto the other shoulder.

Except for Jane—Brooke grins as she watches Jane struggle to don her own pack. At least she's not the only one who over-packed. Brooke can still remember an overnight trip the two of them took from Columbia to Kansas City, when Jane had scored tickets to a traveling production of *Cabaret*. Brooke had packed everything she needed into a small backpack, while Jane showed up at the bus station with a full-sized suitcase. She never traveled without a makeup case, hair dryer, three changes of clothes a day, and a half-dozen fashion and celebrity magazines. *You've got to be ready for anything*, Jane used to say, as if she might be discovered by an agent or producer at any moment, anywhere. Maybe this had been her secret after all—the reason Jane is making a living as an actor while Brooke doesn't have a career left at all, if she ever had one.

She remembers her first college audition—she and Jane both wanted the role of Portia in *The Merchant of Venice*, but they'd have settled for any role, just for the chance to do Shakespeare. More than a hundred women showed up, all theater majors, and the director lined them up onstage, row after row. He arranged them by height, by weight, by hair color, barking out, "You—there," and "You—over there." Someone holding a copy of the play asked, "When do we read?" and the director laughed. He said, "I could ask you to read from the phone book, and that'd tell me all I need to know." Then he began to dismiss them, one by one. Brooke was one of the first women off the stage.

She could think of a dozen reasons why. She was too short, too skinny. Her hair was too straight, too thick, too dark. Shakespearean women were full-bodied, voluptuous, sexy. They had curly hair, pouty lips, cleavage. When she left, Brooke didn't look back, didn't wait for Jane—she headed back to her dorm room, certain that Jane had landed the role of Portia, or at least Jessica or Nerissa. Brooke had already begun mourning the fact that directors wanted women of a certain type, and that she'd never be their type.

But afterward she learned that Jane, too, had been dismissed, and they commiserated over their rejections and vowed never to give up. But Brooke had not kept her vow.

Brooke watches as Bryan walks around, adjusting straps and making sure everyone is well balanced. "Whoa," he says as he feels the weight of Jane's pack. "Did you go ahead and bring your own wine?"

"Well, I'd hate to run out," Jane says, drenching him with her most charming smile.

When Bryan comes up for air, he turns to Brooke. He appraises her for a moment, then reaches around her waist to tighten the straps. Brooke enjoys the feel of his hands there, brief as it is, and then breathes a big sigh as the weight is lifted from her back.

"Better, hey?" he says. "You want the weight to be carried by your hips instead of your shoulders."

She watches him walk away, pulling a long-sleeved shirt off over his head, revealing a snug, short-sleeved T-shirt underneath, and part of a tattoo that disappears into the sleeve. She wants to see the rest of it, especially when she remembers the way he helped her out of the boat, his arm around her waist, her hand gripping his strong biceps. It was the first time she'd touched a man since she left William, and she felt something awaken inside of her, something she was beginning to fear had died but realizes now was only dormant.

"Hey, B., eyes off the help."

Brooke looks back at Jane, whose grin tells her she knows exactly what Brooke is thinking. "Just taking in the scenery," she says.

Bryan returns to the berm and raises his voice. "Okay, everyone, follow me!"

They begin their slow-motion trek over the sand, made that much more challenging by the weight on their backs, toward the thick wall of brush that will take them across the isthmus to the other side of the island.

Brooke falls into step with Jane at the rear of the group.

"I still don't know why we're here, exactly," Brooke says, "but I'm so glad we are. I can't get over how beautiful it is. No trash on the beach, no people on the beach. I'm guessing if this were LA, there'd be resorts from one end to the other?"

"That, and nowhere to park."

"So are you going to tell me?"

"What?"

"What we're doing here."

"All in good time," Jane says with her characteristic mysteriousness. "First, you tell me—are you and Billy Boy in an open relationship now?"

"What?" Brooke looks at Jane. "Where did that come from?"

"I saw the way you were flirting with our hunky Australian guide."

"Oh, him."

"Yes, him."

Brooke feels the pressure to come clean about William, but she can't bring herself to say anything just yet. Then she realizes why Jane is so curious. "Am I, um, interfering with *your* plans for the hunky Australian?" she asks.

Jane laughs. "Hardly. I'm into more mature men these days."

Up ahead, the rest of the group has stopped and gathered around a mound of shells. Surrounded by trees, protected from the ocean breeze, the air is now humid and warm, clinging to Brooke's skin. Flies swirl around her head, and as she waves them away she notices a chorus of birds above.

"We are standing on an ancient Aboriginal meeting place," Bryan tells them. "The Tyreddeme people traveled here from the mainland to fish and hunt. They were part of the larger Oyster Bay nation, and these shell mounds, or middens, are what's left."

Margaret asks a question about rock drawings, and Brooke finds her mind drifting to the sounds coming at her from all directions—the waves in the distance, the buzzing flies in her ears, and, in stereo, birds, all making exotic caws and chirps, recognizable yet enticingly different.

She moves toward Jane. "You hear these birds?" she asks.

"How can I not?"

Just then they hear a piercing caw; it sounds like a crow, but the call is much more drawn out, and there's something mournful about it. "A crow?" Jane asks.

"An Australian raven." They turn to see Ian standing near them. He points into a eucalyptus tree. "Just up there, see?"

Jane looks up. "Where?"

He puts his hands on her shoulders and repositions her, then hands her his binoculars and guides her arms until she sees it. Brooke notices Margaret glancing over at Ian and wonders how long it will be before this leads to an argument or something worse. It wouldn't be the first time Jane got in between a married couple. Toward the end of their senior year, Jane had a fling with their drama professor, who became so consumed with her he left his wife right before graduation. But Jane had no problem leaving him behind when they went to New York. "Love 'em and leave 'em," Brooke had said, and Jane laughed. "Who said I loved the man?"

Men have always been drawn to Jane—or maybe it's that Jane knows how to reel them in—and Brooke has nearly forgotten what it's like to be around her, that old familiar jealousy. It's a waste of time, she realizes, even to fantasize about Bryan; she has no chance, even in her dreams, of competing with Jane.

"Come here, B." Jane waves her over, holding out the binoculars. "Have a look."

Brooke follows Ian's gentle-voiced instructions and finally finds the bird in the trees. It looks just like an American raven. "I wish our birds sounded as exotic as these do," Brooke says. "Ours sound so flat by comparison."

"Must be their Australian accent," Jane says with a glance at Ian. "I've always had a thing for it."

When Brooke lowers the binoculars, she sees that the rest of the group has already gone ahead, with Margaret in the lead next to Bryan. Brooke follows behind Ian and Jane, listening as he tells Jane about the birds he hopes they'll see on the trip, parrots like the swift and the yellow-tailed black cockatoo. As she observes them, she wonders what Jane meant when she said she preferred mature men these days. There's so much about her that is exactly the same, and yet there's also so much she doesn't know.

The trail takes them over a large, grass-strewn sand berm and onto another beach. Impossibly, this one is even more beautiful than the first—it's just as deserted, and the water is calm and glowing turquoise, as if they've just stepped into the Caribbean.

Bryan begins handing out plastic containers; nestled into each one is a salad and a flatbread sandwich. "Can I just spend the night here?" Brooke says to him when he hands her lunch to her.

He smiles at her. "You're welcome to have a go," he says, "but I think you'll prefer our camp. That's where happy hour is."

Brooke notices that Jane has walked to a spot well away from the others. She makes her way over, remembering when she and Jane met, on day one of drama class in college. It was a small class—only fifteen students—and the goateed, bespectacled drama professor, who looked nearly as young as they were, fumbled with the class list and asked them all to prepare a "biological profile" to present to the others. Brooke looked around, yet no one else seemed to notice the verbal typo, that the instructor had meant *biographical* instead of *biological*, and she was thinking she must've heard wrong when she caught Jane's eye from across the room. Jane was smiling, and when she saw Brooke, she raised her shoulders and mouthed, *What the fuck?* Brooke barely caught herself from laughing out loud, and moments later she listened to Jane present her profile to the class: "I'm a mammal, *Homo sapiens*, of Irish and Polish descent. In high school, I performed in . . ." As Jane continued, Brooke felt an immediate bond, during those first moments and afterward, as they went to lunch together, as if the two of them understood each other and the world in a way that no one else seemed to get. And because it was her first week in college, her first time away from home, she was eager for a friend, and Jane quickly became more like family, more like the sister she never had.

Brooke lowers herself onto the sun-warmed sand next to Jane. On a day like this, with only a few tendrils of light clouds crossing the sky, she finds it hard to believe the talk about a storm coming.

Jane stares out at the water as she munches on her salad. Finally, Brooke leans over and bumps her shoulder.

"What?" Jane asks.

"Spill it. What brings us all the way down to the Southern Hemisphere? Are you wanted in eight states or something?"

Jane smiles and gives her a dramatic eye roll. "For one, I thought it was time we reconnected. As for why this trip, this place—well, if you must know, there's a man involved."

"I knew it," Brooke says, both intrigued and disappointed at the same time. Everything has changed—but nothing has changed. "Who is it—Bryan?"

Jane shakes her head. "Bryan is all yours, sweetheart."

"Ian?"

Jane laughs. "Why Ian?"

"Because he's clearly into you."

"Well, he's cute and has a nice body for an older man. But"— Jane shakes her head—"no."

"Then that leaves Malcolm." Brooke tries to be inconspicuous as she glances over at Malcolm, who's sitting next to Charlotte. "Well, I guess some things never change. You've never let a guy's marital status get in your way before."

Brooke turns back to Jane, hoping to see some sign in her elusive eyes that tells her she's wrong. Jane only gazes back at her, that familiar sly grin on her face.

"So, you and Malcolm—really?"

Jane nods.

"How did this happen? How long? Tell me everything."

"He's a media executive, runs his own agency, does a lot of work in LA. He's big now, ever since he appeared as a judge on this Aussie reality show, and my agent got me on his radar since he's doing a lot of TV work these days. He hired me to do a client video in Sydney, and it was a great contract; I couldn't resist. He flew me down under and then, well, we proceeded to go down under."

Brooke glances again at Malcolm, seeing that he noticed the two of them talking. He shifts in the sand, angling toward them while staring down at his lunch, as though he's trying to keep an eye on them without anyone noticing.

"I'm confused," Brooke says. "He hasn't said a word to you. It's like he doesn't even know you."

"Exactly. He's fucking freaking out."

"So I take it he didn't invite you along?"

"Why would he do that? His wife is here."

"He didn't even know you'd be here?" Brooke shouldn't be shocked—this was the sort of thing Jane used to do all the time—but still, it's further than she'd ever gone before, at least as far as Brooke knew. "So, you decided to create a reality show of your own," Brooke says. "This is a total surprise to him?"

"Damn right, it's a surprise. Remember when we got in the van and he was stuttering out his name when we pretended to meet?"

"But, Jane. His wife."

"Yeah, so?"

"What am I missing? How did you even plan all this? When?"

Jane sighs, as though she can't believe she has to waste time on tedious backstory. "Two months ago, I flew down on my own dime—well, my own frequent flyer miles—and surprised Mal at work. We hooked up in his office, it was totally hot, and then he had to go in to some meeting, so I'm there all alone and, well, I happened to glance at his email and see that he was booked on this trip."

"How does one *happen to glance* at someone's email?"

"I wasn't snooping."

"Yeah, right. Did you know he would be here with Charlotte?"

"Of course, but who cares? And I know this is going to sound like every Lifetime Movie of the Week you've ever seen, but he doesn't love her. He doesn't. He wants to be with me."

"Oh, Jane. That's Lifetime 101."

"He's a public figure now, and he's terrified of doing anything controversial. He just needs the right encouragement. A nudge in the right direction."

"So that's why you're here? You're going to tell Charlotte all about it?"

"No—he's going to tell her. He just doesn't know it yet."

"And how do you plan on arranging that?"

Jane doesn't answer, looking past her instead, and Brooke turns to see Bryan approaching. Behind him, the others are donning their packs again.

"Okay, ladies, another few hundred meters, and we will have tea and cake waiting for us in camp."

"Cake—now that's proper motivation," Jane says, hopping to her feet. She shoulders her pack with much more confidence this time, and as Brooke struggles with her own pack, she feels as though she's now weighed down even further by Jane's secret, as if by telling her, Jane had transferred a heavy, physical load onto her shoulders. It had often been like this between them, with Brooke acting as Jane's conscience because Jane herself rarely felt remorse for anything. Whether it was married men, or the little trinkets Jane would steal from fraternity parties—from letter sweatpants to leather jackets—Jane treated her like a confession booth, then went about her life as before, absolved of her sins, while Brooke was left to mull them over, to feel the guilt on her behalf because Jane herself never felt any.

In the past, it had never affected their friendship, perhaps because Brooke was so very straitlaced and law-abiding; she loved the wildness in Jane, the fun and slightly dangerous side that only she knew about, as Jane's most trusted friend.

They begin walking again, and Brooke says, "So, what are you thinking, that you'll announce your love affair over dinner?"

"No, of course not. That's too obvious, even for me. I'm going to channel my inner Shakespeare toward our Malcolm. You leave it to me. By the time we reach Saltwick, he'll be a single man—well, if not completely single, at least between wives."

The idea that Jane wants to marry him is overshadowed by only one thing, which stops Brooke in her tracks. Jane keeps walking, and Brooke has to wait for Jane to stop and walk back to her, giving them some space between the others.

"So where do I fit in?" she says. "Why'd you invite me along?"

"In addition to avoiding the single supplement fee?" Jane laughs. "To protect me from Charlotte."

"Very funny," Brooke says as Jane begins walking again. "Something tells me Charlotte's the one who's going to need protection," she adds, but by then she's not sure whether Jane can hear her.

CHAPTER 4

KERRY

As she walks under the forest canopy, breathing in the tangy scent of the gum trees, honeyeaters and silvereyes dart from branch to branch, her avian welcome committee. She keeps her eyes focused on the edges of the trails, eager to see any sign of a devil—and, though she wouldn't admit it to anyone but herself, also keeping an eye out for snakes—but all she notices is the ubiquitous, square-shaped scat of the wombats. At least the travelers will be able to check wombats off their lists; it's the one mammal she can guarantee everyone will see.

As she gets close to camp, a movement in the bushes ahead catches her eye, and she slows until she sees an echidna, foraging for ants in the dirt with his long, dark brown nose. She kneels for a moment to observe the creature, his light-colored, spiny fur nearly blending in with his surroundings. She watches his narrow, pink tongue dart out to capture ants from a dead tree branch, and when she straightens up again, he hears her and freezes, making himself smaller and smaller until he's nearly indistinguishable from the forest floor. She tiptoes away.

Perhaps if she had chosen the echidna as her research project back in graduate school she would not have ended up like this— knackered, single, essentially homeless, an introvert leading tour groups. Yet the echidnas don't have it much easier than the devils—like every other animal in this state, they, too, get run over by the maniacs who drive too fast or recklessly, and they, too, are terrorized by bogans whose idea of fun is to drink beer and shoot things. But at least they don't suffer from an incurable, contagious disease that's killing them off like a mass extinction. She has never seen echidnas with lesions covering their faces, making them unrecognizable even to those who know the species backward and forward. Not like the devils, whose tumors ravage the skull, turning it to mush, like rotting meat, even the eyes, leaving them wandering crazed and disoriented in their final days, following whatever smell makes it past all that sickness, ultimately taking them to the middle of a dark road to scavenge. The only good thing about so much roadkill is that sometimes, for the sickest of the devils, death is a mercy.

When she began working at the sanctuary, while she was still in school, the disease was known but not believed to be widespread. An *isolated infliction* was how one of her professors labeled it. Yet, over the following years, more and more devils arrived at the sanctuary's doorstep, delirious, usually injured by a car, always near death.

It wasn't long before the sanctuary felt more like an emergency room, and Kerry herself felt like a triage nurse. And if she had any idea then of the magnitude of the disease, perhaps she would have pursued another line of work, or another species. Though deep down she knows she could never have given up on them.

Too many still blame the devils for any number of the world's ills. Farmers and ranchers blame them for taking sheep, though this rarely happens; it's more typically a dingo. Others say they are a disease risk, spreading it to the stocks, another unfounded rumor. And then there are those who simply detest anything that keeps them up at night.

The European settlers feared them and resented them for making them afraid. But Kerry thinks the real reason these poor animals were hated so much was that they reminded the settlers of how far away from home they were. For two hundred years, it was all these people could do to fashion these lands after the lands they once lived in: Ireland, England, even America. And it wasn't until recently, when the public became aware that the devils were close to extinction, that the government began to fund research into a cure. But it's possible that they're too late. That this creature will join the much-larger carnivore marsupial, the thylacine, or Tasmanian tiger, as Australia's two most famous extinctions.

The day she met Paul, he called them *overgrown rats*. Why she went out with him that night still mystifies her. But she was trying so hard to be normal. That is, to act human around other humans. So much of her life to that point revolved around these calf-high marsupials. She spent more time with them during any given week than with her own species. At the sanctuary she'd balance her days between bottle-feeding the youngest, pulled from the pouches of their dead mothers, and the older devils, dangling pieces of meat on bungee cords to keep their world complex, to keep their scavenging instincts sharp. Her goal, and their destiny, was to free them to join the others out in the bush. But as much as she wanted them to thrive out there, a part of her hated to let them go to places where she could no longer protect them.

Paul had arrived at the sanctuary one day with a dozen of his hiking guests. He had promised them a devil sighting, and this was the only guaranteed way to see them. Normally, Kerry's manager played the role of animal ambassador, but he was out with the flu, and Kerry was the only one available.

She took the group around the various enclosures, pointed out the king snake, the emu, the playful kangaroos and wallabies. She handed out small cups of oats that the guests could hand-feed to the roos. While she didn't like that they allowed this at the sanctuary, it was a huge draw for guests, and she did enjoy seeing the way people would light up whenever the roos gently wrapped their black claws around visitors' hands and pulled them close to eat from their palms.

That day, she saved the devils for last. The sanctuary had four devils that the public could view, and she allowed Paul's group to help with a feeding. She let Paul hold the stick of wood that held the leg of a wombat, a road-kill victim, and the moment he dangled the leg over the waist-high enclosure wall, a devil approached at full speed, quicker than they could blink—Rodney, the alpha of the group.

Everyone snapped pictures as Rodney gripped the leg with his jaw and pulled hard, clinging to his feast as he was lifted off the ground when Paul raised the stick. By the time Paul placed Rodney back down, the other three devils had arrived, and within seconds Paul lost his grip on the meat and the devils were playing tug-of-war with it, shrieking and braying in a blur of black fur and teeth.

Kerry explained how the noises the devils made varied in intensity based on their scavenging. The more vocal the cries, the more food had been discovered; this saved the other devils from having to wander aimlessly for food. By sharing in this manner, they helped the entire species thrive. "Amazing, aren't they?" she concluded with a sigh, even as she noticed the looks on the visitors' faces, which ranged from nervous to bemused as they'd watched the four devils devour their meal in a frenzy. No one seemed to appreciate these creatures quite the way she did.

That included Paul. "I thought they were solitary creatures," Paul told her as his guests were piling into their van.

"Most of the time," she said.

"Are you as solitary as they are?"

She laughed. "More so."

"What if I promised you a leg of meat? Only at a restaurant this time."

"It would be lovely," she said, "if I ate meat. Which I don't."

"Oh."

He said nothing else, and she began walking away. Then he called after her. "I know a great veg place down in North Hobart."

She stopped and turned to face the man with whom she would share five years of her life and too many hopes and dreams to count. She should have known better then, but she was living on hope—hope for the devils and for some normalcy in her own life: dinner out, a real date, a boyfriend.

Instead, she is on a remote island surrounded by more animals than humans. And she has to admit, as she continues on toward camp, that she prefers it this way.

When she arrives at camp, she drops her rucksack on the wooden planks of the outdoor patio and unzips the flaps to the dining tent. She lights the stove, puts the kettle on, unlocks all the storage cupboards and the solar-powered cooler. She rummages through the cooler, checking on the cheeses and butter, taking a look at what wine and beer is available for tonight—Chardonnay, shiraz, and an ale, all Tasmanian, of course. Resisting the temptation to open a bottle for herself, she takes out the recipe for the evening's dinner, which Bryan will get going while she leads a group to Haunted Bay, and then they'll finish it up together while the guests enjoy happy hour. Every hour of every day is well planned, down to the last detail, and though she's only done it once before, it's good to know there's a routine in place. This she can deal with.

On the patio, she wipes down the wooden benches and the large table in the middle, where she'll have tea and coffee set up by the time the others arrive.

Then she grabs her pack and heads to the nearest tent. The guides usually share, but with only six guests on this journey instead of the usual eight, she'll have the luxury of her own tent, which she otherwise wouldn't bother with—it means a bit more cleaning in the morning—but she's so irritated with Bryan she can't fathom trying to sleep only a few feet away from the lazy bludger.

When she leans down to find the tent's zip, she stops. It's already halfway open.

Her pulse quickens. "Hello?" she calls out.

No sound, no movement—nothing.

Then she laughs at herself. The stress, the exhaustion—it must be getting to her. There's no one within twenty kilometers of here; she or Meg must not have zipped it all the way shut when they were here last.

She unzips the tent, dark inside, and secures the main flap above her before opening a side flap from the outside to let in more light. When she steps inside, she stops short.

The sleeping bags are set up on pads, which in turn are on raised wooden platforms that double as storage bins. One of the sleeping bags, instead of being neatly positioned on the pad, is unzipped and bunched up. Could either she or Meg have been so careless as to leave a tent unprepared for the next tour? Or has someone been here?

Someone like the poacher Mark had warned her about?

"Shit," she says aloud, not sure what to do. She takes out her phone, thinking she should call Mark, then remembers she won't get a signal in this part of the woods—she'd need to return to the beach. There's not much Mark can do, anyhow, and she has too much to accomplish here before Bryan arrives with the guests. She pockets her phone and returns to the dining tent.

She checks the food stores again—everything seems in its place. Whoever was here—if anyone was here—hadn't taken anything that she can see. She inspects the cupboards, the small shelf with books, sunscreen, and insect repellent, looking for any other signs of disturbance and finding nothing.

So she gets the tea service ready, then checks the dinner recipe for what ingredients she'll need to gather from the other tents. As she goes from tent to tent, opening them up, airing them out, collecting cans of tomato sauce and olives and white beans, she inspects each one for signs of visitors, but they all look clean and untouched.

She opens up the washroom and each of the composting toilets—these areas, too, are as pristine as they should be. She and Meg must've somehow overlooked the one tent when they left.

She returns to the tent and takes another look around. She shakes out the sleeping bag, then looks for footprints, both inside and on the ground around the tent. She sees nothing unusual, nothing to tell her who it might've been.

It was probably no one, of course. The Marbury Island Track Co. has an exclusive permit for these camps and keeps them occupied all season long—if anyone other than one of their tour members spent the night here, he would have had to either happen upon the camp accidentally, or know ahead of time when it would be empty. Both options are virtually impossible; they are too far off the beaten path from Saltwick, where the ferry runs, and they are too often occupying the campsites at this time of year.

Unless it's someone like a poacher. Someone here illegally, someone who needs to stay out of sight, someone who knows the tour company's routine—possibly even better than she does.

She hears voices approaching and makes her way over to the patio, arriving just as Bryan approaches, followed by the others.

"Welcome to camp, everyone," she says, forcing cheer and energy into her voice. "Before you claim your tent, let me give you a tour."

She takes them to one of the two toilets and shows them how to toss sawdust down into the well after each use, how to use the makeshift tap to wash their hands. She reminds them that all the water is rainwater stored in tanks, and to use it sparingly. Outside the three-sided shower stalls, she explains they can ask for a heated tub of water to take a quick outdoor shower if they'd like.

As the guests settle into their tents, she pulls Bryan aside. "I've taken the tent to the far right," she says, pointing. "You can take whatever unclaimed tent you want."

"I thought we were supposed to share," he says. "What, are you a snorer?"

"Right," she says. Then she glances over toward her tent, wondering if it's a mistake to be there alone tonight. "You know, the bedding was all messed up when I got here. Like someone had slept there."

"That's what tents are for."

"No, I mean—someone else. Not one of us."

He gives her a look of mock panic. "Did they steal the beer?"

"They didn't take anything."

"Then what's the problem?"

"Did you know there's talk of poachers on the island?"

"I've heard rumors, sure."

"And you don't think it's weird, that someone slept in my tent?"

"Sounds more like you did a shit job cleaning it, that's all."

She sighs. "Just keep your eyes open. If you notice anything odd, just tell me, all right?"

He shrugs and looks up through the trees at the cloudy sky. "If there are poachers here, at least we can hope all the rain mucks up their plans."

Damn, she forgot to look up the forecast from the Tasmania Bureau of Meteorology while she was on the beach. "Still in the forecast, eh?"

"Squall-force winds. Fifty mil of rain. We're in for a soaker; the whole state's getting smashed."

She follows his eyes up toward the sky. "As long as we make it through this arvo before it hits."

"The bad stuff won't hit until early morning. So they say."

"Good. I'll take the group to Haunted Bay while you start on dinner."

"Fine. Might as well have a cuppa in the meantime."

Bryan joins the travelers who are gathering on the patio and pours himself a cup of coffee, shoving a slice of ginger cake into his mouth as he sits down and puts his hiking boots up on the table.

"Bloody bogan," Kerry mutters, then goes to the dining tent for another pot of hot water.

CHAPTER 5

BROOKE

Inside the tent, Brooke heaves her pack onto her bunk, then looks at it, wondering where she put her sunscreen. It's probably at the bottom, buried under all the things she doesn't need.

She lets out a little sigh, then glances over at Jane, hoping she hasn't noticed. Since Jane's revelation on the beach, Brooke's mind has been almost completely consumed with Jane's plan. She and Jane have always been competitive—how can two drama majors constantly competing for the same roles, the same men, and the same jobs not be?—but Jane's drive seems to have reached a bizarre new level. Sure, given the exorbitant price of traveling solo, it cost only a little more for Jane to bring Brooke along to share accommodations; and yes, it's a chance to catch up after far too long. But if Jane really is here for a man, why does Brooke have to be involved at all? She feels a prickly sensation just under her skin, a not unpleasant tingling of anticipation that's all-too-recognizable as she's once again sharing the same space as Jane: not knowing what's going to happen, or when. Enjoying it and dreading it at once.

Jane has always had a flair for the dramatic, which included making Brooke and others around her uncomfortable, whether it was talking or laughing just a bit too loudly in a restaurant, or flirting unabashedly with someone else's partner, no matter the gender. Jane is hands-on in the literal sense, always touching those around her in intimate ways—curling a finger through a lock of hair, removing a piece of fluff from a shoulder—as though they were her lovers or her children. Anything to keep herself at the center of attention, to keep the eyes and the focus on her.

Moments ago, Jane had chosen for them the tent farthest away from the rest, farthest away from the dining tent and outdoor patio. It wasn't next to Malcolm's, Brooke noticed—but if Jane, for once, doesn't want to be in the center of things, there must be a reason. With Jane, there always is.

Brooke hears Jane rummaging around, and when she turns she sees her pull out a bottle of Jack Daniel's from her pack.

"Holy shit," Brooke says. "No wonder your bag is so heavy."

"Time for a toast," Jane says, pulling out her tin coffee cup with the MARBURY ISLAND TRACK CO. logo on it, which they'd all received that morning. Brooke had affixed hers to one of the straps on her pack, so at least she has one thing that's easy to find.

She holds out her cup when Jane reaches for it. "This is supposed to be a luxury adventure in nature, not a reenactment of our frat-party days."

"We can still party a little, can't we?" Jane says, pouring a healthy shot into Brooke's cup and handing it back. "Where's your sense of fun?"

Brooke touches her cup to Jane's, and after they meet with a light metallic clink, Jane raises hers into the air. "To old times," she says, then downs her whiskey. Brooke follows suit, and she has to admit that the warm, mellow feeling it gives her is exactly what she needs. It also gives her the extra ounce of courage she needs to ask Jane something she's been wondering about since she learned about Malcolm.

"Jane," Brooke says, "I'm starting to worry about—about what you're planning to do."

"What do you mean?" Jane is rummaging in her rucksack again, her back to Brooke.

"Well, I just want to make sure you're not going to spout out something to Charlotte and create a major spectacle. We'll be spending four days with these people, after all."

Jane turns and looks at her. "A major spectacle?" Her expression is half innocent, half defensive. "You mean, like at your wedding?"

"No. That's not what I meant." And it wasn't—at least, not consciously. But now Brooke wonders whether on another level that's precisely what she's worried about.

The wedding. She knew Jane hadn't been thrilled to learn she was getting married—the two of them, Jane mostly, had had plenty of short-lived flings, but neither had been in a serious relationship; no one had ever come between them. Brooke had always known Jane wasn't a big fan of William, but she didn't expect Jane's resentment to come out so publicly, in a drunken speech that started out sweet, all about the two of them against the world, and ended with Jane accusing her of taking the easy way out, marrying for money and stability. *It'll never last, you know*, Jane had said, as she wavered on her feet and Brooke's brother Marty reached for the mic. *I'm the only constant in your life, and I always will be. I'll be there when you move on. I give you two lovebirds about five years.*

"I apologized for that, by the way," Jane says.

"By email. That hardly counts."

"Well, you never apologized to *me*."

"For what?"

"For what? For leaving me high and dry in that apartment when you and Billy Boy flew off to Seattle."

"I found you a new roommate. You never lost a dime."

"You mean that bipolar skank who skipped out on me after two months?"

"She did?"

"Yeah, she did. I lost my deposit—just when I really needed it, too."

"Why didn't you tell me?"

"Like you'd have cared. You were gone. Just like that."

"If we're being honest," Brooke says, "it felt sudden for me, too." And it was true. Meeting William, she realized later, had given her an easy ticket out of New York and into a new life in which she didn't have to be The Failed Actress. Instead, she was The Supportive Wife.

"We were going to make it together, remember?" Jane says. "Whoever got the first role on Broadway would buy front-row seats for the other."

Brooke smiles ruefully, remembering their pact. "But it never happened."

"How could it? You didn't stick around long enough to let it happen."

"I gave it almost four years," Brooke says. "Making a career out of acting is like making a career out of winning the lottery. I wasn't making it, Jane. I knew I never would. You were. You were doing great."

"Until you left town. That's when everything went to shit." Jane pours another shot of Jack Daniel's into her coffee tin. "After you left, I got my dream part. I was all set to play Norma Desmond in a *Sunset Boulevard* adaptation, and then it closed before we even started rehearsals. How's that for irony? I never even got the chance to play a faded actress! At least the fictional Norma got to be a fucking star before she lost it all."

"I didn't know," Brooke says quietly. "Your Facebook posts—they were always so upbeat. All the commercials, the voice-overs—"

Jane lets out a short laugh. "The commercial and voice-over work dried up fast, and that barely paid the rent anyway. What I didn't post was a gig on this cruise ship out of Miami, which was an entirely different sort of hell, and when I finally moved to LA I was already pushing thirty and had every producer and agent telling me I should try stand-up comedy because that's what 'older' women who haven't made it as actresses do, apparently."

Brooke reaches for the bottle and pours herself a little more whiskey. "I'm sorry, Jane. I didn't want to leave. I didn't want to have failed so miserably—but the fact is I did. I guess that made leaving easier."

"There are some things you can't exactly share on Facebook, you know?" Jane says quietly.

Brooke nods. She knows this all too well; her Facebook page says she's still married. "That's why I'm glad we're here in person. So we can catch up for real. I shouldn't have said anything."

"No, it's fine."

"I just don't want to see anyone get hurt, least of all you."

"Don't worry yourself. I may love a good tragedy, but I don't plan on starring in one." Jane swallows the last of her whiskey and stands up. "Let's go get some coffee before the hike. I need a caffeine hit or I'll fall asleep."

"The perfect antidote to all this whiskey," Brooke says, wincing as she drains her cup.

On the patio, it's clear that they've arrived late; there's only one slice of cake left amid a pile of crumbs, and when Brooke pours coffee, only a dribble comes out. She hands it to Jane.

"You ready to see more ravens?" Ian says to Jane.

"I'll settle for one of those hundred-spotted birds," Jane says playfully.

"You mean forty-spotted pardalote," Ian says.

"Yes, that one."

Ian may as well be pointing his gigantic phallus of a camera at Jane's ass, his flirting is so obvious, and Brooke glances at Margaret, wondering if she's noticed. But Margaret is sipping a cup of tea and leafing through a book about the geography of the island, seemingly oblivious—or at least trying to appear that way. And as Brooke goes over to use the sunscreen just inside the main tent, she sees Malcolm shooting furtive looks toward Jane, as if attempting to catch her eye but not wanting anyone else to notice.

Brooke feels as though she's part of an audience, watching a drama, watching Jane as she follows some unwritten script with Ian, her face glowing as if awash in stage lights. Brooke has always felt this way—as if Jane were the real actor, and she herself merely the audience. Yet now, she recalls what a director once told her: that the audience has a role to play, too, and in theater, that role is just as important.

This may not be the front-row seat Brooke had envisioned when she and Jane made their pact, but it's a performance all the same. And Brooke knows only one thing for certain. It's going to be an entirely unpredictable show.

CHAPTER 6

KERRY

The trail to Haunted Bay winds through kookaburra- and cockatoo-filled eucalyptus trees to the southernmost point of Marbury Island, and it is probably one of the most remote hikes on the island—yet Kerry finds her eyes looking past the trees, scanning the brush and bracken fern for signs of another human. When she hears or glimpses movement, her first thought isn't what creature it might be but whether it's the poacher, the lost hiker, whoever it was who slept in her bed the night before.

Most of the sounds she hears are nothing more than eucalyptus trees shedding their bark to the forest floor, and she makes a point of telling the group that there are hundreds of species of eucs in Australia, how the trees will molt their bark as a form of fire protection, and how the oil in the leaves is not only flammable but poisonous to most animals—except for koalas, who know how to eat the least toxic of the leaves, and still sleep up to twenty-two hours a day as if they've been drugged.

"But there are no koalas on Marbury," Ian says, more as a statement than a question.

"Right, Ian. But there are plenty of other marsupials for us to discover." Her eye catches movement, and she stops on the trail and raises her right hand. Behind her, the others stop talking and walking. She whispers, "Like over there, on the right, by the log."

They follow her gaze, silent, until Ian pipes up: "Wombat."

"The koala's closest relative," Kerry whispers.

Cameras whir behind her; they don't know yet that they will encounter many more wombats—entire wisdoms of wombats, even—as they move farther up the island, but she doesn't spoil their fun. One thing she does love about this job is showing off the land and its creatures, offering the feeling that they are co-exploring this wild place together. Until now it's just been her, alone, searching for devils, studying them, with no one to point them out to, no one to share it all with. Being here on the island is so much better, with healthy animals and eco-conscious travelers eager to see and learn.

Now that she's left Bryan behind to handle the chores in camp, she has to admit the afternoon has been positively specky—sun shining high, everyone keeping pace, alternately quiet and friendly with one another. On the last trip, she and Meg had a couple of complainers, tourists from the States for whom nothing was quite good enough—the hikes were too long, the lunches too meager, the breakfasts too hurried. This group is fairly easygoing, happy just to be here. Charlotte decided to stay behind with a book and a writing journal—she's an author, apparently—and there was no discernible tension when her husband, Malcolm, decided to join the hike rather than stay with her. Ian seems just as keen on the tall American as he is on the birds, but his partner seems to take it in stride; Margaret has fallen into step with Malcolm, and Brooke, the smaller American, is trailing behind everyone and seems to relish bringing up the rear, to take it all in at her own pace.

After several kilometers along a gently rising path, they begin a sharp descent, stopping at a wooden sign marked HAUNTED BAY. Kerry points through the trees at the water below. "To get all the way to the bay, we have to take a goat trail," she says. "It's steep and rocky. You're welcome to head back to camp, or if you want to have a go, we can hike all the way down."

Everyone votes to go down to the bay, and Kerry slows her pace to ensure that no one behind her takes it too fast; every step contains the possibility of a twist or fall, a sprained ankle, a broken wrist.

Thirty minutes later, they make it to the large granite boulders that surround the bay, ready for a rest and a drink of water. Kerry instructs them not to disturb the rocks that are covered with rust-colored lichen, and even as she's speaking she watches Margaret step across one of them, lichen crunching under her feet as she peers ahead, as if there might be farther to go. She stands with her hands on her hips, feet apart, as if sizing up a mountain the rest of them cannot see. Kerry sighs inwardly and decides to let it go.

She opens a tin of scroggin and takes out a few bars of chocolate, passing them around as everyone settles in to enjoy the view. A few wispy clouds have begun skidding across the sky, the sun hot and unrelenting when it peeks through, and if Kerry didn't know better, she wouldn't believe how much rain is in the forecast; right now, it doesn't seem possible.

"Why is it called Haunted Bay?" Brooke asks. "Who does the haunting?"

"This used to be a big whaling spot," Kerry says. "And, story goes, the name derived from the sounds of the whales crying as they were forced into the bay to be slaughtered. The whalers corralled them here so they'd be easier to kill."

Kerry hears Brooke suck her breath inward and knows what she's thinking. The glittering indigo beauty of sky meeting water belies that anything that violent could possibly have happened here. She nods, hating this part of the job: revealing the region's wounds, its scars—but it's part of the experience, all the same. "There's quite a bit of tragic whaling history here in Tasmania," she continues. "North of Marbury, in Freycinet National Park, Wineglass Bay—which always makes the lists of the best beaches in the world—is said to be named not only because of its shape but because it, too, was used to corral whales for slaughter. The waters turned red with their blood."

She watches the faces of the hikers turn mournful and thinks perhaps she should've kept her bloody mouth shut. She's a naturalist, not a journalist. Just because she's had a tough go of things, just because she's seen what she's seen and doesn't believe in sugarcoating anything anymore—she doesn't have to bring everyone else down with her. Especially paying guests who are here to have a good time.

Then another voice inside her, a quieter yet more determined voice, reminds her: *Without truth, there is no action.* What if nobody had spoken up about the disease laying waste to the devils? At least now there's a fighting chance of saving them.

A hundred years ago, the Tasmanian tiger could have used a few more voices. Plenty of scientists knew the thylacine was on the verge of extinction, but nobody made enough noise. And how did the last one die? Of exposure. Because the curator refused to let Allison Reid, the woman who knew the animal best, have a key to the zoo. Because she was female. The tiger died because he could not get back to his den, because the door was closed. And so on an unusually cold night in September of 1936, in some shabby private zoo in Hobart, the very last thylacine in the world died, not with the bang of some rifle, but with a frozen whimper.

Just as Kerry feels herself slipping back into that familiar darkness, she makes eye contact with a spotted skink who appears surprised to see trespassers sprawled about on his sunbathing spot. The lizard does a push-up, then scurries into the shady crack of a boulder. Clearing her throat, Kerry tells the group to look for the lizards in the crevices, and she points to the one she's just seen, who's poking his head adorably out of his hiding place. She's relieved when they turn their attention to the lizard, and then out to the water—thinking more pleasant thoughts, she hopes.

From the corner of her eye, she sees Brooke approach. "I didn't realize so much violence happened here."

Kerry inwardly curses herself. "Sorry," she says. "I didn't mean to bring you down."

"No, no," Brooke says. "It's important. But it must be difficult for you, talking about it all the time. Not only the history, but all the animals that are now endangered."

"Yeah, sometimes. But then I remind myself that at least I'm out here educating people. I hope so, anyway." She forces a smile and asks Brooke, "So what brings you to Tasmania?"

"My endangered marriage, for one."

Kerry smiles—a genuine smile, for a change. Guests aren't usually so forthcoming, and in fact Brooke looks rather shocked by her own words; she seems to be scrambling for something more to say—perhaps to take it back. Kerry puts an arm on Brooke's shoulder. "No worries. My own relationship has recently gone extinct, so you're in good company."

Brooke looks relieved, and they both notice that the other guests are beginning to stand, to walk along the boulders, taking photos, gazing down at the azure water, listening to the waves pummeling the rocks a hundred meters below. As Brooke walks off to pick up her pack, Kerry gathers up the scroggin containers and what's left of the chocolate bars.

She looks around, waiting patiently for everyone to get their photos, to feel as though they've had enough time. "Ready to head back to camp?"

Then she notices there aren't as many people as there were when they arrived. "Who are we missing?"

"Malcolm wanted to get back early for a shower," Margaret says.

"Jane wasn't far behind," Brooke says. "The jet lag's catching up with her."

Kerry looks from one of them to the other, sensing something in their voices but not knowing exactly what. Had she made those two depressed enough to ditch the group, or did they really just want to get a head start back toward happy hour and dinner and a good night's sleep?

"Right," Kerry says. "Well, let's see if we make good time heading back. With rain on the way later tonight, we might want to take advantage of the sun and have a swim."

This time, she follows behind as the hikers make their way slowly back up the goat trail. She can't help but think how, every time she considers how much better this job is, how much more optimistic, the opposite feeling follows so closely behind: the knowledge that, at least before, she was responsible only to the animals, who didn't complain, who didn't judge, who were impossible to make unhappy.

CHAPTER 7

BROOKE

During the walk back to camp Brooke feels the clenching of unused muscles in her calves and wonders if she's incorrectly converting kilometers to miles; Kerry says they will be hiking six Ks today, but her body's telling that this has to add up to more than four miles. Either that, or she's even more sorely out of shape than she thought.

When she asks Kerry, Ian chimes in to point out that six kilometers converts to precisely three-point-seven miles. Brooke feels her face flush; it's the same sort of thing William used to do. William—like Ian, apparently—knew a little bit about a lot of things, and he never failed to share his knowledge. He could do amazing feats of mathematics in his head, which first impressed Brooke but later irritated her and made her feel slow by comparison. For William, being right was more important than anything else; there was a sort of cold impatience about him, which Brooke had first taken for a type of genius she didn't understand. When they met, he was one of the company's star developers, and a year later he was lured to Seattle by an incredible offer to head up his own team. She leapt at the chance to leave New York with him, to start over.

She'd fallen for William in part because he seemed so real; unlike the actors she spent so much time with, he put up no pretenses. And he had no expectations of her but accepted her for who she was—not what role she got or didn't get, or what job she did or didn't have.

After spending her childhood being ferried between bitterly divorced parents, it was a relief that she no longer had to act—to play the grown-up, the good-natured girl, the well-behaved child. It wasn't until she met William that she'd even realized she'd been acting all her life—and that maybe this was why she was drawn to the stage, because pretending felt so familiar. Yet with William, she didn't have to pretend. She could just be herself. He was like a blank canvas onto which she could project whoever she wanted to be.

The problem was, she wasn't sure who she wanted to be.

When she met William, she was drawn toward his independence, his competence. She knew she'd be safe with him, that he would never leave her. Sure, he was a little aloof, a bit of a workaholic—but she liked that he had his own life, and she had hers.

But as the years passed, she found herself yearning for a sign or two of dependence—not just on a physical level but an emotional one. She could spend the day walking the city with him, from Belltown to Ballard and back again, and yet never feel like they'd shared the same day. For so long she told herself that this was the mark of a mature relationship, one in which the couples don't need to constantly talk.

She had to learn the hard way that the absence of talking does not mean things aren't being said. In all those quiet moments, she and William said plenty.

She's so lost in her thoughts she stumbles over a fallen tree branch on the trail. She catches herself quickly, relieved that no one else seems to have noticed. As she continues walking, she watches Ian and Margaret, each here for their own reasons, each enjoying entirely different things, as if they hadn't even planned the trip together. But while the Bird Man and Ms. Everest seem to be very well matched in this way, this hadn't been the case with her and William. Brooke remembers a sunny Seattle Saturday when she and William walked through the sculpture park over-looking Elliott Bay. Two young girls were running around the giant Alexander Calder statue, *The Eagle*, shrieking as they hid behind its golden steel wings. Brooke, smiling as she watched them dodge the statue's shadows, looked over at William, who was staring down at his phone. Even when she nudged him and pointed out how cute the girls were, he merely nodded, then returned his gaze to the screen. Choosing work over the brilliant blue sky, the sparkling bay, the art and laughter and conversation surrounding them. Choosing work over her. They'd not yet talked about children, but just then Brooke realized she couldn't picture him as a father. His technical smarts and talents, it seemed, came at the expense of wisdom and warmth, and she knew, suddenly and just as certainly, that raising kids with William would be like raising them alone.

Now, while the others peer to both sides of the trail looking for animals, Brooke thinks of Jane and Malcolm having conveniently left the group early and keeps her eyes anxiously ahead, wondering around every turn whether they'll come across the two of them—locked in an embrace, or in an argument. Or maybe they're already back at camp, making use of one of their empty tents. This would be the best-case scenario, Brooke decides—she can already tell that

Jane is wavering along a slim edge between manic and morose. Sex has always been the most effective mood enhancer for Jane; it's better that she go for it than end up angry or depressed.

Brooke feels the grip of their old dynamic taking hold. She and Jane enabled each other, in both good and unhealthy ways. Jane gave Brooke confidence and a sense of adventure, while Brooke injected calm and levelheaded reasoning into Jane when she was at her most scattered. They filled each other's gaps, smoothed out each other's roughest edges; they made each other better versions of themselves. Except when they didn't.

And now? Brooke is the one on anti-anxiety meds, the one with secrets.

As they approach the final descending stretch of trail toward camp, she hears Kerry coming up behind her. She moves aside so they can walk side by side, and at the edge of the trail she feels a dense bracket of overgrown ferns tickle her thighs.

"If anyone fancies a swim," Kerry says, "now's a good time. If the weather turns, this arvo may be our only chance."

"A swim sounds great." Brooke is in no hurry to go back to her tent if there's even the smallest chance that Jane might be in there with Malcolm. Would they dare to be so bold, knowing that anyone could catch them? Well, Jane would.

Then it occurs to Brooke that Charlotte had stayed behind—so if Jane and Malcolm wanted any privacy, let alone any intimacy, they likely wouldn't be anywhere near camp. Where was it even possible to have torrid extramarital sex in this wild place, with venomous snakes lurking everywhere?

As they approach the crossroads where the beach trail meets the track back to camp, Ian announces he'd prefer to go into the bush to look for birds.

Margaret scoffs. "Knackered already, are you?" she says to him, then turns to Brooke and Kerry with a smile that doesn't quite take the sting from her tone. "Ian doesn't have the stamina I do. Not to mention, an ocean has to be the temperature of a bathtub for him to have a go."

They part ways on the trail, with Ian heading through a copse of trees and Brooke and Margaret following Kerry along the grass-strewn sand to the beach. Once there, Brooke sees a blonde woman, fully clothed, sprawled facedown on an array of towels, and even in their seclusion it takes her a moment to realize it's Charlotte, who'd apparently been snoozing and looks up as she hears their voices. She doesn't look pleased to see them, and when she attempts a smile, it looks more like a grimace.

Brooke lowers her day pack onto the sand, then realizes she doesn't have a swimsuit. She's not going to risk returning to the tent to get it—with Charlotte here on the beach, who knows where Jane and Malcolm might be?—and she considers skipping the swim when she sees Margaret strip down to her bra and underwear without a trace of self-consciousness. Probably because there's nothing to be self-conscious about: Ms. Everest's body is lean, a bit on the skinny side but extremely fit, with muscles that are well defined while still being feminine, and not a trace of fat or sagging skin. Brooke realizes that while her sun-spotted, wind-worn face belies it, Margaret is closer to her and Jane's age; she must be at least ten years younger than Ian.

Brooke glances around and sees Kerry looking at her. "Forgot your bathers?" she says with a smile.

It takes her a moment to realize Kerry means bathing suit. "Yeah," she says. "Are you going in?"

Kerry shakes her head. "I don't have mine, either, but that's not why," she says, holding up her phone. "I'm hoping to make a quick call if I can find a signal."

"I'm glad I'm not the only one who forgot."

"I didn't forget," Kerry says with a laugh. "Mine—how shall I say this? Well, it's a long story."

"Now I have to hear it," Brooke says.

"It was on the last trip actually, before—" Kerry pauses, then seems to shake off an intruding thought before continuing. "Anyway, we'd had a swim one afternoon, and I set my bathers on a sunny rock for just a few minutes, so they'd dry. I meant to move them and hang them up where the devils couldn't get them, but it got dark and I forgot all about them. The next day I found them a few feet away—there's nothing the devils don't get into, but I was just glad they hadn't eaten them. So I put them on under my hiking gear and went for a swim later on that day. And it turns out the devils had indeed had a bit of a nibble. In a very conspicuous place, as it turned out."

"You don't mean—"

Kerry laughs again and nods, creating a triangle with her thumbs and index fingers and positioning her hands low in front of her. "Meg, my guiding partner for the trip, was the first to tell me—but I'm afraid she wasn't the first to notice. We had a good laugh about it at dinner later. So, if you're worried about having a swim in your underwear—well, I'm here to tell you you'll be far better covered than I was that day."

Laughing, and acting quickly, before she can think too much about it, Brooke takes off her shorts and top, hiking shoes and socks, and runs through the powdery sand toward the water.

She can't help but wonder what William would think if he could see her now, practically skinny dipping off the coast of Tasmania. Despite being a drama major, despite being at home on stage in front of an audience, Brooke has never been nearly as comfortable in her own skin. It's probably the least-known reality of being an actor: that you pretend to be other people because it's so much easier than being yourself. By the time she'd met William, she'd basically given up on her career. He never saw her onstage, never saw her do what she loved best.

She steps into the sea, the water bracing, but instead of retreating she picks up her legs and sprints into the gently lapping waves, diving under as soon as she's waist-deep. She swims away from shore, the movement warming her chilled skin. She feels loose and flexible in the water, in her limbs as well as in her mind, a freeness she hasn't felt in a long time. The last time she'd felt this sense of possibility was when she and Jane had landed in New York, the city and the world wide open to them. As she looks out over the deep green water, she feels that same sense of expansiveness.

Then she feels a twinge, remembering how her great New York adventure had turned out. It wasn't *all* bad—between waitressing and bartending jobs, she'd gotten a couple of small roles, and the fact that she'd met William in the city used to be a plus—but in the end, even though she Facebooked her story in a cheery *Getting married, moving to Seattle!* post, the reality was that she felt as though she'd slunk away from New York a complete failure.

Still, it had remained, until now, her biggest adventure. Jane had a friend in Long Island City whose floor they slept on while they looked for an apartment of their own, and they so loved the views of Manhattan across the East River that they didn't look any farther than that section of Queens. Ten years ago, LIC's low-slung industrial buildings had been giving way to new sky-scrapers, apartment buildings, and a growing hub of bars and cafés, but Jane had found them a railroad flat on the ground floor for a fraction of the rent Jane's friend paid in a newer building. The flat had four rooms, lined up as in a train car, with flimsy doors crookedly hinged between them. At the back was a kitchen and bathroom, in the front a room they used as a living area; they slept in the two middle rooms, not minding that they had to walk through each other's spaces to get to the bathroom or to get out the front door.

They both found it auspicious that a film and television studio had been in Long Island City for decades, often shooting outdoor scenes right there in the neighborhood, and it was a ten-minute subway ride to Manhattan on the 7 train. It was perfect, and in their youthful innocence and optimism—or was it ignorance and stupidity?—they both believed great things were ahead of them.

But Brooke didn't take to New York the way Jane did. She found the city manic and unfriendly, the subway stifling, the tourists ceaselessly annoying. The overstimulation of subway and sirens and sidewalks crammed her brain until it ached. Yet these were the things Jane loved about New York. She remembers Jane heading out fearlessly into Manhattan for whatever appointment she may have had, barely glancing at a map, while Brooke herself studied both the subway and Google maps obsessively, thinking that if she could learn her way around the city, perhaps she might navigate her own future just as easily. But she's never been good with directions.

Most of all, she'd never managed to gain a foothold in the theater. She'd known for a long time that she didn't look the way many directors wanted, but she also knew that every actor heard this at some point, even Jane. You just had to persevere. And so she did. But an audition for *Romeo and Juliet* changed everything.

She was thrilled to receive a callback—in her career so far, callbacks were rare, and she finally felt as though she were making progress. And though at first she couldn't wait to tell Jane, in the end, something stopped her, and she ended up keeping it to herself. Somehow, her small victory felt sweeter this way.

After her second audition, which she thought had gone very well, as she was heading down the theater hallway to find a restroom, she overheard voices and paused. One of them, she knew, was the casting director. "Brooke Sanders? Yeah, she's all right, but she's not Juliet. She'll never be a Juliet."

And with that, her newly burgeoning confidence vanished. She stumbled back out into midtown, the cold air stinging her eyes. She'd endured rejections before—too many to count—but this one felt especially brutal, probably because she'd actually felt as though she'd been on the verge of real success. She'd already been daydreaming about the wigs and makeup, the Elizabethan costumes, which of the beautiful men would end up playing her Romeo.

She could've stuck with it, taken a smaller role, but in that moment, she didn't see the point anymore. Why continue acting if she would never be leading-role material? It had never been part of the dream to get by on bit parts in small performances.

Her only clear thought on that icy day was that she was glad she hadn't told Jane. Her disappointment would have felt nearly overwhelming if she couldn't bury it, and bury it she did—along with her hopes of ever becoming a working actor. She knew then that she just couldn't keep going through this, that she didn't have what it takes.

Yet over the years she regretted giving up so soon—and when she received Jane's unexpected invitation to come here, she leapt at the chance to start over. To become the person she'd left behind years ago, in New York. To see, finally, where life might've taken her if she hadn't given up. Jane had always made her feel brave, and she needed this courage now more than ever. The minute she boarded the flight to Sydney she told herself that this would be the beginning of a whole new life. And, right now, immersed in emerald water off a pristine stretch of white sand, she can't think of a better place to begin anew.

"How you going?"

Startled out of her flashback, Brooke looks over to see Margaret treading water nearby, her light-brown hair darkened by the water, a few tendrils clinging to one cheek.

"I'm going—fine," she answers. "You?"

Margaret shrugs. "It's not my idea of a dream trip, but then Ian and Malcolm concocted it. These posh tents are about as outdoorsy as those two get. If I had my way, we'd be trekking Southwest National Park. No trails there. Just bush and bugs and one reasonably sized mountain."

"Sounds like fun," Brooke says, feigning enthusiasm, though sensing it's not even necessary. People like Margaret don't need others to be enthused for them. "Maybe you'll get your wish next year."

"Next year, I plan to summit Aconcagua."

"Where's that?"

"Argentina. It's the tallest mountain in South America."

"Wow. Is Ian going?"

"No. We typically keep our passions separate—he and his birds, me and my mountains."

"An open marriage," Brooke says, amused at her joke.

But Margaret only stares at her, as if trying to decode the expression on her face. "What brought you here?" she asks.

"Jane did," Brooke says. "She's the adventurous one."

"A woman who wears that much makeup isn't what I'd call adventurous."

"You try lugging a hair dryer across this island."

But Margaret doesn't take the bait. No smile, no hint of humor or even friendliness. Brooke rubs her arms as though she's cold and says, "Well, I'm going to head in. Maybe catch a shower before dinner." She turns and begins to swim away before Margaret can say anything more.

Back onshore, Kerry is still on the beach, her eyes and fingers on her phone, and Charlotte is sitting up, writing in a notebook propped on her skinny knees. Brooke shivers in the cooling air, realizing she hadn't put her small camping towel in her day pack. She's about to slip her shorts on over wet skin when she hears Charlotte's voice behind her.

"Here, darling, use one of mine."

Brooke turns to see, at the end of Charlotte's thin arm, a towel—a full-sized, thick towel. "Really?" she asks.

Charlotte smiles. "I loathe those flimsy camping towels," she says. "I would rather have several good towels and one change of clothing on a trip like this, packing instructions be damned. Go on, you look frozen."

Brooke takes the towel and wraps it around her shoulders, pulling it tight around her. "Thank you," she says, relaxing under the towel's soft warmth, the slight grit of fine sand. "This feels heavenly right now."

"Enjoy your swim?"

Brooke nods. "It's cold but worth it. You're not going in?"

Charlotte shakes her head. "I prefer water from a comfortable distance."

"Sorry if we disturbed you earlier," Brooke says. "It looked like you were having a nice nap."

"I wasn't napping," Charlotte says. "I was plotting."

"Plotting—what?"

Charlotte laughs. "My next novel," she says. "I'm a psychotherapist by trade, but a few years ago I wrote a book—on a whim, really. I always loved to write and just thought I'd have a go. And then it got published, and here I am—three books later."

"Wow," Brooke says. "I'll have to find a bookstore before we leave. What sort of novels?"

"Psychological thrillers, I suppose you'd call them. Though I actually loathe such categories."

"Are they based on your patients?"

"No, not my own clients specifically," Charlotte says. "But I get called into court as an expert witness on occasion, and that was what first inspired me to combine the criminal and the psychological."

Brooke pulls the towel around her more snugly as a ripple of wind washes over them. "I admire anyone who can write. In drama school, we had a project to write and perform a one-person play, and I found it so hard."

"Did you?" Charlotte says. "Writing's not so difficult. All it takes is a bit of imagination."

Brooke laughs. "Maybe I'm not that imaginative."

"If you went to drama school, darling, then surely you are," Charlotte says.

"So what's your new book about?"

Charlotte's eyes skip out to sea for a long moment. "Have you ever heard the term *l'appel du vide?*"

Something about the way Charlotte speaks makes Brooke shudder even under the warmth of the towel. "No, I haven't."

"It's French," Charlotte says. "*The call of the void.* The lure of the unknown."

"I'm not sure I understand."

Charlotte seems to come back to her then and looks her in the eyes. "Have you ever been driving along a bridge and thought about steering yourself right over the edge? Have you been hiking on a mountain trail and thought about stepping off into the abyss?"

Even knowing the questions are hypothetical, Brooke answers quickly, instinctively: "No."

Charlotte looks at her for a long moment, and Brooke has the eerie feeling Charlotte can tell what she's thinking. That she's remembering an evening when she was nine and her mom had not come home from work, when Brooke had waited after school and past dinnertime and late into the evening. Her mother had finally come in, tossing her keys on the kitchen table and sitting down, looking shaken. "What happened?" Brooke asked, going to her and climbing into her lap—she was too big for that, but her mom let her anyway. "Are you okay?" Her mother had sighed, then spoke softly into Brooke's hair, her voice so muffled that to this day Brooke still wants to believe she'd heard her wrong. "I almost drove the car off the road. I just thought it might be easier, you know? Just to be done with it." Brooke froze in her mother's arms and didn't move or speak, and then her mom got up and took a shower and went to bed, where she stayed for nearly two days, lost in another one of her "spells."

"It's not a new phenomenon, by any means," Charlotte continues, "but I read a paper about it in a psychology journal a few years back. Some people gravitate toward the positive, others toward the negative, toward the truly dark places. I'm intrigued by those who find their instincts can be so dangerous."

"Interesting," Brooke says, hoping her voice doesn't sound as shaky as she feels. She's thinking of her mom again, who was drawn toward the light as well as the dark—despite her spells and moods, her illnesses and migraines, she was also fun and spontaneous, sneaking Brooke out of school to go ice skating, or keeping her out past midnight at the county fair.

And Brooke is also thinking of Jane, why she is still so inescapably drawn to her friend. Why their friendship has always felt so seamless—so unpredictable, dangerous—and yet comfortable, and entirely familiar.

She shakes off her thoughts and turns her attention back to Charlotte. "That's a great premise for a novel," she says. "Will it be set on a remote Tasmanian island?"

Charlotte smiles at her. "No, darling, it's set in suburban Sydney. Believe it or not, that's where most of the world's drama happens. Right in our backyards." Then Charlotte shifts her focus and nods toward the towel. "Nice and warm, isn't it?"

"Yes, thank you." Brooke unwraps herself and hands the towel back. "Thanks again. I really needed that." As she puts her clothes back on over her still-damp underclothes, she sees Margaret emerge from the water.

"How you going, guys?" Kerry calls out. "About time for a bevo?"

Brooke looks up and sees that the clouds have tarnished and thickened overhead. Moments later, they're following Kerry back to camp. Brooke hears laughter even before they arrive, and when they reach the wood-planked patio, happy hour is in full swing. Malcolm and Ian are sitting around a well-stocked table of beer and wine, crackers and cheese, presided over by Bryan, who's got a bottle of beer in one hand and a cheese-smothered cracker in the other. Brooke glances around, but Jane's not there.

Then she notices Bryan staring at her, and she looks down to see the wet spots on her clothing: two on her chest, the outline of her underwear showing through her shorts. She may as well be naked—but to her own surprise, she finds she likes the feeling. She meets Bryan's eyes and holds them, and a slow grin spreads over his face.

Then Kerry barks out his name, and he turns, his smile fading when he sees Kerry's face. Brooke watches him follow her into the main tent.

Margaret, who has wrapped a bright blue sarong around her body, sits down next to Malcolm and pours herself a glass of red wine. Ian gives her a look. "Don't you want to change?"

"Why?" Margaret asks, leaning back and stretching her long, bare legs out in front of her. "I'm perfectly comfortable." She raises her glass. "Cheers."

"Cheers," Malcolm echoes. He seems much more relaxed than earlier, and Brooke wonders whether it's from sex. She watches Charlotte sit down next to Ian, across from her husband.

"I don't know how you do it, Margaret," Brooke says. "I'm freezing. I have to go change."

"Very few things can get between me and a glass of shiraz," Margaret says.

Brooke returns to her tent, where she finds Jane, lying on her sleeping bag, staring up at the dark-green canvas.

"Jane? What happened?"

Jane doesn't move, doesn't look toward Brooke, as she begins to talk, slowly, in monotone. "He said he doesn't love me. He has no intention of leaving Charlotte. He said he'd end my career in a heartbeat if I said a word to anyone about us."

Brooke sits down on the edge of the platform, forgetting about her wet clothes. "I'm sorry, Jane."

"It's okay."

"No, it's not. I know he's surprised and probably pissed off that you're here—but he's the one who's married, not you. What an asshole."

Jane doesn't respond. She still has not moved, and Brooke has a sudden recollection of a time in college, when Jane caught Tyler, the Beta Theta Pi she'd fallen for, kissing a sorority girl in the alley behind Harpo's one Friday night. Jane spent the next two days in bed, looking just the way she does now—her face blank, her eyes dead—and Brooke had brought her everything from soup to potato chips to tequila, trashy magazines and movies, anything to get her out of her trance. Then, the day she arrived at Jane's dorm room with the student crisis hotline number programmed into her phone and ready to dial, she found Jane dressed and putting on makeup. There was a party, Jane told her, and they were going.

They went out, got drunk, danced and flirted and ordered late-night pizza as if nothing ever happened. Brooke didn't learn until later that Tyler's car had been keyed, the windshield bashed in with a brick, and the air let out of every tire. When she told Jane about it, Jane smiled, unsurprised, and said, "Vandalism is so common in college towns. Shame, isn't it?"

Now, Brooke can only wonder what Jane is contemplating doing to Malcolm during the next four days of this journey.

She stands up and digs out dry underwear and clothes from her pack. "For what it's worth, you're not alone."

She turns to see Jane looking at her.

"William and I—we've separated." Brooke turns away again as she peels off her wet clothing and gets dressed. "We're probably getting a divorce."

"What?" Jane sits up.

Brooke sits down on her own bed so they're facing each other across the small space. "I moved out last month. We haven't talked about it, but it's over." She finds she doesn't know what more to say. She'd rehearsed it in her head so many times—*We fell out of love . . . We were never in love . . . We want different things*—and all of it, and none of it, sounded true. Which is partly why she hasn't told her mother, whom she talks to every few weeks but hasn't seen in years, or her father, now remarried and whom she hasn't seen since her wedding. The freedom of this silence— of, for once, not having an audience—feels like something she'd been missing in her life for a long time.

"Wow," Jane says. "I was right on the money, wasn't I? Almost five years exactly." A moment later, she adds, "Why didn't you tell me?"

Brooke sighs. "Maybe I didn't want to admit how right you were. I know you thought he was a work in progress, but I really did think he was going to be a great partner."

Jane lets out a short laugh. "Women always marry men expecting them to change," she says. "And men marry women expecting them not to." She leans back on her bunk and props her feet on the tent wall. "I always pictured you marrying a handsome doctor. Someone who'd support your acting career."

"William would've been supportive, if I'd kept it up." Brooke isn't sure why Jane is making her feel like defending William. "Besides, doctors don't get stock options, or retire at forty-five."

Jane sits up again. "Just because he's rich doesn't make him any less weird. I told you that years ago. The way he barely acknowledges anyone else in the room? And how he's so intense about the littlest things, like the water temperature of his freaking dishwasher? And he never closed his mouth when he chewed."

Brooke has to laugh. "I hardly noticed any of that. I guess I got used to it."

"You shouldn't have *had* to get used to that. Fucking techs think they're smarter than everyone else, and for some reason they think this makes them perfect. Trust me, I know the type. They're just like media executives who get too famous for their own good."

"Are there any men who aren't assholes?"

"I doubt it." Jane pulls out the whiskey bottle and takes a drink. "I think we need our own little happy hour before going out there."

Brooke reaches for the bottle. "Definitely."

Then she remembers her medication. She removes the prescription bottle from her pack and palms one of the pills into her mouth.

Jane snatches the bottle from her hand. "What's this?"

"Nothing. Just for anxiety."

Jane's reading the label. "Sertraline? That's for depression, sister."

"How do you know so much about it?"

"I did a commercial for Zoloft. It was national—didn't you see it?" Jane adopts a sober expression and deep voice. "Side effects may include nausea, diarrhea, dry mouth, headache, insomnia, and/or weight changes." Then she relaxes her features and, in her normal voice, adds, "Anyway, my point is, it's a crutch."

"And this isn't?" Brooke holds up the whiskey and echoes Jane's TV voice. "People taking Zoloft should avoid the use of alcohol." She takes a long swallow.

Jane leans close. "You need to find your inner courage again. Billy Boy drained what was left out of you."

"Maybe I never had much to begin with."

"I disagree. And by the end of this trip, you'll see."

"I hope you're right."

They pass the whiskey back and forth a couple of times in silence. Even though it's been so long since she's seen Jane, in the quiet space between them Brooke feels close to her again.

"What do you do for work now?" Jane says.

"I'm at a nonprofit cultural center in Seattle," Brooke says. "Sort of an office-manager thing, but it's full-time. Decent benefits. Lucky for me—I'll need health insurance with William out of the picture. I like it, actually. It keeps me at least tangentially connected to theater."

"Don't you miss acting?" Jane asks.

Brooke takes another drink before answering. "I'm acting all the time," she admits. "You're the only one I've told about William. My family doesn't know. I've spent the past month pretending everything is just the same."

She sighs. "But, to answer your question, I do miss acting—real acting. Being onstage. Being someone else." She laughs. "It's weird, but being someone else is what makes me feel most like myself." She looks at Jane. "You're so lucky you've made a career of it. No—it's not just luck; I don't mean to sound glib. It's talent. Perseverance. I didn't have enough of either."

"You have more than enough talent," Jane says. "I think Billy Boy got in the way. I think he gave you the excuse you needed to give up."

Brooke mulls this over as she takes a long drink and hands Jane the bottle. "I just don't know anymore."

"That's what friends are for," Jane says, raising the bottle as if in a toast. "To remind each other what's real and what's not."

"I'm glad you invited me here," Brooke says suddenly, meaning it.

"I'm glad you came, B. And not just because it's nice to know I'm not the only one unlucky in love."

"I think the best revenge is to spend the next four days having as much fun as possible. I'm a world away from William. As for Malcolm—"

"No such luck."

"You just need to ignore him. Pretend he doesn't exist. Show him what he's missing by having much more fun than his wife seems to be having."

"You noticed that, too? I mean, she couldn't care less about being here."

"I know, it's weird. She was on the beach all afternoon and didn't even go into the water."

"I wonder if she resents him," Jane muses.

"Malcolm? For what, if she doesn't know about you two?"

"She's a published writer," Jane says, "but it's all because of him. He sent her first book to a friend in publishing, and it tanked, but

Mal convinced them to publish the second anyway. It did slightly better, but still. That's gotta hurt."

"She seems confident nonetheless. Besides, it's only a side thing. Doesn't she work as a psychologist, too?"

Jane stands up. "How about we *not* talk about how accomplished she is?"

"Sorry."

"Anyway," Jane says, "I don't even know why she came. From the email I read, the trip was Ian and Malcolm's idea."

"That's what Margaret said. Is anyone glad to be here besides us?"

Jane puts the whiskey bottle down. "Let's show them what a good time really is, shall we?"

Brooke watches Jane change into a black T-shirt with a dipping neckline and put on lipstick, and she wonders as she pulls on a fleece pullover exactly what Jane means by that. She doesn't ask.

Jane wraps a gauzy, emerald-green scarf around her long hair, pulling it back from her face. A light rain begins to patter the top of their tent, and they zip it shut before walking to the deck.

CHAPTER 8

KERRY

In the kitchen, Bryan is fumbling around with the stove, a plate of sloppily chopped vegetables on the counter nearby. Kerry looks at the mess and, realizing that dinner is going to be quite late at this point, takes another bottle of wine and an extra wedge of cheese out to the patio. The rain, fortunately, is intermittent, and no one has yet made a move to come into the tent, though she knows it's only a matter of time.

She takes a quick glance at her phone again, wishing she'd been able to get a connection. The only place she'd got reception today was at the narrowest part of the isthmus, and she won't have time to go back, unless it's very late. She was hoping to call Meg, to see how she's feeling, and most of all to apologize for her role in what happened. She must've uttered the words *I'm so sorry* a thousand times when Meg was in the hospital, but she can't be sure Meg remembered any of it, thanks to the painkillers. Most of all, she wants to hear Meg's voice, to absorb some of her calm and be reassured that she can get through these next few days without anyone asking for their money back.

"Fuck," Bryan mutters, yanking his hand from the stove, where he'd just grabbed the hot handle of a large pan.

"Go chat with the guests," Kerry tells him, nudging him away from the small, two-burner stove. "I'll handle this."

It's his night to cook, and it's the last thing she wants to do, but she can't trust Bryan not to stuff it up, and they're already thirty minutes past the time when dinner should be served.

"You sure?" Bryan asks over his shoulder as he pulls a beer from the cooler.

"Yes, go," she says.

She takes out the guest information sheet and is immediately glad she's sent Bryan away; meals are going to be complicated. Margaret is paleo, Ian is vegetarian, Charlotte is gluten-free—and with her luck, the other guests probably also have restrictions that they forgot to mention.

It's ingenious, the way camp works, with the guides carrying in freshies and the tents and coolers stocked with everything else they'll need for the four-day journey. Nigel, the owner, created a recipe book with modifications for virtually every type of diet and food allergy, so Kerry doesn't have to think too much about it; she simply has to follow directions. She got familiar with the recipes during the last track, and now all she has to do is figure out how to fix tonight's meal in a way that doesn't poison anyone.

She puts the risotto on the stove to cook and begins to re-chop the vegetables Bryan has butchered, cutting them into much smaller, but at least much more attractive, pieces. The rhythm of the task sets her mind free, and she finds herself thinking of where she might otherwise be at this time of evening—in her closet-sized office at the sanctuary, at Veg Bar having a drink, at home with Paul—if she hadn't left. Left her job. Left her partner of five years.

Left years of research and experience and half-written grants that would now never be awarded.

It happened three months ago, but it had begun long before that—the night she found an injured Tasmanian devil crawling along the side of a road on the outskirts of Hobart. She can no longer be in a car anymore without scanning the shoulders, looking for the tiny victims of hit-and-runs, pulling over and getting out to see if they can be saved and, even if not, to check for a joey nestled in the pouch. That is the saddest part of all sometimes—when a roo or wallaby or wombat gets hit and left for dead and has a joey who is left to die of cold, starvation, fright.

She shakes her head and tries to focus on the vegetables, on the simmering risotto. This is why you're here, she reminds herself. To forget about all that.

But it's hard to be here without remembering how she ended up here; she can hardly separate her presence here from the reason.

When she rescued this injured devil and brought her to the sanctuary, the other animal caregiver, Matt, suggested euthanizing the creature rather than putting her through any more suffering. But Kerry convinced him otherwise, including offering to pay for the emergency veterinarian, and they assisted during the late-night surgery as the vet cleaned the devil's wounds, tweezed out bits of gravel, and sutured the lacerations on her belly, back, and head. Under sedation, the devil could have been mistaken for a family dog; she was the size of a Boston terrier, with short legs, the rear legs longer than the front.

By the time the rest of the staff arrived, Boomer (named for the boomerang-shaped swath of white fur across her black chest) was asleep in a towel-lined kennel. Kerry was still there, having spent the night on a pallet of donated birdseed. Later that morning, Boomer's rat tail twitched, and Kerry leaned in. The devil looked up at her with her small black eyes. Kerry reached in and stroked her shaved and bandaged head, knowing full well this was neither safe nor appropriate—but she couldn't resist, and Boomer did not flinch or move away, keeping her steady eyes on hers.

Two weeks later, she and Matt and an intern drove fifteen kilometers south of Edith Creek, then another twenty on a pockmarked dirt road. They released Boomer on private land, far from homes and people and, most important, far away from the four-wheeled instruments of death. Devils live six years, if they're lucky, but don't breed until after two. It's such a narrow window for keeping a species—a culture—alive. But it had been enough for thousands of years. Just enough. Until now. Until this disease. Boomer, at less than a year old, wasn't quite ready to find a mate, yet Kerry was hopeful. Since the disease has spread, they've noticed that many devils begin breeding earlier than ever before.

The area was one in which they'd released other rehabilitated devils, including a few males, all without the facial tumor disease that plagued their species. They didn't have the budget to tag and track the animals, but volunteers went out there a few times a month to observe anything they could, from scat to actual devil sightings. They rarely saw much.

So it felt like a miracle when, weeks later, one of the volunteers saw Boomer during a site visit one evening; she recognized her by her boomerang marking. She looked well, the volunteer said, the excitement in her voice contagious, her photos far away but clear enough to see her assessment was spot-on.

The next report, some six weeks later, was entirely different: Boomer had a bright red swelling above her left eye, and while they couldn't get close enough to confirm that it was the disease and not a random injury, there was little room for doubt. When Kerry heard the news, she felt a part of her soul scurry and hide. She knew the following weeks would break her heart, in slow and painful pieces, as Boomer's lesion spread like a bloodstain.

Kerry went to the property immediately but couldn't find her anywhere; she knew better than to think Boomer would remember her as her rescuer, her lifesaver, but a part of her hoped she would. She waited all day and late into the night, flashing her torch around, looking hopefully for two eyes to shine back at her. Instead, she had to leave without ever seeing her again, knowing the tumors would cover her face, would prevent her from eating, would blind her, that she'd starve or die of organ failure.

But something made her return the next night, despite Paul urging her to rest. And that's when she found Boomer, wandering in drunken circles near the location where they first set her free. Kerry recognized the behavior and knew that there was not much time left.

She took Boomer back to the apartment she shared with Paul. She couldn't leave her to die alone out there in the cold night. It was madness to bring Boomer home; she knew as much. But the sanctuary was nearly an hour away, and Boomer might've died along the way.

And so she sat with Boomer in her lap, tuning out Paul's plea to take her to the sanctuary. Eventually, Paul gave up and retreated to a pub. Boomer had only one eye left, and with it she looked up at Kerry with a wary but hopeful expression, almost as if she thought Kerry could help her. That Kerry's species, which for so long slaughtered devils with abandon—by poison, trap wells, dogs, and bullets—that this species so well versed in the art of killing would somehow be able to save one of them. Just one.

Kerry watched her tears fall and dissolve into the matted fur of Boomer's belly. And when Boomer closed her eye for good, Kerry felt the world go silent. She remained on the floor, counting the rings in the wood, thinking how many trees died to build this apartment building. How much death was all around her, death at the hands of humans. In her own hands. In her lap.

Suddenly she felt movement and looked down. Boomer's body shuddered from the inside, jolting Kerry into action. She reached inside Boomer's brood pouch to find three joeys squirming to feed from dry nipples.

She rushed them all to the sanctuary, calling Matt along the way. Together, they carefully extracted the three joeys from their mother, tiny red creatures, the size of baby rats. The look on Matt's face said everything.

"We have to try," Kerry said.

They used eyedroppers to squeeze formula into the joeys' hungry mouths. When Matt could keep his eyes open no longer, Kerry took over, staying with them the next day and through the night, refusing to admit defeat when the joeys' skin turned ashen and they stopped reaching for the eyedropper. The following morning, Matt found her staring at three thumb-sized corpses.

In a stupor, Kerry returned home and went to bed. She didn't make a conscious decision to stay there; she just saw no reason to move. When the alarm on her phone sounded the next morning, she simply reached over and turned it off, then rolled over. As daylight crept through her eyelids, she pressed them closed. At some point, Paul shook her shoulder and asked if she was going to work. She didn't respond. "Are you sick?" he asked, and finally she told him she was, and he went away.

She tried to stay asleep—it was only then, and in the first second or two upon awakening, that she felt the glimmer of hope those babies had given her—only then that everything in her world was, all at once, as she wished it could be. She was still in bed when Paul got home from work himself, and she was still there two days later. She could hear the faint murmured sound of footsteps on the hardwood, felt him sitting next to her on the bed, waiting, then getting up to leave again, leaving her to fall back into a merciful nothingness. She began to dread consciousness, the resurfacing memories of what happened to Boomer, to her babies, the knowledge that what happened to them was happening everywhere, and she was powerless to stop it, even to help.

Paul didn't seem to know what to do. She knew her behavior was not in the unwritten contract couples sign when moving in together. For better or for worse: it's all abstract until your life turns to worse. He pleaded, then scolded, perhaps thinking this would galvanize her into action, into anything. But nothing he did gave her either inspiration or solace. He was in tourism, not rescue. She convinced herself he didn't understand, that he cared only about the animals as props for his work.

She wanted to weep, to scream. Yet she couldn't move; she feared something within her would break, or explode. The ache in her chest spread upward and enveloped her entire head. When Paul brought her aspirin, she shook four tablets into her hand, then dry-swallowed each one. She fell back to sleep with bitterness on her tongue.

On the fifth day, Paul called her sister in Port Arthur and asked her to come.

It's all a blur to her now, but she was vaguely aware of being checked into the Psychiatric Intensive Care Unit at Royal Hobart Hospital, given an IV and medication. She remembers the concerned faces of her sister, Paul, a handful of colleagues and friends, and the expressionless faces of doctors, but very few other details surfaced through the fog, until the afternoon that Matt showed up and they walked through the garden in silence. It helped to be with her colleague, with someone who truly understood. She looked up at a pair of cockatoos in the trees, in the middle of some riotous squabble. Matt stopped and looked at her. *You have to find a way to separate yourself from the death*, he said. *Or it will eat you up and you'll end up like Boomer.*

How do you do it? she'd asked. *What's your secret?*

Secret? She thought she saw a shadow of something in his eyes before he turned away. *If you find it, be sure you tell me.*

It was another two months, with antidepressants and twice-weekly therapy, before she began to feel as though she could cope with a world so cruel, that she could find a place for herself in it again. That she could accept her own helplessness, tolerate the notion that she could not fix everything, that some things would never be fixable. Including herself.

She couldn't go back to her work at the sanctuary—her therapist advised against returning too soon anyhow—but she wanted to stay close to nature; she didn't know any other way to be. So she worked on finding something new, to remain part of the same world but in a positive way, a way that wouldn't knock her off her feet again. Her education and experience as a naturalist made her overqualified for this job as a guide, and her lack of guiding experience made her underqualified—something in the end that was easy to overcome, her employers thought. She'd told them only that she'd decided to take a break from research and rescue; none of them knew that she was still weaning herself off high doses of psychiatric drugs.

And if she ever had any doubts about her abilities, the antidepressants masked them; they masked everything. Paul didn't like it—*You're not you*, he said; *you're not the woman I used to know*—but this was exactly what she depended on. She could no longer be the woman she was, the one who knew how little hope was left for the devils, for so many animals, for the planet itself. She needed to be a woman who knew this only in some vague and faraway place in her mind, and who no longer cared too deeply. Who could look the other way. Who could pretend it wasn't happening. It was the only way she could get up in the morning and live like a normal person.

The voices on the deck seem louder, closer, and when Kerry forces her mind back to the present, she realizes the rain has picked up again—they are preparing to move the party inside.

She looks down at the counter and sees that she has prepared nearly the entire meal without realizing it, as if hypnotized. This both reassures her and terrifies her, that she is capable of this—of doing what she needs to do, of so cleanly separating her mind from her body, of living without even being aware of the moments ticking by.

Then it occurs to her that maybe this is what Matt was talking about. Maybe this is what progress looks like.

CHAPTER 9

BROOKE

The light mist that has been sprinkling off and on for the past hour quickens suddenly, and by the time they stand up and begin to gather the glasses, bottles, and plates, the rain is pelting them like hail. No one seems to mind; they step inside the tent, which is warm and fragrant with Kerry's cooking, laughing as they shake out their dripping hair and clothes.

"Is there anything left on the deck?" Charlotte asks as she deposits a handful of wine and beer bottles on a short table adjacent to the counter.

Malcolm laughs. "You sound like a Kiwi," he says, affectionately, putting his arm around her.

Brooke glances at Jane, whose mouth is set in a straight, unamused line, and then turns to Malcolm. "What do you mean?" she asks. Anything to deflect Jane's attention from her lover's arm around his wife's shoulders.

Charlotte rolls her eyes, making Brooke wonder whether she may one day need corrective surgery—it's such a constant action following just about everything her husband says, and she can't quite discern whether it's more mocking or affectionate. "Don't mind him," she says. "He's being rude, making fun of New Zealand accents."

Margaret is smiling. "It's true, though," she says. "When a Kiwi says 'deck,' it sounds like 'dick.' And it's quite humorous in some contexts, you have to admit."

"I've decided to extend my deck," Malcolm says.

"I had a party last night on my deck," Margaret adds.

Brooke can't help but laugh along with the others. "That is pretty funny," she says, with another nervous look at Jane, who is gazing at Malcolm with an expression Brooke knows all too well.

"I have a client," Jane says, "who spends a lot of time on my deck." Her face breaks into an innocent smile that only Brooke knows is dangerous. "She can't get enough of my deck."

Jane turns to Malcolm. "You're right. It's hilarious."

Now it's Malcolm's lips that flatten, his smile disappearing, and there's a moment of awkward silence before Kerry says, "Okay, guys, come sit down. Dinner is served."

Relieved to have the strange quiet broken, the group all but rushes toward the table, and Brooke notices for the first time that the tent's warm glow comes from lit candles on the long wooden table.

Kerry is putting the last plate down at the head of the table, placing a napkin across the plate. Brooke pulls out the chair next to it, but Kerry touches her arm. "Bryan needs to sit here," she says, "so he can help me serve. Just move down one, if you don't mind."

She does, sitting next to Jane, who is directly across from Malcolm. Jane stares directly at him as he tries to avoid her eyes. Bryan puts four more bottles of wine on the table, two whites, two reds—a shiraz and a chardonnay, both from mainland Tasmania. Brooke fills her glass, then hands the shiraz bottle to Jane.

"Tonight's menu," Kerry says, "begins with white bean pâté on fresh bread or rice crackers." She and Bryan go around the table placing small plates in front of each guest.

Brooke spreads some of the creamy pâté on a slice of warmed, crusty bread and takes a bite; it's thick and garlicky and delicious. She feels a pleasant buzz in her head from the wine, and as she savors these first bites of food she lets the sound of the rain, now heavy, relax her.

"So, Malcolm," Jane says.

Brooke turns her head sharply toward Jane. She relaxed a moment too soon.

Malcolm raises his head in response.

"I have this overwhelming feeling we've met before."

Brooke feels her lungs freeze. Another awkward silence settles over the group.

"If you've happened to turn on the telly since you've arrived," Charlotte says, "then you probably saw him there."

"Oh, right." Jane snaps her fingers. "That reality show."

"Not very real," Ian chimes in. "It's all scripted, isn't it?"

Malcolm nods, focusing very closely on spreading pâté on a piece of bread.

"What do you do in the States, Jane?" asks Charlotte.

"I'm an actress."

"Oh, you and Brooke both, then," says Charlotte. "Did you hear that, Malcolm?"

"Yes."

"He hires talent for lots of the production companies in Australia," Charlotte adds.

"Is that right?" Jane says.

"Well, I'm a former actress, really," Brooke says.

"Oh, don't be modest," Jane says, then turns back to Charlotte. "We used to perform in New York together."

"If you mean performing in front of a mirror." Brooke gives a nervous laugh. Jane is up to something, but she doesn't yet know what.

"In front of other audiences, too," Jane says. "Way, way off-Broadway, you might say. We performed what we called *Lifetime dramedies.*"

"Which are?" Margaret asks, eyebrows raised.

"Lifetime is a TV network in the States," Brooke says. "Kind of soap-opera stuff—catfights, obsessions, deadly love affairs, you name it."

"We spent the better part of our college years watching Lifetime movies," Jane adds. "We knew some of them by heart and could act out entire scenes."

"There was a bar in the East Village," Brooke says, feeling apologetic about Jane's embarrassing tangent into their silly hobby. "They had karaoke night, stand-up night, and we got known for Lifetime Night."

"So many good films," Jane says, as if fondly reminiscing about childhood summers. "*Stalked by My Doctor. The Psycho She Met Online. Dirty Teacher.*"

Margaret bursts out laughing at the same time Bryan repeats, through a mouthful of pâté, "*Dirty Teacher?*"

"That was a fun one," Brooke says, quickly, as if by talking she can prevent Jane from doing whatever it is Jane plans on doing. "Jane played the dirty teacher, and I played the high school girl whose boyfriend had an affair with her."

"Who *writes* this stuff?" asks Charlotte. "Even my books aren't this melodramatic."

"Sometimes we made it up," Jane says. "If we couldn't remember all the dialogue, we'd just come up with our own lines." Jane turns to Brooke. "How about it? A scene from *Stalked by My Lover*?"

"Now?" Brooke wants to put a stop to it, even as she feels a tingle of anticipation, the lovely, exhilarating jolt through her veins that she used to feel just before going onstage.

"Give it a burl," Ian says. "A bit of dinner theater."

"Yeah, have a go," Bryan says. "Though if you're taking requests, I vote for *Dirty—*"

"Bryan," Kerry interrupts. "Why don't you begin serving the risotto." As he gets up, she turns to them and says, "For our main course, we have mushroom risotto, with optional scallops, and a mixed vegetable salad with . . ."

As Kerry recites the menu, Brooke whispers to Jane, "What are you doing?"

"Having fun. Come on, it's just like *Hamlet*. 'The play's the thing,' remember?"

"But I've never even heard of *Stalked by My Lover*. Did you make it up?"

"Just follow my lead."

Before Brooke can protest any further, Jane turns back to the table and says, "Brooke will be playing the role of high-powered business executive Jack Roloff, who is happily married with a wife and three children. I will be playing the role of Simone, the flight attendant Jack had a wild layover with one stormy night in Denver."

So, this is what Jane was heading toward all along.

Bryan places a plate of beautiful, steaming risotto in front of her, and Brooke stares at it. Part of her wants to pick up her fork and eat in peace; another part of her wants to inhabit Jane's creation, Jack Roloff, to inhabit the role of a character in a doomed marriage. She's halfway there already, art imitating life.

"The scene is a restaurant," Brooke adds. This way, she may be able to eat a few bites of dinner.

Jane stands up as if to better address their audience. Dramatically, she unfurls her green scarf from around her hair and loops it around her neck, as if by doing this she is getting into character. "Simone has shown up at a restaurant where Jack is having dinner with his wife. When the wife gets up to go to the ladies' room, Simone sits down at his table."

Brooke pretends to loosen a tie around her neck as she takes a drink of wine, then a bite of risotto. Jane pulls out her chair, sits down, then pulls it in again in an exaggerated motion.

Brooke looks up and adopts a look of surprise, then dawning horror. "Simone," she whispers, looking around. "What are you doing here?"

"You won't answer my calls, my texts. What am I supposed to do?"

Brooke glances at the tent doorway. "You need to leave."

"Oh, Jack." Jane leans forward. "I've been watching you all night. You don't love her. It's so obvious. I know you've been thinking of me the whole time."

Brooke pushes her chair back. "No. This isn't going to happen between us. Not tonight, not ever again."

"You promised me you'd leave your wife."

"It's not that easy."

"It's as easy as you want it to be. You love me. Not her."

"Don't get hysterical."

"I'm tired of waiting for you to make up your mind."

"What are you saying, Simone?"

"I'm saying you had better tell her. Or—"

"Or what?"

"Maybe I'll tell her myself."

Brooke feels a spike of adrenaline akin to stage fright as she resists the urge to look at Malcolm, and she wonders how far Jane plans to take this little performance. But she stays in character—what choice does she have? And does she dare admit, even to herself, that this is a little bit fun?—and clears her throat, looking again toward the tent opening, the fictional ladies' room. "You can't do that, Simone."

"You're in no position to tell me what I can and cannot do."

"Is that a threat?"

"It's just a fact."

Brooke stands up, half acting, half not, as she realizes this moment needs to end before it goes too far. "You need to leave. Now. She'll be back any second."

Jane laughs, a high, manic chuckle Brooke remembers from the nights they drunk-performed in the Village.

"I'm not afraid of her," Jane says. "And, since I'm having your baby, she'll find out about us eventually."

"What?" The surprise in Brooke's response is real—this is a twist she doesn't expect. And she has no idea if Jane's line is fact or fiction.

Jane doesn't help matters by not feeding her another line; she just sits there, a smug smile on her face. Is she a better actor than Brooke remembers—or is she really pregnant?

Brooke stutters out her next line. "You're—you're *pregnant*?"

"Maybe." Jane smirks.

"Don't *maybe* me," says Brooke, the irritation in her voice completely authentic.

Jane looks around before leaning in and hissing out her next words. "Yes, I'm pregnant. That time in your office, two months ago? When I assured you I was protected? I lied."

"You bitch." Brooke picks up the butter knife from her place setting.

Jane laughs again. "You're going to kill me?"

"I'll do anything to protect my family." Brooke raises the butter knife.

"You can't kill me, Jack. And even if you do, I'll haunt you. I'll—"

As she hovers over Jane, Brooke hears a violent coughing from across the table. She looks over to see Malcolm hunched over his plate, Charlotte's hand on his upper back. "Are you all right, darling?" she asks.

He nods. "Fine. I seem to have swallowed wrong. Sorry."

"Don't let us interrupt," Charlotte says.

"We're done anyway," Brooke says. "Unless you really want to see me dismember Jane with this butter knife."

Ian laughs, then begins to applaud. "Well done," he says.

"I'm just drunk enough to see how this might be marginally entertaining at a bar in the States," Margaret says. "Is American television really this absurd?"

Kerry stands up and motions to Bryan to clear the plates. "The evening's entertainment will be followed by a quinoa chocolate pudding for dessert. Anyone fancy a tea or coffee?"

Malcolm stands up. "I've eaten way too much already," he says. "Better turn in and get ready for tomorrow."

"I'll come, too," Charlotte says.

Bryan places bowls of pudding in front of Brooke and Jane. "Bravo," he says. "You two should take this on the road—tour Oz and make a go of it."

"You think?" Jane grins.

"Better than that reality show rubbish." He stops and looks over at Ian.

"You can't offend me on that one, mate," Ian says. "I think even Malcolm knows it's shite. The money's what he likes."

Jane stands and stretches. "I'm off to bed, too," she says. "Exhausted."

Brooke's tired, too, but she isn't leaving until she's finished every bite of her pudding. "I won't be far behind."

Jane leans down and kisses her cheek. "That was fun. Like old times."

Brooke laughs. "I guess."

"Love you, B."

"Love you, too." Brooke looks at her, wanting to ask about the pregnancy line and whether it was all just for show, so curious that she considers giving up the pudding and following Jane to the tent, but Jane is already halfway out the door, hips swaying in that way she walks when she's happy and confident, and Brooke simply watches her go.

The conversation turns to a discussion of Australian television, and when Brooke finishes her pudding, she takes her coffee to the mouth of the tent, peering into the darkness. The rain is still falling steadily, if not quite as heavily as earlier, and she steps outside, leaning her head back to soak it in—Tasmanian rain, cold and sweet, the air so clean and pure. She breathes deeply and lets herself relax.

When she turns back toward the tent, Bryan is there. "More coffee?" he asks.

"No, thanks. I might take a shower though. Can you get me some hot water?"

"Sure. I'll meet you over by the showers."

Brooke goes to the tent to fetch her camp towel and a change of clothes. She tries to be quiet, so she doesn't wake Jane, but when her headlamp accidentally flashes across Jane's bed, she stops, then shines the light directly on it. No Jane.

Jane's pack is there, leaning up against the foot of the bed, and Brooke shines the light all around, wondering where she could be in this dark, this rain. Maybe she went to one of the toilets, or to the little washroom to brush her teeth.

Brooke digs her towel out of her pack but decides to leave the clothes since they'd only get wet. She hurries over to the showers. There's no sign of Bryan yet; he's probably still warming the water, which won't stay warm for long in this cold. She begins to undress quickly, so she can get under the water as soon as he brings it and run back to her tent before freezing again.

She doesn't realize until her clothes are in a wet pile on the wooden planks at her feet that her camp towel barely covers her. In fact, it actually doesn't cover her—she needs to choose whether to leave exposed several inches up top or down below.

She's still deciding when Bryan shows up with a steaming plastic bucket. "Ready?" he asks.

"Yes, thank you." She steps back so he can lower the cylinder and fill it. Then he hoists it up again and tests the lever that starts the water flow.

"Anything else you need?" She sees him discovering her skimpy towel, and she feels a sudden rush of desire—a sensation she hasn't felt in years, and it suffuses her whole body, even as she shivers in the cold air, that adrenaline spike again, this time a completely different sensation, a completely welcome one. Bryan's tousled hair. That accent. The sense of possibility.

The wine still swims deliciously through her veins, erasing her inhibitions. She takes a step toward him. "As a matter of fact, there is something more I need."

Warm bodies in cold air. Hot water mingling with icy rain. The wind whisking through Bryan's tent above and around them.

CHAPTER 10

KERRY

She is with her, walking alongside her, watching her follow her wet nose, black fur shining, ears glowing red with blood, a sliver of boomerang visible in the moonlight. She stops and raises her head, detecting a new scent, foreign yet familiar. And now she is running toward it, through fern and flax, manic in her pursuit of an odor that can mean only one thing. And now Kerry is looking down on her as she arrives at the kill, no longer alone. Others have gathered around the carrion, and a tug-of-war ensues, the growling and whining, voices rising as limbs and fur and flesh and tendon and bone of what was formerly a wallaby are fought over and devoured.

Another shriek rises up, and she jolts awake in the dark. She takes a few deep breaths. It was such a vivid dream, so real—especially the eerie screams of the devils. Sometimes their cries sound almost human.

She blinks into the darkness, her heartbeat rivaling the pounding of rain on the tent. She is still half in her dream, and she wants to return to it, to those otherworldly sounds that most people find terrifying but that she loves more than almost anything—the sounds of healthy animals, the sounds of survival. A serenade, a lullaby.

Paul accused her once, near the end, of loving the devils more than she loved him. She said it wasn't true, but he knew she was lying.

She lies still, wondering if perhaps the sounds came from the woods, filtering past her ears, past her subconscious, into her dreams. She knows that they are surrounded by healthy, active devils, even if they never see them.

She sits up in bed. Perhaps this is what she needs: to go out, even in this rain, to find them, to bear witness. If she can glimpse even one devil living free of that ghastly disease, maybe she, too, might be cured. She has absorbed their sickness, and it feels as though it's taking over her own body, her entire brain.

Suddenly she freezes in place, angling her head.

A rustling sound, very close to her tent.

Quickly, hopefully, she slides out of bed and pulls on her hiking pants, boots, rain jacket. She grabs her hat and torch and slips out of the tent as quietly as she can.

The rain falls persistently, straight down; the wind has eased a bit. Still, she steps slowly and carefully, and she doesn't turn on the torch, not just yet, so she doesn't scare the creature, or perhaps even creatures—she can't tell yet whether she'll be fortunate enough to see more than one devil. She can still hear the rustling sound, now about fifty meters away, past the toilets. She follows the raised wooden path from her tent across the deck and past the guest tents until she reaches a dirt path, nearly hidden by the bracken fern.

She stops and waits. Even here, on the outskirts of camp, she can hear snoring emanating from Bryan's tent, and she shakes her head. How he sleeps at all, let alone so well, is beyond her—not only did he leave dinner prep entirely to her, he disappeared afterwards, in the middle of cleanup. He claimed someone wanted water for a shower—why, in this rain, anyone felt the need to have more water pouring down on them seemed dubious to her—and then left with a bucket of hot water, never to return.

A part of her thought it was better this way; he'd have mucked something up anyway. The sooner she accepted her position as a solo guide, the easier it would be for both of them. So she washed and dried the dishes, silverware, pots and pans. She cleaned the table, stove, and counters, and mopped the floor. She sliced up fruit for breakfast and finally zipped the tent closed. By then it was nearly one in the morning, and the camp was quiet and still.

Now, she hears another sound, this one closer, coming from just past the bend in the trail ahead. She turns on her torch, dimming the bright light with the dark sleeve of her fleece sweater, as she walks ahead nimbly, as stealthily as she can. Normally devils lie low in the rain, so she'll be surprised to actually see one, but the noise, especially at this time of night, indicates something quicker and more active than a wombat or echidna, the only other suspects. She feels her excitement rising at the idea of coming face-to-face at last with a healthy devil. She has not seen an unscarred devil face in years. Just one look, that's all she needs, and this job, her worthless fellow guide, this crap weather—it will all be worth it.

The sound continues, louder, a scuffling noise, almost like feet shuffling through leaves.

She steps past the tree where the trail turns and sees a large figure, a man, coming in her direction. She rips the fleece off her torch and blasts him with the light. He puts a hand over his eyes, and in that instant, she recognizes him.

"Ian?"

She lowers the torch and studies him. He's dressed in rain gear, and what she supposes is his camera is in his other hand; it's obscured, covered with layers of rainproof material. Ian lowers his hand from his face and seems, for once, at a loss for words.

"Ian?" she says again. Something about his quietness, his very presence out here, sends a sudden chill through her body. "What are you doing out here?"

"The usual," he says with a laugh—an odd, nervous laugh, she thinks—holding up his camera. "Looking for birds."

"At this time of night? In the rain?"

"I'm hoping to glimpse the masked owl."

"Did you hear one?" she asks. Masked owls have been sighted on Marbury, but they're endangered and quite rare. She is certain she'd have recognized the sound if there was one nearby—a distinctive, hissing screech.

"No," he admits. "I was just hoping to get lucky."

"You'd be right lucky to see one in this kind of weather," she says, and she can't help but look overhead, shining her torch, scanning for a hollow that would indicate a nest. She wouldn't mind seeing one herself; the owls are beautiful, their heart-shaped faces rimmed with black.

"I suppose I should get out of the rain," Ian says.

"Sounds like a good idea."

"Good night."

She watches him amble back to camp. While the rain has let up a bit, Ian's raingear is soaked, as if he's been out for a while—thirty minutes, an hour, maybe more.

Something tells her it's not the birds that drew him out here, but she's not really sure what else it could be. Maybe, like her, he was simply hopeful. He's a city dweller, after all, and she's seen how the city folks come alive when they first land here, in the rare place free of cars and the electrical buzz of modern life. The euphoria of finding yourself alone with nature can make you do some pretty crazy things.

A gust of wind whisks past, and the rain begins to hit her sideways. She hurries back to her tent. Inside, she strips off her wet clothes and hangs them up, hoping they'll dry at least somewhat before her day begins, in just a couple more hours.

She puts on dry fleece and leggings and climbs into her sleeping bag. She is nearly asleep when she hears them—a gathering chorus of grunts and growls, diabolically wild.

It's like music. A symphony.

She's tempted to put on her wet clothes again and try to find them, but she stays where she is; she doesn't want to scare them off. Instead, she tries to count them by their voices—three, four, five? Even with her years of experience, it's hard to tell.

She closes her eyes, the sounds soothing to her ears, and she remembers a weekend in Sydney with Paul, a night at the Opera House, letting the music wash over her. It was years ago, a time when they were happy, and in this moment she feels a fraction of that bliss return to her—a moment of peace, of being immersed in beautiful sound.

"Good night, guys," she whispers, and as their vicious cries reach her through the dark, it feels as though they're answering her back.

CHAPTER 11

BROOKE

When she wakes, she keeps her eyes closed so she can relive it. She sees light at the edge of her eyelids, but she wants to linger in last night for just a few minutes longer. Remembering.

How they used both of the bunks in Bryan's tent. How she struggled to stay silent, grateful for the occasional crack of thunder overhead. No words, just lips to body, hands to hips, the salty taste of his chest, the feel of his thick blond hair between her fingers.

Afterwards, spent, they lay together on top of his sleeping bag, damp with sweat, impervious to the temperature outside. Whatever dropping degrees Celsius or Fahrenheit it was by then, all Brooke felt was heat. It was one of the best nights of sex she could remember.

She opens her eyes and listens—it's still quiet, still early. She'd slept well after finally sneaking back into her tent, during one of the lighter periods of rain. To avoid waking Jane—she wasn't ready to answer questions—she'd turned off her headlamp before climbing carefully into her sleeping bag, and fortunately it had worked—Jane didn't stir as Brooke zipped up her sleeping bag and drifted to sleep.

She still isn't ready to talk about it, Brooke realizes, closing her eyes again without moving. Maybe when Jane wakes, she'll keep pretending to be asleep.

She and Jane never had secrets, least of all about sex. And Brooke knows the minute Jane sees her face, she'll know everything. She'll know Brooke got laid, she'll know it was Bryan, and she'll want all the juicy details. Details that used to be so much fun to discuss and dissect over weekend brunches.

That all changed when Brooke became serious about William. The first few times they'd slept together, she freely offered details—mostly about certain skills he possessed, so finely tuned it was as if he'd researched and studied them as he did everything else—but her openness changed quickly, and Brooke knew it was one of the reasons Jane didn't like him. After all, because of William, Brooke had shut her best friend out of one of their favorite activities: dishing about their sex lives.

Yet she couldn't tell Jane the details that had become so precious to her, those intimate nights with the man she was falling in love with. For one, she was afraid Jane would make fun of her, or of both of them. Sex had always been something they never took too seriously, at least emotionally speaking. But for Brooke, falling for William had a lot to do with how they were in bed together—not only was the sex good from a purely objective standpoint, but it was the one time he opened up, the one time he lost his reserve. In bed, he was fully present; he saw her and felt her and touched her. It made her wish he were more like that all the time, and she convinced herself he would be, in time.

Bryan, of course, is only a fling, but it's the wrong time and wrong place—not for her but for Jane. This trip, in Jane's mind, is supposed to be about winning over her lover, not watching Brooke find one.

She could lie. She could say that she was simply up late talking with Bryan, unloading about her soon-to-be ex-husband. It would be better if Jane thought she, too, was nursing her wounds rather than having hot midnight rainstorm sex with a younger man.

But Jane would see right through her; she always had. And given Jane's already strange mood, Brooke doesn't want to go there. Not that she has a choice.

She sighs and opens her eyes, then turns her head toward Jane's bed.

It takes her a second to realize that maybe she does have a choice, after all.

Jane's bed is empty.

Brooke sits up and looks around. Jane's pack is where she remembers seeing it last night, propped up against Jane's bunk. The sleeping bag looks untouched, as if Jane never slept in it, or got up early and straightened it as Brooke slept.

Had Jane even been here last night when she snuck in?

Brooke tries to remember. It was pitch-black, and she couldn't see a thing; it was raining lightly, just enough to obscure the smallest of sounds, like Jane's breathing. She honestly can't say whether or not Jane was here when she returned.

Maybe their little Lifetime skit over dinner had an effect on Malcolm, and Jane had been having her own night of passion elsewhere.

Or maybe she just got up early and went to breakfast.

Brooke reaches into her pack for her water bottle and the aspirin and swallows two. She can't remember when she'd last had so much to drink. William wasn't much of a drinker; they enjoyed a good bottle of wine every now and then, but not to excess, like last night. Her last wild, drunken night out had probably been with Jane, ages ago.

Feeling a sudden chill, Brooke retreats inside her sleeping bag. She hears a man's laugh coming from the main tent—it sounds like Ian. He strikes her as the early bird type. And now that she thinks of it, Jane sometimes had the occasional manic morning, getting up at first light and cleaning the apartment, or getting up to go for a run. Brooke would awaken to Jane's annoying cheeriness—*About time! You're wasting the whole day!*—but at least there was always fresh coffee made. She did wish, on those occasions, that Jane herself had switched to decaf.

Shivering as she leaves behind the cocoon of her sleeping bag, she gets dressed, and as she unzips the tent, a cold blast of wind nearly rips it from her hands. The rain has slowed, but the winds are fierce, and the temperature has dropped. She feels a throb in her head and wishes they didn't have a long day of hiking ahead.

She heads first for the toilets. Out of the corner of her eye, she sees that someone had just entered one of them, so she tries the door to the other one. It's locked.

She hears no movement from within, and suddenly she wonders whether Jane had been as drunk as she was, whether she could've passed out in there. It certainly wouldn't be the first time she found Jane the next morning in front of a toilet.

"Jane?" she asks. When she's met with silence, she repeats her name, then knocks.

The door swings open to reveal Margaret's bemused face. "Do I look like Jane?"

"Sorry, I was—I thought she was in here."

"Rehearsing for another brilliant night of theater?"

"No." Brooke watches Margaret walk away.

After using the composting toilet and the makeshift sink with its trickle of water, she dodges rain as she hurries to the main tent. It seems darker outside than when she woke up not half an hour ago.

Inside the tent, the two couples and Bryan are seated at the table, with Kerry standing at the stove.

"Morning," Ian says. "Where's your fellow thespian?"

"I thought she'd be here," Brooke says. "Has anyone seen her this morning?"

"Maybe she went to the beach," Malcolm says without looking up from his coffee.

"In this ungodly rain?" Charlotte asks.

"I quite fancy hiking in the rain," Kerry says, putting a tray with thick slices of toasted bread on the table.

"I'm glad someone does," Charlotte says. "You can leave me behind."

"I'm afraid we can't," Kerry says. "We have nearly ten kilometers to our next camp."

"That's nothing," Margaret says.

"Speak for yourself, Maggie," Charlotte says with a laugh.

"I realize the weather is not ideal," Kerry says. "But much of the trail is inland, so the trees will give us good coverage."

Kerry gestures to Brooke to take a seat at the table. "We've got eggs if you want them, fruit and toast are on the table, and there's cereal over there, so just help yourself."

Brooke looks at the others, occupied with their breakfasts, and feels a prickly sensation run down her back. Malcolm still hasn't made eye contact with her. "Just some coffee for me," she says.

Charlotte looks up. "Are you that worried? I'm sure she'll turn up eventually."

"Let's not hold our breath," Margaret says under hers.

"Excuse me?" Brooke says.

"Is everyone chockers already?" Kerry looks over the empty plates as she sits down. "There's plenty more." She says quietly to Brooke, "You really do need to eat. We've got a long day ahead."

"I'm just a bit distracted, that's all."

"Is Jane an early riser?" Kerry asks.

"Sometimes."

"I reckon she got herself some coffee and went for a walk," Kerry says. "Some of the paths around here are so well covered you'd hardly get wet if you had a rain jacket on."

Kerry's voice is so reassuring that Brooke lets out a sigh and relaxes a bit. Kerry is probably right—of course Jane got up early; everything that happened with Malcolm yesterday probably put her in one of her manic states. She may not have slept much at all.

Brooke mindlessly nibbles at a piece of toast, vaguely listening as others begin talking, the sounds of a normal morning floating past her ears, even though her mind is still focused on the empty seat next to her.

CHAPTER 12

KERRY

From the corner of the dining tent where she's standing with Brooke, Kerry looks toward the others, still at the table with second and third cups of coffee, beginning to glance in their direction as Brooke whispers to her about Jane with barely concealed panic.

Kerry has been nodding reassuringly even though she doesn't feel the slightest bit confident. She's starting to wonder whether she'll ever have anything but shit luck as a wilderness guide. On her first trip, she gets her entire group lost. Her partner gets bitten by a tiger snake. Then she ends up with a bogan more interested in rooting his guests than guiding them.

And now this. A missing person.

Perhaps her idea of a career change would have been better left an unformulated, unrealized idea, instead of metastasizing into a never-ending series of mistakes and misadventures—now punctuated by a missing woman. A woman who shouldn't be missing because they haven't even gone anywhere yet. And where would someone disappear to in all this weather?

She is not at all surprised that Bryan has played a role in this latest disaster. If Brooke hadn't been in his tent all night, maybe she'd know where her friend is instead of cornering Kerry while she's trying to do the washing up.

But Kerry listens as Brooke tells her everything. That she spent the night with Bryan and didn't see Jane when she snuck back into their tent. That Jane wasn't there in the morning, that it looked as though Jane never slept in her tent at all. That Jane is now nowhere to be found.

"I checked the tent again, the toilets, the showers, the washroom," Brooke says breathlessly. "I even went down to the beach. I can't find her anywhere."

Brooke's hair is wet from the rain and plastered to her face, pinched with worry.

"Okay," Kerry says, infusing her voice with a confidence she doesn't feel. "When did you last see her, exactly?"

"Last night. Right here."

"So you didn't see her in your tent after dinner?"

Brooke shakes her head. "I figured she was brushing her teeth. I went to have a shower, and then—I didn't get back until late. I thought she was asleep, and I didn't want to wake her."

"Okay," Kerry says again. "Look, I'm sure she's right and there's no need to worry. You have a seat and get yourself some more coffee, and I'll take a crack at finding her, okay? It's easy to get turned around out here. I'm sure she just went out for a walk and ended up going a bit farther than she expected."

Brooke nods reluctantly, and Kerry taps Bryan on the shoulder and points to the sink, its murky water jammed with dirty dishes. Then she retrieves her rain jacket from her tent and sets out into the steadily falling rain. She doesn't mind having a slow start this morning; no one seems eager to set out walking in this weather, and maybe in time the rain will slow a bit.

First she circles the dining tent, with futile glances down for footprints; the ground is all soaked fern and puddles. The voices inside seep through the canvas in the high tones of questions, probably asking Brooke about Jane. Though she's only known the guests for twenty-four hours, Kerry can guess their reactions to the news. Margaret will be annoyed at having to wait; Charlotte will be relieved not to rush out into the rain. Ian and Malcolm probably don't care either way, though Kerry senses that Ian has a wee crush on Jane and that Malcolm, for some reason, doesn't like her very much.

Jane herself is one of those guests who can be fun but more high-maintenance than they're worth. Their "Lifetime dramedy" of the night before was welcome entertainment; it took the pressure off Kerry to do all the talking. But guests like Jane, the ones who love to be the center of attention, don't care who waits for them and for how long. They don't realize the trip is not planned around them and their whims.

After searching all of the common areas and finding them empty, Kerry goes from tent to tent, trying to unzip the front flaps as quietly as she can. She hates to think Jane might be in another couple's tent, but she has to check everywhere—and who knows? She could be a kleptomaniac or just really nosy. Meg had warned her, during that first trip, *Be ready for anything. People are odder than you can imagine.* She'd said it with a laugh, and Kerry had laughed, too, but now she's failing to find the humor in the oddness that is Jane. Where is she?

She gets to the last tent, Jane and Brooke's. Brooke had left in a hurry, not zipping it closed, and the flaps sway violently in the wind. Kerry steps inside, using her torch to illuminate the room. Everything here looks like all of the other tents: two backpacks, two sleeping bags, shoes, hats, rain jackets. Nothing out of the ordinary at all.

She's tempted to open Jane's backpack and have a quick look, just to see if there might be a clue inside as to where she's gone—but she knows they're not quite there yet. If Jane indeed has only taken a long walk and returns to see one of the guides rummaging through her rucksack—well, that's not good for business, or for her future as a guide.

Kerry exits back into the rain, pulling her hood down tight over her head. The winds are blowing the rain nearly horizontal now; she puts an arm up in front of her to keep the stinging drops from hitting her in the face.

She looks right and left. If she turns left, she will return to the beach they landed on yesterday. If she turns right, she'll be headed into the woods, toward Haunted Bay.

Then it occurs to her: Jane could be trying to make a phone call. Americans live on their phones, and she remembers that one of the first things Jane asked in Triabunna was whether she'd get any cell coverage, mentioning she'd purchased a local SIM card at the airport.

Brooke said she'd checked the beach, but maybe she hadn't looked hard enough, or long enough, or in the right spot. Galvanized by her relief, Kerry jogs to the beach through jabs of rain, then climbs a steep berm that offers a panoramic view of the area, including the narrow strip of sand where there's a barely perceptible signal. She scans the full expanse of sand from south to north.

Nobody.

The winds on her back nudge her forward, and she has to lean against them. Just ahead, the waves are white-tipped and a sickly shade of green. She looks down, hoping for footprints. But the wind and the retreating tide have glazed the beach smooth.

When she finally turns from the water, she feels a force shove her from behind, and the next thing she knows, she's fallen face-first onto the rain-hardened sand. She pushes herself to her knees, brushes the sand off her needled face, and looks behind her. It felt like a person, like hands on her back—but it was only a hefty gust of wind. She closes her eyes against flying sand and, using her rain jacket to shield her face as best she can, she makes her way back toward camp.

She walks straight through camp without pausing, past Jane's tent, another twenty meters or so, until she is out of sight. The ground beneath her hiking boots is mucky and littered with eucalyptus leaves. She slows her pace by necessity, which gives her a chance to think. They are already an hour behind schedule, and the rain will slow them even more.

It's a small island, and there are only a few places Jane could've got off to. She's not at the beach, so Kerry can check that off the list. She could have taken the trail to Haunted Bay—a well-marked trail nearly impossible to lose yourself on. Kerry hopes this is what happened; worst case, Jane forces them to wait, but even if they set out after lunch they can make it to the next camp by dark if they skip the scheduled stops and breaks. And if Jane is even later than that, they'll spend another night here. Some guests won't like it; others may be glad not to hike in the rain. Either way, they'll blame Jane, not Kerry or the Marbury Island Track Co., which at this point is only a minor relief.

There's another possibility—a short trail that leads to nowhere, and this is what Kerry fears most, that Jane might've thought this was a trail she could follow for a stroll but instead had gotten lost. It would take a search party to find her, if this were the case—a search party they do not have, with time they do not have.

Reluctantly, Kerry begins moving forward until the trail disappears. By then the ferns close in, forming a knee-high canopy, so it's hard to see much on the ground. Kerry looks anyway, just in case Jane had come out this way and tripped and fallen.

A color catches her eye, a brighter green than the surrounding ferns, and she uses her foot to push the vegetation away. Her boot catches on the remnants of some sort of wispy material, something definitely not a plant.

She reaches down and picks it up, then drops it almost as quickly.

Whatever it is, it's bitten to shreds and spotted with black. Dirt, maybe?

Kneeling on the ground, she uses her hands to spread apart the ferns, to see what else is here. What she finds next nearly stops her heart in her chest.

A smartphone, or what is left of one. Its bright pink case is tattered and pierced. The screen is shattered, bits of electronics showing through like ribs.

Kerry takes a deep breath and looks around. Even as she feels the fast rush of blood pounding through her veins, she forces herself to remain calm as she methodically moves forward, pushing aside more plants to see what else is here.

Under another fern, she stops again: fabric, dark, spread across the muddied ground. She uses the toe of her boot to brush the fern aside and finds herself staring at the shredded remains of a black cotton shirt. She puts it all together—the green material: Jane's scarf. A phone. Now a shirt. What happened out here?

She picks up the shirt carefully, with the tips of two fingers, and she jumps to her feet when she sees what's underneath—slivers of white bone and gristle—and she barely manages to suppress the gasp that bursts from her throat.

She's standing in the middle of a crime scene.

And she thinks she knows exactly who the perpetrators are.

The sounds last night, the cries and growls that serenaded her to sleep. This was no dream. This was a pack of devils, six, seven strong, maybe more.

She looks down at the remains. The black substance she thought was dirt, she realizes now, is blood, and now she sees it everywhere, even as the rain dilutes it. If it were not for the clothing and phone, she might be able to believe these are the remains of an animal. But even if it weren't for these human artifacts, if the victim had been a roo or a wallaby, there would likely be nothing left at all. When Tasmanian devils descend upon a body, they rarely leave anything.

Unless it's something they normally do not ravage, like a human.

Kerry turns around, trying to listen over the sound of the rain, trying to see beyond the ferns and gum trees. But she knows she won't see the devils—they are long gone, sleeping off their feast.

She feels her breath quicken and tries not to panic as she attempts to piece together what might have happened. Devils are ferocious and mad with hunger, but she's never known a devil to attack a human. Ever.

But the devils are increasing in population on this island, competing for food. If they came across a dead or badly injured body, they would not hesitate. She thinks of the urban myth about a hiker out in the bush who gets pinned under a fallen tree. The next day the rescuers arrive to find only boots and pieces of leg.

But could something like this have actually occurred? It's true that devils will devour a carcass of any size—a sheep or cow. So why not a human?

Given the amount of wine she consumed, Jane was certainly pissed beyond belief last night. Could she have passed out drunk here among the fern, unable to defend herself?

Kerry stands motionless, her brain scattered and manic. Who to call first? Her boss, Nigel? No. Not yet. The police? Yes, probably, but they are on the mainland, and what could she tell them that would make sense?

Mark. He'll know what to do.

She high-steps her way back to camp and then races to the beach. She finds the sweet spot where she can access a weak signal, then fumbles with the phone in the rain and wind until she manages to successfully press Mark's number.

"Morning, Kerry." Mark's chipper voice comes across as if from another planet.

"We've got a problem."

"Yeah, I know. This storm is giving us all sorts of problems. The visitor center is flooded, the dorms—"

"No. Mark. I've got a problem up here. A—a dead body."

"A what?"

"A body. A guest. She's dead."

There is a long pause. "Did Meg put you up to this?"

"What? No, Mark, listen. I'm not bloody joking."

Then silence on the other end. "You're serious."

"Yes!" Kerry feels her voice rise on a note of hysteria. "I've got a dead woman here, and I haven't a damn clue what to do next."

"Who is it?" Mark's voice is instantly professional and calm, and Kerry takes a deep breath.

"One of the Americans. Jane Pearson. Her friend—well, it's a little unclear, they've been playing musical tents—but she thinks Jane could have gone missing as early as last night."

"What happened? A tree branch?"

"No. I didn't find the whole body, just—some remains." Kerry sighs and feels tears collecting at the back of her throat. "I can't believe I'm saying this, but—it looks like the devils got to her."

"The devils? That's not possible." She hears a waver of doubt in Mark's voice.

"She's gone, Mark. And her clothing is scattered all over the woods, torn to shreds, and blood. Oh, God. The blood is everywhere."

"Shit."

She hears crackling over the line, echoed by a splinter of lightning overhead. Instinctively, she ducks down.

"Mark? Can you hear me?"

"Yeah, I'm here." She can tell his mind is spinning, probably in the same endlessly hopeless loop as hers. Wondering how a creature that rarely kills anything larger than itself has somehow devoured a human being. Thinking of what a nightmare this will be for their guests, for Brooke, for Jane's family. Looking ahead to what might happen with the media, the government, the park, desperately hoping already that it won't destroy the work being done here, the pristine image of this island. Things like this are not supposed to happen here.

"What do I do?" Kerry asks.

"I need to get down there. I'll leave now."

"What about the police? Will you call them for me? I worry my connection won't last. I can barely hear you."

"I'll phone them straightaway."

"How fast can they get here?"

"Don't hold your breath."

"What do you mean? Won't they want to investigate?"

"Jetty's closed. Ferry's not running. No one can come and go in this storm."

She looks up at the waves—whitecaps as far as she can see. Of course; she should've known when she saw the sea's wildness before. They are trapped, completely cut off from the rest of the world.

"When's the storm passing?"

"What?" His voice is cutting out.

"The storm! How much longer?"

"This is just the beginning," he shouts back. "Just try and hang on. I'll be there soon."

"How soon?"

"Couple of hours, if I don't hit any washouts."

"What do I tell everyone here?"

"Just tell them I'm on my way." His voice suddenly sounds clearer. "To help with the search. Okay? One step at a time."

He's right. One step at a time. His rational words, the soothing balm of his voice, calm her down, and suddenly she wonders whether she's jumping to horrible conclusions far too soon. Mark is coming to help with the search because—because she didn't find anything, not really, now that she thinks about it. Some clothes, a phone. They look like Jane's things, but she realizes now how absurd this sounds. The devils consuming a human body? Mark must think she's insane.

"Mark, maybe I'm wrong. I hope I'm wrong. I mean, this has never happened before, has it?"

"Not since I've been on the island. Tourists get bit from time to time, but only the daft ones, dangling food and all, trying to get a photo."

"I must be wrong then." There's a void on the other end of the line. "Mark. Mark?"

The call has dropped. She holds her phone up for a signal, but the rain is coming down harder, so she pockets it and tries to even out her breathing. She has to remain levelheaded. *The guide sets the tone for the entire group*, Meg told her. She needs to be relaxed, in control, in charge.

She heads back to camp, completely soaked through. It doesn't matter. She'll change into dry clothes, make another pot of coffee. Tell the others that they're going to wait for the park ranger to come help with a search. One step at a time.

She allows herself, for a few moments, to imagine that Jane will waltz back into camp in her dramatic way, complaining that the devils stole her clothes and her phone. They will all have a good laugh about it, and she'll call Mark and invite him to dinner at their next camp.

Yet this island has a history of death, its terrain cluttered with bodies. The people of the Oyster Bay nation once lived here in peace, until they were removed from the island, every bit of their land stolen, pestered and pushed around until the last native died a meaningless death. And then the prisoners arrived, the English and Irish, sent from overseas to work the land or die trying. Who is she to think she will be spared one more death of so many?

She feels as if the dark clouds above have descended into her head, the blackness she spent months conquering again invading her thoughts, dissolving her hard-won optimism into negativity.

She forces a breath out of her lungs and looks up, toward the green tents of camp just ahead, rattling in the wind.

She hears Paul's voice in her head. *Being pessimistic is like waiting for a train you know will never come.* He was the positive one in the relationship; he thought he could bring her into step with his own worldview. It was one reason she chose guiding, in hopes of getting closer to that worldview. Paul, who himself ran a tour business, thriving with increasing tourism to Tasmania, would be gone for weeks at a time during high season, returning for a day, maybe two, when they would make love like teenagers and laugh at all of his stories.

But there was another side to tourism, and she'd grappled with it before taking this job. More tourists means more rental cars, more urban drivers from mainland Australia and other countries, drivers unaccustomed to the narrow roads and the tiny creatures who roam them after dark. Lumbering wombats and asphalt-black devils. Roos and wallabies who are attracted to the headlights. Even if she didn't ever look at a calendar, Kerry would know high tourist season by the number of dead and dying devils arriving at the sanctuary every day, some in cardboard boxes, others in plastic grocery bags. She often felt the place was little more than a rubbish dump, with her and the other staff and volunteers custodians of the dead and dying.

And now she has to hope what she saw in the ferns was a mirage, a misinterpretation, a mix of the wrong things in the wrong place. If the devils were involved in any harm to a human, great or small, they would be vilified by the media, even if today most people want them saved. All it takes is one incident to turn it all around. After all, too few people know what she knows— how maternal the devils are, how devoted to one another, how playful. The funny way they walk, with the hind legs slightly longer, giving them a stilted gait. How they sun themselves when awake and alone in the forests. How they roll in the dirt like dogs, then sit with their legs folded underneath. So wild and yet so familiar.

Just outside the dining tent, she stops. She can hear Margaret talking about her summit of K2. Malcolm's laughter. Charlotte's low voice. Everything sounds so normal, and she is about to shatter it with the announcement that Jane is still missing. And none of them will know that this is only the very least of what's happening.

ACT II

CHAPTER 13

BROOKE

Brooke watches Kerry as she stands, dripping wet and shivering, in front of the table in the dining tent, where they've all been waiting. Breakfast is long over, the coffee is gone; Ian has been back and forth to the tent's opening a half-dozen times, as if to check on whether it's stopped raining, and Margaret's twice gotten up and done a series of pre-hike stretches. When Kerry walked in, Margaret was the first to point out that it was almost eleven o'clock—two hours past the time they should've left for the next campsite. Almost lunchtime, Malcolm joked, to half-hearted laughter.

It's obvious, with Kerry standing before them, the water from her jacket puddling around her feet, that they won't be going anywhere.

"I'm afraid we'll need to change our plans for today," she says. It looks to Brooke as though she's struggling to keep her voice steady. Her face is very pale.

"Why?" asks Margaret, with a not-so-subtle glance in Brooke's direction, as if she's to blame.

"The park ranger is on his way," she says, "to help us look for Jane. She—she seems to have gotten lost, somehow, and we can't go on ahead until—until we find her."

"Lost?" Ian says incredulously. "Where is there to go?"

"I don't want to worry anyone," Kerry says, "and I—I hope we can continue on shortly. I just ask that you please bear with me. I don't have all the answers you want right now. We just need to be flexible for the moment."

"Fine by me," says Charlotte. "I wasn't keen on hiking in this weather anyway. As long as we don't run out of tea or wine."

"We've got plenty of both."

"Well, then," she says, tossing up her hands and smiling. "I have no problem with sitting and reading all day." She turns to Malcolm. "Be a love and run get me my book, will you?"

Brooke studies Malcolm's face as he rises from his chair. He shows no emotion whatsoever—no irritation, like Margaret and Ian; no relief, like Charlotte. He certainly doesn't seem worried about Jane. His expression looks a lot like Bryan's—as if this news is of no concern to him at all—but Malcolm's demeanor is even cooler.

Ian speaks up again. "Why can't Brooke stay with you or Bryan and wait while the rest of us go ahead?"

"That seems reasonable," Margaret agrees.

"We need to stay together as a group," Kerry says.

"Why should we all pay the price for her negligence?"

Brooke looks at Margaret and grinds her teeth together in the effort not to lash out at her. If the situation were reversed, if Jane were the one whose friend was being insulted, Margaret would have been read the riot act or perhaps even had a cup of hot coffee "accidentally" spilled into her lap. Jane wouldn't have let it go.

But Brooke isn't Jane. And Jane isn't here.

As Kerry explains that they all need to sit tight until the park ranger arrives, Brooke's eyes wander, as does her mind—back to last night, back to wondering where Jane could've gone off to in all this rain.

Then she straightens with a shock. Her eyes have settled on Kerry's feet, on her hiking shoes, which are stained dark. She first assumes it's water or mud, from walking in the rain, but Kerry's socks reveal otherwise; they are smudged with red, which, mixed with the rain, gives the impression that she'd walked through watercolors, splashing pinkish-red paint all over her shoes and socks.

Brooke forces her eyes upward again, to Kerry's face, noticing again its pallor, the tension gathered there, tightening her features.

"Are we just going to postpone this trip indefinitely then?" Ian asks.

"We can't wait here forever," Margaret adds. "What if she decided to go ahead to the next camp herself?"

"She wouldn't do that," Brooke snaps.

"If you know her so well, then you tell us," Margaret says. "Where is she?"

Kerry takes a step forward, raising her voice a notch. "Okay, guys, I know this is frustrating. Between the weather and other unforeseen circumstances, this trip is having its challenges. I'm asking you for your patience, and in the meantime I'll do all I can to get us back on track." She looks at her watch. "It's coming up on lunchtime. Until then, we have a wonderful lending library here, a lot of great books about the island. I'll put out some snacks, and the bar is officially open."

"Now we're talking," Bryan says.

"Bryan, you're the bartender, not the guest," Kerry says.

"Right."

Kerry takes Bryan aside and appears to be giving him instructions regarding food and beverages. A moment later, Malcolm walks in and places a book on the table in front of Charlotte, who sits back in her chair and folds her legs underneath her, as if settling in to read on any ordinary rainy afternoon. Bryan puts two bottles of wine on the table and begins to rummage through the cooler.

Brooke watches Kerry exit the tent and waits a few seconds before following. She's taking the wooden walkway toward the far edge of camp, and Brooke continues to follow, as quietly as she can, though she knows Kerry probably can't hear her footsteps over the rain.

When she reaches the end of the walkway, Kerry stops. Still several yards behind her, Brooke stops, too, watching as Kerry lowers her head and brings a hand to her face.

Suddenly a cockatoo screeches in the trees above, and Kerry raises her head, looking startled to see Brooke standing there. "What are you doing out here?"

"I'm worried about Jane." Brooke steps forward. "What are you not telling us?"

"Sorry?"

"I feel like you're hiding something." Now that she's face-to-face with Kerry, up close, she can tell something is most definitely very wrong. "What is it?"

"There's nothing I can tell you at the momen—"

"What's that on your shoes?"

Kerry looks down at her hiking boots, then closes her eyes. She doesn't raise her head, and her voice is so soft Brooke has to lean in to hear her. "I can't say anything."

"About Jane? What do you know?"

"Please understand, Brooke. I'm doing my best here."

"She's my oldest friend. We're traveling together. I need to know what's going on."

"I realize that." Kerry looks up at last. "But I'm responsible for this entire group, and I can't do anything that might cause panic."

"Do you think I'm the only one who has noticed those bloodstains on your feet? Even if I am, I won't be for long."

Kerry looks down again, staring at her boots and socks, as if she's weighing the possible responses to Brooke's question.

"We're all grown-ups here," Brooke says, though the panic welling inside makes her feel as vulnerable and needy as a child. "I don't care what you tell the others," she continues, "but I need to know. Have you seen Jane? Has she been hurt? What is going on?"

Kerry winces, as if even the thought of talking about it pains her, and Brooke feels her stomach clench.

"I don't know if you should see it," Kerry says. "It wouldn't be—"

"See what? Whatever it is, just show me."

Kerry looks at her for a long moment. "All right," she says finally. "Come with me."

Kerry turns and steps off the walkway, onto a dirt trail leading away from camp. As Brooke follows, her eyes scan the forest floor, as if she might find Jane down there somewhere. Is this what Kerry is implying—that Jane is out here? Or was?

Kerry stops up ahead and waits for Brooke to catch up. "Stay close to me," she says, "and please don't touch anything."

Brooke nods, feeling her legs go weak. Kerry looks as if she's going to be sick, and the same queasy feeling roils Brooke's stomach as she steps carefully after Kerry, both of them moving slowly among the ferns. Brooke pauses for a moment, taking a deep breath and looking around. She can no longer see their camp. They are, essentially, in the middle of nowhere, where they can't be seen or heard.

What could be out here that has anything to do with Jane?

She turns to Kerry, whose eyes are on the ground. Brooke moves forward slowly, carefully, taking care not to step past where Kerry is standing. Then she sees it. The gauzy green material.

Jane's scarf.

She sees it in her mind, in bursts of memory snapshots, images of last night. That thin, fine green fabric, pulling back Jane's red hair. Wrapped around Jane's long, elegant neck.

Now, it's crumpled on the ground, rain-soaked, dirty with—with what, exactly?

Brooke leans over and stretches out her hand, then feels Kerry close behind her. "Please, don't touch anything."

"I just want to make sure it's hers."

"Is it? Hers?"

"I think so. It's kind of hard to tell." Brooke looks around. "What's it doing out here? Why would she have come out this way? Do you think she got lost?"

Kerry's eyes dart forward, toward another parting in the lush green blanket of ferns. As Brooke inches forward, she sees what Kerry was so reluctant to show her. On the muddy ground are the remnants of a black T-shirt, Jane's crushed cell phone.

"Oh, God." Brooke covers her mouth with her hand, her stomach lurching. "Is that—blood? What happened? Where is she?"

"She's here."

"What do you mean?" Brooke hears her voice rise shrilly. "Where?"

"I should say she *was* here," Kerry says quietly. "She's—gone, I'm afraid. At least I think she is."

Brooke stares at her, a blurry, wan face before her in the rain, unreal as a dream. "What do you mean, gone? Where could she have gone?"

"Brooke, I'm so sorry," Kerry says. "You can see what's left of— of her things. I think that's all there is. I think something happened to Jane out here, and—and the devils got to her."

"The devils?" Brooke struggles to understand. "You mean, Tasmanian devils?"

Kerry nods.

"You're saying they killed her?"

"No, I'm not saying that. They don't kill people. But I know they were here—I heard them. Last night. And if something happened to Jane, and they came upon her—" Kerry pauses, her voice shaking. "All I know is that if they found her lying here, they wouldn't—" She pauses again, taking a breath. "They wouldn't have cared whether it was a wallaby or a human being. They would have been hungry. They're scavengers. They eat what they can, and everything they can."

Brooke feels as though her brain's gone rotten; she can't make any sense of Kerry's words. She takes a step backward, resisting the urge to flee, to get as far away as possible from Kerry and from Jane's things and from the very notion of what Kerry is trying to tell her. "You're not saying—"

"I'm saying—it looks like Jane was their victim."

"That's impossible." Brooke feels a sudden relief. This is all too strange, too absurd, to be real. "If you haven't actually found Jane, you don't know that anything happened to her. She's just lost, like you said before."

Kerry shakes her head, slowly. "I'm sorry, Brooke. I know it sounds crazy, but I think I'm right about this. I've spent years studying these animals. It's my life's work. I've seen four devils consume a one-hundred-kilo kangaroo in a matter of hours. When they find a carcass, they go positively mad, fighting over it, tearing it to shreds. They eat the bones, hair, teeth, everything."

Brooke turns away, swallowing hard, trying not to throw up her meager breakfast. She feels Kerry's hand on her shoulder.

"I'm sorry to be so direct, but I need you to understand. This is what I think happened. This is why Mark is coming from the ranger station. We need to investigate."

Brooke turns back around. "What we need to do is look for Jane," she says evenly. "This is ridiculous—it's insane. And meanwhile Jane's out there in the rain and cold, and we're doing nothing to find her."

Kerry looks at her sadly, as if Brooke is the one who's insane. "It's not as crazy as it sounds. Trust me, I wish it was."

"Then where's the rest of her stuff? Where's the rest of—the rest of her body?" Brooke's voice breaks as a sliver of this reality slips through a crack in her mind.

"We may never find it," Kerry says. "What they don't eat straightaway, they can drag up to a kilometer away."

"I don't believe you." Denial. The first stage of grief, and the one she needs to cling to right now. Anything else is incomprehensible.

Brooke turns again and takes a few steps away, but as she looks down she realizes she's stepped into another muddy puddle, and she sees the red-tinged mud soaking into her shoe.

"Oh God," she whispers and kneels down. There's just so much blood. Could this wild theory of Kerry's possibly be true?

She feels her stomach twist and heave; she needs to get out of here—now. But as she straightens up, her foot slides on the muddy ground, and the next thing she knows, she's lost her balance, both feet flying out from under her, and she lands on her back in the soft, wet ground, falling through a tall patch of bracken fern, head connecting firmly with the sodden earth below her.

When she opens her eyes, she's looking up at the underside of the ferns, a lacy veil of green that, for the moment, protects her from the rain. As she hoists herself up, she feels something tangled under her hand, and as she tries to shake it off, she looks at it—a thick, clingy spiderweb, red with blood. With Jane's blood.

Then, as she desperately uses her other hand to disentangle the web, she's hit with a gut-wrenching realization. It's not a web; it's too thick, and there's too much of it, and it sticks to her hand as she tries to shake and pull it free. Finally, she pulls the strands from her hand with the other, and the realization dawns on her. It's hair. Jane's hair.

Kerry is standing next to her, hand out as if to help her up, and Brooke hears her gasp as she, too, realizes what Brooke holds in her hands. "Holy shit," Brooke whispers. At the ends of the long red tresses she sees bits of skin. As if the hair had been yanked violently from Jane's scalp.

She feels Kerry's hand on her shoulder and jumps. Her whole body is shaking; sweat is mingling with the rain soaking her clothes, and she feels tears joining the raindrops sliding down her face.

Kerry gently takes the tangle of hair from her and lets it fall. "I think we need to leave everything as we found it," she says.

That's when Brooke fully comprehends what's happening. It's a crime scene, and Jane is the victim.

But she still can't understand the crime itself. "These devils are small, right?"

"Yes."

"And they kill humans?"

"No. Never to my knowledge. But if Jane was drunk and she passed out, or—"

"Or what?"

Kerry shrugs helplessly. "I don't know. Was she depressed?"

Brooke feels a bitter almost-laugh rise in her throat. *No, that would be me*, she's tempted to say. "Are you suggesting she killed herself? That's ludicrous."

"We should consider all—"

"No. She'd never do that."

"Okay. Okay."

Brooke can tell Kerry doesn't believe her. But then it occurs to her that there is another possibility. "Did you know Jane was having an affair with Malcolm?"

Kerry's eyes widen in surprise. "Was she? No. I had no idea."

"They've been seeing each other for a year. He didn't know Jane was coming on this trip. She planned it all without telling him. Without telling me, even, until I got here."

"Does Charlotte know?"

"Nobody knows, except him and Jane. And then me. And now you."

Kerry still looks wide-eyed, as if she's replaying the last day in her mind, trying to put it all together.

"I'm telling you this," Brooke says, "because Jane is not one to give up on anything. Not Malcolm, and especially not her own life. It may not have been her smartest move to plan this trip to confront Malcolm, but before you start insinuating that she was suicidal, you should take a look at the one person in that camp that might want her silenced."

Kerry's face pales even further, and Brooke can see a smattering of freckles she'd never noticed before, standing out against the ghostly white skin. For a moment, Brooke feels bad for implying that one of Kerry's guests has murdered another one, but then she shakes it off. What she regrets more is feeding Kerry's imagination, falling into this theory and then adding to it. They have no evidence of anything other than that the devils ran away with a few of Jane's things, which apparently got mixed up with whatever creature they did eat.

"I think we need to keep looking," Brooke says. "I know what you think, and you're right—Jane was drunk last night. She could've dropped her phone, left the tent open for the devils to take her clothes. There are lots of explanations for this. I mean, this blood could have come from a wallaby, right?"

Kerry looks doubtful, but Brooke doesn't care. She turns and starts walking back to the trail, calling out for Jane. She calls her name over and over, shouting until her voice cracks, and it feels good to scream, to release her pent-up energy, her fear and anger, all her own doubts and hopes floating out there on Jane's name in the wind.

She sees something move in the bushes to her right and whirls around. Her heart nearly stops. It's a tall figure, dressed head to toe in black, peering out between tree branches.

Ian. Brooke's blood is pounding wildly through her veins, leaving her too startled to speak.

"Sorry to frighten you," he says. He looks ahead as Kerry approaches through the ferns. "Did you find her?"

"If we did, would I still be yelling?"

"Where are you off to, Ian?" Kerry asks.

"Thought I'd get some birding in." He holds up a pair of binoculars.

"I don't know if that's such a good idea," Kerry says. "There won't be a lot of birds about, and with these winds you could get hit by a falling tree branch."

"I'll take my chances," he says.

"I'd prefer you didn't."

Ian gives her a cold stare. "What happened to the customer being right? This trip is not inexpensive, and if you're not letting us leave for the next camp, the least I can do is look for birds."

He turns and walks away. Kerry begins to speak, but apparently changes her mind. He's heading in a different direction from where they'd found Jane's things.

Brooke looks at her. "Are you worried about the devils attacking anyone else?"

"No," she says.

"Why can't we go on the assumption Jane is alive?" Brooke says.

"We can," Kerry says. "That's why Mark is coming, to help me figure this out, one way or another. If she's out there, we'll find her." She looks at her watch. "I need to get back to help with lunch. And you need to get out of those wet clothes." Then she looks directly at Brooke. "You'll keep this between us?"

Brooke nods. She watches Kerry disappear into the ferns, until all she sees is green, and all she hears is rain. Then the deep rumble of thunder in the distance.

Jane can't be dead. Just the idea of it—Brooke stops herself from thinking further, but she can't stop the wave of guilt that rolls through her, the years lost, the way she'd abandoned Jane in

New York. Her jealousy over Jane's success—it was as much behind her motivation to leave as her commitment to William—and the crushing disappointment over her own failures. So much promise, so many dreams, all of it left behind, and she's ashamed to admit she was glad to learn that Jane finally left New York, too. That she wasn't the only one who'd given up.

Brooke follows the path slowly back, her eyes still searching, hoping for a clue to prove Kerry wrong. They'd barely caught up, she and Jane, and she can't accept that they'd never get the chance again.

When she gets to her tent, she stops. Though her teeth are chattering in the cold and she does want to change out of her wet clothes, what she needs to do more is talk to Malcolm. Maybe he knows something no one else does.

She walks over to the dining tent but doesn't go in; instead, she peers in through one of the mesh screens on the side. Charlotte is still nose-deep in her book on an Adirondack chair she has brought in from the outside deck. Bryan is at the little stove, preparing food. Ian, she already knows, is out in the woods. She doesn't see Kerry, but with any luck, she'll find Malcolm in his tent, alone, and she can confront him there.

She goes to Malcolm's tent and pauses outside, listening. It's completely quiet, almost as if no one is inside. She looks around, wondering what the etiquette is. She can't exactly knock, but she can hardly just walk right in either.

She opens her mouth to say his name when she hears it in the air, coming toward her from somewhere else. She spins around. The nearest tent is Ian and Margaret's.

She hears the name again—*Malcolm*—a woman's voice, breathless, hushed.

Brooke tiptoes over toward the other tent. The front is zipped shut, and the flaps have been pulled down on either side, covering the mesh screens. She hears low moans, two voices, a raspy sound, like movement on a waterproof sleeping bag—and then a sharp, brittle, muffled laugh she recognizes instantly.

Margaret.

In the tent she shares with her husband. Only she's not with Ian. She's with Malcolm.

CHAPTER 14

KERRY

As she starts back toward camp, Kerry feels her mind whirl, threatening to spin out of control. She hears her therapist's voice in her head and doesn't want to ask herself the obvious question— *Are you sure you're ready for this?*—and instead tries taking deep, calming breaths as she walks through the bush in the rain.

It doesn't work.

Suddenly she veers right, into the woods, unable to return, unable to face anyone. She walks slowly, giving herself time to think, but still her breath comes fast, as if she's running at a sprint.

She reminds herself again to take one step at a time, literally and figuratively. Maybe Brooke is right; maybe they're dealing with a missing person instead of a dead woman.

But Kerry knows better. Even though she wishes more than anything that she's wrong, her hopes just don't stand up to her years of experience, to everything she knows. If the devils got to Jane's body—and all evidence says they did—then Jane is gone. Long gone.

And assuming that she is, it's one thing to have a woman die on her watch; it's yet another to have a woman murdered on her watch. And here of all places, with an apocalyptic storm upon them, being unable to leave, with the police stuck on the mainland.

Which means if it was murder, they are stranded here with whoever did it.

Kerry thinks about Malcolm. She didn't know about Malcolm and Jane's affair, though she has to admit it does make a certain sort of sense—Malcolm doesn't seem terribly engaged with his wife, and he was uneasy during that performance Jane and Brooke put on last night.

But it's a big leap from cheating on one's wife to murdering one's lover.

Or is it?

A part of her is willing to believe Malcolm did it, if for no other reason than to give the devils a break. The poor creatures get blamed for everything. They invade, they annoy, they pester, they pollute. Like all wild animals, they are allowed to exist—to a point. Should they get too close to civilization, should they dare to interact with the human species, they are afforded no compassion. The humans keep shrinking their homes, razing their habitat, leaving them less room to roam, fewer opportunities to live as they're meant to live. Even here, at the devils' last refuge, travelers tramp across the island, camping and biking and swimming. Something has to give.

Maybe it already has.

It's no accident that Kerry ended up a defender of an endangered species; she should've known early on she'd end up living her life outdoors. She grew up in suburban Hobart with an accountant father and stay-at-home mother, both of whom were longtime apartment dwellers who'd previously lived in Sydney; they'd never had pets and had no interest in getting any for their children. While her bookish sister didn't seem to mind, Kerry—a tomboy through and through—couldn't stand being inside the family's pristine home, where she felt she had to creep around on tiptoes, not making a sound or touching a thing, lest she leave fingerprints on tables or footprints on her mother's finely groomed carpeting. She spent most of her young life outside, in places where no one could see her footprints—and, as it turned out, being a quiet observer served her well later, when she spent her time tracking and studying wildlife.

She's never had pets as an adult either, other than the occasional wombat or devil baby who needed temporary home care—with Paul, it was impossible; he had allergies, or so he claimed. She wondered, even in the beginning, whether it was just a convenient excuse; he traveled all the time and didn't have time for pets, but it bothered her that she couldn't at least adopt a few shelter cats. It wasn't only that there was a great need for homes, but she also felt lonely when he was away for weeks at a time. It made her wonder if she should move out, just so she wouldn't have to live alone.

If only she'd realized sooner that the allergy wasn't to animals but to her, to their relationship, to each other. It turned out there was something in him that reacted, strongly and inevitably, to something about her, and there was no cure for it.

She's beginning to wonder if there's a cure for anything about her, or whether she's doomed to a life of anxiety, of living on this edge of human and animal existence and wishing more and more that she were on the animals' side.

The best thing she can do for the animals right now is to find out what happened to Jane—to place the blame where it belongs, not on the devils but on whichever human caused her to be found dead or unconscious in the woods.

It could be Jane herself, passed out drunk or dead from suicide.

It could be Malcolm, a lovers' quarrel gone wrong.

She pauses mid-step as another thought comes to her: the poacher Mark had mentioned. She remembers the sleeping bag that looked slept in, the footprints Brooke thought she saw on the beach. Could it be they are not alone here?

She keeps walking, turning back toward camp. The rain is still coming down, steadily, and she wipes water from her eyes, stopping short again as she remembers something else.

Ian. Out in the middle of last night—birding, or so he said.

But Ian has no reason to harm Jane; he seems to have a crush on her, in fact. Or maybe that was what happened—he made a move, she rebuffed him, he killed her.

Kerry draws in a shaky breath. She's rather fond of everyone on this trip, and it's hard to imagine any one of them hurting another. Ian's a bit full of himself, but he's not a bad sort; she actually doesn't mind him playing tour guide, as it takes a bit of pressure off her having to explain everything about the island's flora and fauna. And as different as Ian and his wife are in terms of their interests, Margaret is cut from the same cloth as her husband; she, too, can't seem to resist sharing her knowledge and experience, no matter whether people care to hear it.

As for Malcolm—he's a pseudo-celebrity and, like his mate Ian, a bit full of himself, but in a more genial way than either Ian or Margaret. Most of all, he has everything: a beautiful wife, a successful career, time and money to travel—why would he risk it all? Then again, celebrities are a species unto themselves, driven by a need to be adored. If Jane had threatened to come between him and his wife, him and his fans, who knows how he would have reacted? Those who have the most also have the most to lose.

Especially his lovely wife. Kerry reckons she likes Charlotte most of all because she's quiet and easygoing, happy to go with the flow as long as she has a book to read or a journal to write in. She also reminds Kerry a bit of herself; Kerry, too, is usually happy with very little—for her, it's nature instead of books. Still, as a wilderness guide, she has to be grateful for a person who doesn't bore easily or get restless too quickly.

And then there's the oddest couple of all: Jane and Brooke.

What had Brooke called Jane? *My oldest friend.* That, Kerry thinks, is interesting—not *best friend* or even *close friend*; that's different. She has no doubt they've known each other a long time, but she's not sure how close they are.

Brooke had resisted any suggestion of Jane committing suicide, but how well does she still know her so-called oldest friend? The only time Jane has appeared even moderately stable was during the unstable boat ride over. And now that Kerry knows the real reason Jane signed on for this trip, it's become very clear why she can't be considered the most reliable person among them. Jane wanted something—romance, vindication, revenge—and whatever happened, it obviously backfired on her.

The problem is, the way her apparent plan blew up doesn't point to how she ended up in the woods, vulnerable to the devils.

Kerry wants to believe whatever happened was accidental—too much alcohol; wrong place, wrong time; anything to simplify what is already becoming alarmingly complicated. But she knows that even accidents aren't always accidents.

Paul had an incident on one of his guiding trips years ago, before they met—Kerry can't believe she's nearly forgotten about it, until now. He'd been guiding a married couple on a custom fourteen-day hike across Southwest National Park. The weather was piss-awful, he told her over cocktails in Hobart: rain and leeches, impenetrable understory, blisters. The couple were arguing every step of the way, to the point where Paul said he found himself half-contemplating up and leaving them.

Then, on day eleven, as they were halfway to summitting Federation Peak, one of the most challenging hikes in all of Oz, the woman slipped, breaking her leg in three places. She had to be airlifted to the hospital, and while the three of them waited for help, clinging to the side of the mountain, Paul made her as comfortable as he could, and she grew delirious with pain and exhaustion. She began mumbling that her husband pushed her, that he was trying to get rid of her.

The husband brushed it off, attempting to soothe her as if she had gone mad. Paul himself attributed the crazy talk to shock—yet apparently it had continued at the hospital, and the police were called by the staff. Yet with no evidence—and the woman by then being under the influence of strong painkillers—they didn't investigate, and nothing came of it.

Until the following year, when the woman went missing on a cruise she and her husband took to New Zealand. She was believed, at first, to have fallen overboard somewhere on the Tasman Sea, but this time, the husband was arrested, and this time, his story didn't hold up under the slow, quiet eyes of the law. He was ultimately convicted of murder.

It's a fact, Kerry recalls, that most murders are committed by those whom the victims know well. And the only people Jane knows well are Malcolm and Brooke.

The green tents are now visible through the trees. As she walks into camp, all is silent except for rain pattering on canvas. Inside the main tent, Bryan is stacking the lunch dishes in the sink, and Charlotte is lounging in a deck chair with her novel and a glass of white wine.

Bryan looks over when she enters, abandoning the dishes. "Where have you been?"

She slips out of her wet jacket and looks past him at the sink. "I've had a shit morning, so don't even think that I'm going to tackle those dishes."

"Hey, I've been busy trying to keep the peace around here. So don't look at me like I've been doing fuck-all while you go off and disappear for hours."

"What are you talking about?"

He steps close and lowers his voice. "Ian and Margaret got into quite a row. Not sure how it started, but it ended with them both cracking the shits, screaming at each other, and finally storming out of here. I hope they haven't killed each other."

"I saw Ian," she says, "so he's still alive. Where's everyone else?"

Bryan shrugs. "They all scattered after the row. Drunk, mostly, which is probably good. They're getting restless, want to know what the plan is." He pauses. "Do we have one?"

Kerry shakes her head, not trusting her voice to speak.

"Well, no sense in going anywhere if we don't have to. It's pissing wombats out there."

Kerry glances at Charlotte before asking him, quietly, "Did you notice Jane doing or saying anything strange last night?"

"Besides that little show those two put on?"

"She seemed awfully wound up, didn't she?"

"Yeah, but you know," Bryan says. "Americans. They always talk twice too fast and listen half too slow. You think something happened to her? Or did she do a runner?"

"I don't know." Kerry suddenly feels unbelievably knackered. She looks at her watch. "Mark should be here in another hour. Maybe he'll have some insight."

"He's coming in this piss? I'll believe that when I see it. What'd Nigel have to say?"

"I haven't talked to Nigel."

"You're serious?" Bryan looks at her. "Nigel of all people needs to know that everything's gone tits up over here."

"Why? So he can get a head start on sacking me?"

"I'm just saying."

"There's nothing to tell him right now. Mark's on his way, we'll get it sorted, and we can fill Nigel in later." She catches his doubtful look. "How long have you worked for him, anyway?"

"Six years, off and on."

"Has anything like this happened before?"

"Crazy things happen all the time."

"Like what? People disappearing?"

"Well, no—not like this. People get lost, but not for long."

"Has anyone ever—died? On one of these trips?"

"No, 'course not. Why?"

Her mobile rings. She sees Mark's number flash on the screen just before it goes silent again.

"I have to find a signal." She puts her wet jacket back on, and without another word to Bryan she leaves the tent and makes her way to the beach. Though she's slightly sheltered by the eucalyptus branches above, she can tell by the winds and the dripping leaves that conditions are getting worse, not better.

When she emerges from the shaking ceiling of trees into the open, the wind seems to grab at her from every direction, whipping her jacket against her skin, sending her hair flying. She hunkers down behind a sand dune, getting more sprayed with sand than protected from it, and calls Mark. The signal is weak, and she has to shout to make herself heard.

"Bad news," he shouts back. "I'm not going to make it."

"What happened?"

"Tree branch fell, slammed right into my windscreen. Nearly flattened me along with the ute."

She can barely hear him over the wind. "Are you okay?"

"Shoulder's killing me, but it'll be right. I'm headed back to Saltwick. Sorry about this, Kerry. Not sure whether the roads would be passable anyway."

"Oh, shit." Kerry looks up at the sky, angry and roiling with dark clouds. "I'm sorry, Mark."

"How're you going?"

"Not good. People are upset, getting restless."

"Keep everyone together."

"I'm trying!"

"This storm is getting scary," Mark shouts. "Don't take it lightly, and don't let anyone else either. You've got food. You've got a generator. You've got to hold tight one more day."

"There's something else."

"What's that? Kerry? Hello?" Mark's voice is cutting out.

Silence. "Mark? Mark?"

He's gone again.

"Fuck!" Kerry shakes the sandy, waterlogged mobile and feels the urge to chuck it into the waves.

That's when she sees a figure standing on the beach, near the water's edge. Through the rain, it's hard to tell who it is. She stands up and holds up both hands over her eyes.

It's Brooke.

Kerry heads toward her, the wet sand forcing her into slow-motion as she begins to panic, wondering what Brooke could be doing out here. Has she found Jane?

She screams Brooke's name over the wind, and Brooke turns. Her face momentarily fills with fear until she recognizes Kerry.

"What are you doing out here?" Kerry yells at her.

"Looking for Jane," Brooke yells back, "since no one else seems to care what happened to her."

Kerry stops next to Brooke, pausing to catch her breath. "I do care, Brooke. You know that. But look, it's not safe to be out here right now."

As if to prove her point, a wave crashes hard in front of them, soaking them further with a wall of sea spray. They both back up, and just then a bolt of lightning hits the water, followed fast by a loud crack of thunder as the sky flashes white. Kerry takes Brooke firmly by the arm and begins to lead her back toward camp.

"Who were you talking to?" Brooke asks, pointing toward Kerry's phone as they enter the relative shelter of the woods.

"The park ranger."

"When's he getting here?"

"He's not. A tree fell on his truck. He has to go back to Saltwick."

Brooke looks at her. "What does that mean for us?"

"Just that we have to stay here and wait out the storm," Kerry says, as calmly as she can manage.

"But what if Jane's still out there somewhere? We need to search for her."

Kerry wants to scream at her again, to get it through to her that her friend is dead, that they can't waste their time and risk their own lives trekking through the woods during a lightning storm.

Instead, as the main tent comes into view, she says, "Bryan and I will take care of things, okay? You need to just relax, stay dry, and we'll figure this out."

Brooke is shaking her head, and Kerry can't be sure whether it's in response to what she's just said or to the laughter coming from inside the tent. How can anyone be laughing at a time like this, she wonders. Then she remembers that none of them know what she and Brooke do.

They enter the tent to find Malcolm, Charlotte, Margaret, and Bryan sitting at the table, wine and beer bottles in front of them.

"Picture a reality program about guides in the wild," Malcolm is saying. "Actually, I rather like how that sounds: *Guides in the Wild.*"

"Yeah, and not just the easy tracks," Bryan adds. "Tough slogs. So there's lots of getting lost, getting pissed. Running out of water and food."

"Speaking of food," Kerry interrupts. "Bryan, we've got to get dinner prep started." Then she looks at Margaret. "Is Ian not back yet?"

Margaret shrugs. "Do you see him?"

"He's been out there a long time," Kerry says.

"It's just a little wind and rain," Margaret says. "I thought you Tassies were tougher than that."

"It's a bit more than a little wind and rain," Kerry says. "I'd like you all to stay inside, under cover, for the rest of the evening. Ian included, when he gets back."

"You can't be serious," Margaret says.

Kerry ignores her and turns to Bryan. "Can I have a word?"

"Fire away."

"Outside."

"Uh-oh, mate. You're in trouble now," Malcolm says.

"You just said we need to stay inside, under cover," Bryan says.

Kerry gives him a withering look, then turns and walks out, heading toward her own tent, the closest one. She stands just inside, holding the flap open, letting in the rain as she waits for him. Finally he appears, jogging over the wooden planks barefoot, using a tea towel as an umbrella.

"Before you yell at me," he says, squeezing into the tent beside her, "you did want me to keep everyone calm, and I have. It just took a little more booze, that's all."

"For them, Bryan, not you."

"I'm fine," he says. "Perfectly sober. I'm deso for the night, after all—I've got to run the generator. With no solar, we're going to lose our lights unless I fire it up tonight."

"What about dinner?"

"We've barely finished lunch."

"But you should have had everything prepped by now. We've got to stay organized."

"I thought it was your turn."

"We don't take turns, Bryan. I'm the senior guide. When are you going to figure that one out?"

"Did you bring me here just to tell me that?"

"No. I need to ask you something."

"What?"

"Were you with Brooke last night? All night, I mean?"

"Why, did she tell you that?"

Kerry sighs. "Look, I don't care about your sex life, and I'm not going to report you to Nigel. I just need to know where everyone was."

"Yeah, we were together."

"In your tent?"

"In my tent. In various positions in my tent."

She wants to smack his grin right off his face. "When did she leave?"

"I don't know. Early morning, I reckon."

"So you were asleep."

"Yeah. What's this about?"

"I just want to be sure Brooke wasn't involved."

"Involved?" Bryan looks genuinely confused. "You think she knows where Jane got off to?"

Kerry pauses. She has to tell him, she realizes. She needs someone to share this with and, despite his numerous flaws, he's the only one she can confide in. She certainly can't keep talking about it with Brooke; already she wishes she hadn't said anything to her.

"Look, what I'm about to tell you," she begins. "You have to keep this between us."

"Sure."

"I think Jane is dead. I think she was taken by the devils."

He looks at her, all traces of his grin vanishing. "You're joking, right?"

"I'm dead serious. There's a five-meter-square scene of blood and torn clothing just off the trail around the bend."

"Jesus," he says, and he looks so perplexed she almost feels sorry for him. "Devils don't kill people."

"I know. I think Jane either passed out—or something worse—and that's when it happened."

Bryan is looking at her as if he's trying to gauge her mental state. "Something worse? What do you reckon that would be?"

"If somebody else was involved."

"You mean—" He hesitates, then lets out a short laugh. "You realize you sound like that play Jane and Brooke made up last night, don't you? You think someone did something to Jane and left her out for the devils to clean up? Thereby committing the perfect crime?"

"Bryan, this isn't a reality show."

"Exactly," he says. "That's what I'm telling you. There's got to be a reasonable explanation."

"You've been getting pissed with the guests all afternoon and you're talking to *me* about being reasonable? Please." She isn't sure, at this moment, whether she's more disgusted with him or with herself. "I know what I saw out there."

"Okay, okay." He holds up his hands as if in surrender. "You're the wildlife expert, not me."

"Look, just promise me you won't say anything. Okay?"

"How long are you planning on keeping this a secret?"

"Brooke knows," she admits. "But she's the only one, and I want it to stay that way."

Just as he's about to respond, the world goes flame-white, and Kerry pitches violently to the ground as the earth rumbles around her and her mind goes numb.

It feels like both seconds and hours before she finally raises her head, her mind foggy yet oddly alert, fully aware that what just happened was a lightning strike, dangerously close, and yet not believing what's right in front of her: a large browntop stringy-bark, its branches in flames, splintering into pieces and falling onto the dining tent.

CHAPTER 15

BROOKE

Brooke stands on the deck with the others, staring through the rain up at Bryan, who's in the tree above them dousing the last of the flaming branches with a wet towel.

Moments earlier, just after the nearly instant flash-and-boom that jolted her to the core, he and Kerry had run into the dining tent, grabbing brooms and flipping them handle-side up, then jumped onto the table, knocking over bottles and glasses as they jabbed at the smoking red objects on top of the tent, sending them flying. The burning objects were tree branches, Brooke saw, as they hit the ground outside the tent—and more were falling.

That's when Bryan took a towel from the kitchen and rushed outside, climbing what was left of the tree to extinguish the other branches before they could fall. Now he carefully climbs down, the tree's trunk beige on the inside, where it was split open. Its dangling branches and thick, ropy bark are black with smoke. Brooke grips her elbows with her palms, holding her arms close to her body to stop them from shaking. No one speaks.

Thanks to Bryan and to the pouring rain, the fire is out now, the air smoky and wet. Brooke can see that the tree was nearly halved, and the smaller, upper part fell just to the right of the tent, missing the canvas wall by less than two feet. It did, however, land on a piece of equipment that looks like a generator. Brooke catches the faint scent of diesel as she watches Kerry drain the remaining fuel into a plastic container.

In her peripheral vision she sees Malcolm shaking his head, and she's about to ask him what's the matter when he calls out to Bryan, "Here's your reality show, mate. Shame we didn't have cameras running."

"Darling," Charlotte chastises him. "We should all just be grateful no one was hurt."

"He's right, though," Margaret says. "This is turning into an episode of *Survivor*."

"Glad you've got your survival spirit," Bryan says, "because it's going to be a very dark evening."

"Why?" Charlotte asks.

"The lights in the main tent and over the deck—not to mention our coolers—run off of a solar-powered battery," Bryan explains. "Without much in the way of sun these past couple days, we planned to flip on this backup generator tonight. And now that's stuffed up, as you can see."

Kerry straightens up and looks at them. "We have our headlamps," she says, her voice higher than normal. "We've got battery-powered lanterns in the main tent. And candles are nice at dinner anyway, right?"

"Right, of course," Charlotte says. "We'll be just fine, won't we?" She squeezes Malcolm's arm, as if to urge him to agree.

But Malcolm pulls away, and Brooke's thoughts return to earlier, when she heard him and Margaret together, and she involuntarily shudders.

"We should all get back inside," Kerry says, holding her arms wide to usher them into the tent. "Bryan and I are about to get dinner started, and we'll open up another bottle of wine."

"Or two," Bryan adds.

Brooke follows the others inside. Kerry hoists up the side flaps as high as they will go, in an attempt to let in the last of the day's light. The tent is still fairly dark, and shadowy in the corners, like a cave, which makes Brooke feel as though they're about to enter a more primitive existence—as if things could possibly go further downhill from here.

Kerry lights the candles on the dining table, and then she begins to clean up the overturned bottles and broken glass from the table and the floor. When she's done, Bryan plunks down a bottle of wine onto the center of the newly cleaned table.

Brooke stands in front of the tent's "lending library," a small bookshelf where she can pretend to look at books while she sneaks peeks at the others. Charlotte pours herself another glass of wine, oblivious to the fact that her husband's eyes are on Margaret, who's sitting across the table, her face illuminated by her iPad, looking entirely unconcerned with anything happening around her.

Bryan, another bottle in hand, pauses next to her. "Can I get you a glass of something? Two glasses of something?"

Brooke musters a smile. "Thanks. But I'm fine." She turns toward the deck, watching the water drip off the burnt leaves, splattering the wood inky black. After the recent lightning strikes, the air smells so fresh and alive. She still can hardly believe that Jane is gone. Missing, dead—she still can't imagine either scenario. And she can't stop thinking she should be out there looking for her. Would Jane be standing here, obeying Kerry, if Brooke were the one missing?

She sneaks a glance back at Malcolm, his attention now on Charlotte, who's talking to him in a rather animated way, as though she's telling him a story, but he doesn't appear very interested. Margaret's face is still bent toward her iPad, but Brooke wonders if she's really reading or instead listening to Charlotte. How do they manage such an affair? It's one thing for Malcolm to sleep with a client, someone from work—but the wife of one of his best friends? And what Brooke overheard didn't sound like their very first encounter, which means Malcolm has probably been cheating on his wife with both Margaret and Jane at the same time.

Yet the big question about Malcolm is not whether he's capable of cheating but whether he's capable of murder.

Brooke remembers a night in college—one of those weekday nights when she and Jane took a study break that involved, naturally, beer and cigarettes—and she'd pulled her philosophy notebook from her desk to read Jane some of the questions the professor had posed to the class earlier that week. One of them was, *Would you kill someone if you knew you would never be caught?*

Jane had laughed. "Would you?"

Brooke had already thought about it. "I would," she said. "A mercy killing. If someone needed it."

Jane took a long drag on her cigarette, blowing smoke up to the cracked, yellowed ceiling of their dorm room. "Wow, you're a good person," she said. "I would just kill people I hate."

It was Brooke's turn to laugh, but even through Jane's mischievous smile she could see there was some truth in it. Not that Jane would ever actually do it, she knew—but what if she really, truly thought she could get away with it?

Was that how all this started? Perhaps Brooke had it wrong; perhaps it was Jane who'd threatened Malcolm, and that's when things got bad. Somehow, Jane ended up left in the woods, and then—

Suddenly, Brooke is brushed aside as Margaret breezes past her, pulling the hood of her dark-green rain jacket over her face.

"Excuse *me*," Brooke says, annoyed, at the same time she hears Malcolm call, "Margaret!"

Then Kerry is standing next to her, at the tent's entrance, watching Margaret as she strides across the deck.

"Where's she going?" Brooke asks.

"To find Ian," Margaret calls out. A few paces away but apparently still close enough to hear, she stops and looks back at them.

"Margaret, please." Kerry steps forward. "Get inside. Let me or Bryan go find him."

"I climbed the world's tallest mountain at minus sixteen degrees Celsius, with winds at fifteen knots," Margaret says. "I think I'm quite capable of finding my own husband in a bit of rain."

She turns away again and walks off. Kerry sighs.

"I'm surprised she's even bothering to look for Ian," Brooke mutters.

"Sorry?" Kerry asks.

Brooke looks at her. For a moment she's tempted to tell her about Margaret's extramarital activity, then decides against it. "Do I have time to go back to my tent before dinner?" she says instead. "I still need to change."

"Sure," Kerry says. "Just come right back. We really do want to keep everyone together."

Brooke waits until Kerry is back inside the tent before taking the walkway past her tent, past all the others, out of camp.

Stepping back out into the rain is a comfort compared to being in that humid and stuffy tent, with strangers who don't care about Jane being missing—who seem far more irritated than concerned, in fact. But Brooke can't sit still. She isn't sure where to look, and she also isn't sure she wants to return to the gory scene she saw earlier.

She slows her pace as she steps off the walkway. The trail will end soon, and then what? The sky is dark with clouds, but the sun hasn't set—it's still out there somewhere, buried in folds of thick, angry gray. While her headlamp is in the pocket of her cargo pants, she doesn't want to get stuck out here when it gets dark.

She doesn't want to go back, either. Not only does she not want to be among any of these people—the peculiar, loveless couples; the man she slept with while her friend went missing; Kerry and her nervous energy—she can't trust herself not to say something she shouldn't. As if possessed by Jane's ghost already—Jane, who always spoke her mind, who never held anything back—Brooke has found herself wanting to blurt out inappropriate things. Things like, *What have you done to Jane, Malcolm? And was it because she threatened to break up your so-called marriage?*

If only she dared say what she's actually thinking—but she's spent her whole life doing the opposite. Telling her mother that, yes, her father's child-support check arrived when it hadn't, which it rarely did—passing off her secondhand clothes as new, since it was all she could ever buy. Telling her father that, yes, her mother was doing well, when she was nearly always on the verge of losing her job for taking too many "sick" days in a dark room with yet another "migraine." Brooke was so good at telling people what they wanted to hear, needed to hear, was it any wonder she'd ended up on the stage?

Perhaps she and Jane had connected due to a strange sort of *folie à deux*, in which they shared the same talents for lying and manipulating—only for Jane, it was for fun, or for revenge, or for adventure. For Brooke, it had been merely for survival.

She can't say anything to these people, anyway, she reminds herself, or they will think she's insane, which she knows people often think of Jane. Brooke has always loved Jane's lack of inhibitions, but most others don't appreciate it, especially if Jane speaks a truth they don't want to hear. Jane makes people uncomfortable; she always has. And now, whatever happened, it seems she may have taken it a bit too far.

Brooke stops as she reaches the end of the trail. Up ahead, she can see the trampled-upon ferns that mark the way to the last signs of Jane. She wonders if she should have another look, whether she might find a clue as to where Jane went. But what worries her is that she might find something else, something that only confirms that Jane died there.

She decides to skirt around that spot, to avoid the scene of the mayhem but to look for other clues. Most of all, she needs to do something, to keep moving, to feel a little less utterly helpless.

She hears a sound amid the trees and stops. Heavy footfalls, audible above the rain. Straining to see through the branches, she sees a tall figure. She doesn't dare move, holding her breath as she waits for the figure to move first. They are practically facing each other, about twenty yards apart and obscured by the trees, and the other person hasn't seen her yet.

Then the figure takes a step closer, and Brooke lets her breath out in a whoosh. It's only Margaret. What's up with that jacket of hers, Brooke wonders—the same deep, leafy color of the forest, as if she's trying to camouflage herself.

She watches as Margaret looks left and right, apparently trying to decide which way to turn. Is she wondering where Ian might be, or is Ms. Everest actually lost?

Then a strange thought occurs to Brooke. Could Margaret have found out about Malcolm and Jane?

This could have any number of consequences, she realizes. It could have led Malcolm to hurt Jane, or perhaps even led Margaret to hurt her—to confront her, at the very least. Margaret has disliked Jane from day one, and Ms. Everest isn't the type to let herself be humiliated. If she knows, then she, too, has a motive to be rid of Jane.

And Brooke now is here, alone, in the woods with her. In very much the same spot where Jane's things were found.

Brooke takes a step backward, her heart pounding, and that's when Margaret looks straight ahead and locks eyes with her.

A look of irritation flashes across Margaret's face. "Oh, it's you," she says flatly.

"Any sign of Ian?" Brooke asks.

"No," Margaret says.

"Does he know? Is that why he took off and hasn't come back?"

"Sorry?"

"I'm guessing he found out," Brooke continues. "About you and Malcolm."

Margaret gives her a look that could melt the ice off the top of a mountain. "I beg your pardon?"

"I mean, it was hard not to hear you two in your tent," she says. "I'd be surprised if everyone in camp doesn't know by now."

Margaret's eyes darken, and she takes a step toward Brooke. "What the hell do you want from me?"

"I want to know what happened to Jane."

"And how on earth do you think I would know that?"

"For one, you were both fucking Malcolm."

Margaret laughs that humorless laugh of hers and tilts her head to one side. "Excuse me?"

"Oh, you didn't know he was screwing Jane, too?" Brooke injects false innocence into her voice. She feels a sudden boldness, a sudden courage: she's onstage again, playing a role. It allows her to continue, without breaking character, under Margaret's unrelenting glare. "Mmm-hmm. Hot item, those two. It's been about a year now."

Margaret waves her hand in front of her as if to shoo away a fly. "I don't think so. Malcolm has better taste than that."

"Ask him yourself. Better yet, let's both go back and ask him. Because I can't help but think that Jane disappearing has something to do with her sleeping with Malcolm."

Margaret's face goes stiff and serious, and she stares at Brooke. "You honestly think he had something to do with Jane going off and getting herself lost?"

"Her being gone is pretty convenient for him, don't you think?"

"Please." Margaret snorts. "That bitch wasn't a threat to him."

Brooke feels her heart thud in her chest as the words sink in. Margaret just referred to Jane in the past tense.

Brooke summons every last rule she'd ever learned about acting. About stage fright. She takes a deep, surreptitious breath; she floods her voice with confidence. "Maybe it was convenient for you, then. To get *that bitch* out of the way so you could have Malcolm all to yourself."

"Are you joking?" That laugh again. "If you are even coming close to insinuating that I had anything to do with—"

"Did Jane know about you? Did she threaten to tell Ian the way she threatened to tell Charlotte?"

Margaret moves forward so quickly, so suddenly, that Brooke nearly falls over in her haste to step away. "If you say one word, to *anyone*, about this—"

"What?" Brooke demands. "You'll what?"

In the rain, in the dim light of the forest, Margaret is terrifying. She's taller than Brooke by half a foot, and her expression holds a fury that Brooke has never, in all her years of studying acting, seen on anyone's face before.

"You bloody Americans," Margaret says at last. "You really do think the world revolves around you." She takes a deliberate step back, eyes on Brooke, and then after a few more steps turns around, walking away in the direction she came from.

Brooke lets her breath out in a long, shaky sigh. She waits until Margaret disappears into the woods before she retraces her own steps, finding her way back to the trail, back to the wooden walkway.

There, she pauses, still trying to breathe, to make sense of what just happened. It seemed as if Margaret really didn't know about Malcolm and Jane; her surprise looked genuine, and unless she's a better actor than Brooke, she truly had no idea.

But now she does. Things are sure to get interesting between her and Malcolm, but even more concerning is that Brooke may have just put herself in danger.

She hears movement and freezes, listening. It's coming from the right, the direction from which Margaret would be coming if she returned. Brooke steps behind a tree and crouches down, trying desperately to see through the growing darkness. The sound of rain on branches makes it hard to hear—and then, there it is again. A shuffle.

She leans forward, trying to see around the tree without making any sound herself. She hears it again—the shuffle, like tentative footsteps—and this time it doesn't sound like Margaret, though it's definitely not a wombat. It's something large, the size and weight of a human.

It's now dark enough that she can't see anything but shadows; she can't even see the walkway, which she knows is only a few feet away, but she'd gotten herself turned around and can't remember which way to go. She feels her breath come faster as she begins to panic—then she remembers her headlamp. She pulls it out of her cargo pants and holds it in front of her. Whoever's there—Margaret, Ian, Malcolm—she'll blind them and then run for it.

Two eyes gleam back at her through the dark.

She stares straight into them—huge eyes, unblinking, right at her level where she's crouching behind the tree. Then the eyes jump sideways and disappear, and she realizes, in the following thumps through the bush, that it was a kangaroo.

Her first thought is that she's safe.

Her second is that Jane isn't here to see it. That she may never see another one of the wonders of the Australian wilderness.

Her third thought is that she's getting paranoid, imagining one of her fellow travelers is out to get her. Imagining that one of them hurt or killed Jane. That option is so much more extreme— and unlikely—than Kerry's original theory. Suicide.

Brooke believes what she told Kerry—that Jane isn't the type to give up—but she now wonders whether she also needs to acknowledge Jane's flair for the dramatic. Years ago, in New York, Brooke had been backstage during a tech rehearsal at a community theater in Brooklyn when she got a text from Jane. She'd just taken *half a bottle of pills* and wanted Brooke to know she was her best friend and *I've loved you more than anyone.*

When she got to the apartment, Jane was facedown on the floor. The pills, she learned later, were ibuprofen, and she'd taken maybe a handful of a mostly used-up bottle. But in those first moments, Brooke panicked; she shook Jane awake, and Jane clung to her, weeping and apologetic, then blearily insisted she didn't need to go to Emergency. It was too expensive, she claimed; she'd never be able to pay the bills. *Besides, all I need is you. To know I'm not alone.* Brooke held her, let the adrenaline rush subside, made them both tea. Jane never offered a reason, just apologized over and over for the meltdown, for feeling so weak and hopeless. *I'm not as strong as you, B.*

Yet once the initial scare was over, Brooke began to suspect that it had been nothing more than a ruse to get her home, jealous that Brooke had gotten a part and she hadn't. It was signature Jane—faking a suicide attempt but not going through with it, calling Brooke home in a panic during a tech rehearsal but not on opening night. She did things that got her close to the edge without having to actually go over it.

Until this trip, Brooke hasn't let herself feel just how much of a relief it had been to leave Jane behind in New York—the same relief she'd felt when leaving her mother behind for college. Yet when Brooke left the drama of being friends with Jane, she also left behind her drama career. After that play in Brooklyn ended, Brooke had a harder time getting roles; she felt, on some unconscious level that affected her auditions, that she could not be more successful than Jane—or else Jane would take more pills, or do something even worse. Just as she'd played the good girl in hopes of keeping her mother's darkness at bay, she was now playing the less successful, loyal friend in an attempt to manage Jane's moods. A weariness settled over her, like a thick cloud, and she began to think she wanted to be done with acting, that she should try just being herself for a change.

And so she began skipping auditions, cutting off the oxygen to her budding career, until her searches for open calls became searches for actual jobs. And when she saw the ad for a marketing assistant, she applied. What was the difference, she reasoned, between selling yourself to a casting director and selling software and apps? And she had to admit she liked the idea of working at one of those tech companies she had always read about, ones that handed out stock like candy, offered up free meals and loaner bikes and the latest Mac laptops. And when she acted her way through the interview, then another, then another, she realized that she could do it—that it was like any role; if you rehearsed enough, if you devoted yourself to it completely, you could nail it. She did, and her employers agreed.

The energy of all those people at their stand-up desks and reclining on bean bags gave her such a rush, as if she had entered a new world, one in which she could start over again. Then, when a serious-looking man in faded jeans and a Superman T-shirt asked if he could share a table with her in the cafeteria, she thought she might reinvent her love life as well. And it wasn't long after William asked her out that the curtain fell on her friendship with Jane.

* * *

Back in the dining tent, the candles have multiplied. There are a half dozen on the table, two near extinction. LED lanterns on the kitchen counter emit a bluish glow as Kerry and Bryan work on dinner.

Ian is back, but Margaret isn't. Brooke helps herself to a large glass of wine as a close lightning strike invades the tent with white-hot light. The ground shakes as thunder cracks overhead.

"Please make this stop," Charlotte says.

"I'm beginning to wonder if we'll see Noah's Ark floating by," says Ian.

"If we're lucky," says Malcolm. "Then we'd have a way off this godforsaken island."

Brooke looks at him over her wineglass, trying to keep her gaze neutral. Again she wonders: even if he'd done nothing at all to Jane, why hasn't he shown the least bit of concern for her whereabouts? Why hasn't anyone?

"Dinner is served!" Bryan calls out, placing plates in front of Brooke and Charlotte. Kerry is right behind him with food for Ian and Malcolm. "Where's Margaret?" she asks, returning with one more plate, holding it up as she looks around the table.

Ian shrugs. "She was in the tent getting changed. You can put her food down. She'll be along any minute."

Kerry relents and leaves the plate at the empty place next to Ian. Then she and Bryan sit down. "It looks like a dog's breakfast," Bryan says of the pasta in front of them, "but keep in mind we're working under difficult conditions here."

"It looks delicious," Charlotte says, "and we appreciate all that you're doing under these—circumstances."

As they take their first bites, Brooke can't help but notice the difference between last night and tonight. They're all probably just as drunk, but everyone is subdued. Kerry checks her phone a few times, then turns it off.

Finally Malcolm clears his throat, and they all look at him expectantly. "Kerry," he says. "I propose that first thing tomorrow morning we push north."

"I'm not sure that's—"

"I realize *you* can't leave," he interrupts, "but Bryan knows the route. And we did pay to see the island, not spend our days under some curious version of house arrest."

"What Malcolm means," Charlotte says, "is that while we are all very concerned about Jane, we do have to get back to the mainland eventually. Especially Malcolm, with his work schedule. We don't mean to be insensitive. Just practical. It's all very unfortunate."

Kerry swallows a mouthful of pasta before answering. "Malcolm, with respect, this isn't one of your reality shows. We're in the midst of a dangerous storm, and with Jane still—missing, we need to stay put. For now."

"And, with respect," Malcolm counters, "you can't keep us here."

Kerry sighs. "You're right. I can't force you to stay. But I hope you will. We can talk about it in the morning."

"I've made up my mind."

Kerry looks around—at Charlotte, at Ian, at Brooke. "Have you all talked about this with each other? Who is planning to leave, exactly?"

"I'm not going anywhere," Brooke says, looking at Malcolm. "And until we find out what happened to Jane out there, I don't think any of us should leave."

"What do you mean?" Charlotte asks. "Do you know something about Jane?"

"Jane is not just missing," Brooke blurts out. "She is presumed dead."

Silence falls across the table. One of the low candles flickers out.

"Dead?" Charlotte says at last, her voice small. "Why do you think Jane is dead?"

Kerry raises her hands. "We don't know for sure. We found evidence of—of a death. That's why we need to stay. We need to wait for investigators."

In the dim, flickering light, Brooke struggles to read Malcolm's expression. As Kerry tells the others what they found outside of camp, what she thinks transpired, Malcolm remains motionless.

Charlotte pushes her plate away. "Darling, I need to lie down. Walk me back to the tent?"

Ian rises as well. "I'll go check on Margaret," he says.

Brooke glances at Kerry, whose face crumples as she looks down at her food. "I'm sorry," Brooke says. "I didn't mean to tell anyone. Especially like that."

Kerry looks up. "It's okay," she says quietly. "I couldn't keep this from them forever. Maybe at least it'll convince Malcolm to stay." She stands up and says to Bryan, "Let's get this mess cleaned up."

"Do you want some help?" Brooke offers.

Kerry shakes her head. "No, thanks. You'd better get some rest."

"Want me to walk you to your tent?" Bryan says.

"No, I'll be fine."

But she walks to her tent on shaky legs, wishing Jane hadn't chosen the farthest one. She passes the other tents, seeing lights inside, hearing murmured voices. When she reaches her own tent, zipping herself inside, she quickly changes into dry clothes and gets into her sleeping bag.

She turns off her headlamp and hangs it on the nail above the bed. Just then she realizes she hadn't taken her medication; she forgot about it last night, too, the night she spent with Bryan— she certainly hadn't needed it then. She reaches into her pack and rummages around, but she can't find the narrow prescription bottle. Not by touch, anyway.

She dons her headlamp again and points the light toward her bag as she opens it up, searching with both her eyes and her hands. The light of the headlamp skitters with the motion of her head, and the darting shadows make it impossible to see anything. She feels her breath coming a little faster as she begins to take items out of her pack, suddenly desperate to find the pills.

The first panic attack had happened a few days after she'd left William. She'd made her decision quickly but resolutely—after following him after work that night, after seeing what he'd been doing while "working late," there'd been no doubt in her mind that their marriage was over. And the fact that her friend Serena had gotten a movie role and needed to sublet her apartment indicated to Brooke that leaving William was the right thing to do just then. She called Serena that night and offered to take the three-month sublet.

But after the initial rush of the decision—which felt at once both heart-wrenching and revitalizing—she began to regret acting so impulsively. After packing a couple of suitcases and seeing Serena off, instead of feeling empowered, Brooke ended up feeling more alone than ever. Not only was she not in contact with William, but Serena, her only real friend in Seattle, was now on a remote movie set in Canada. Serena had accepted Brooke's flimsy reason for wanting to sublet the space—*I'm going to try writing a play, and I need a writing studio*—but Brooke could tell she didn't believe it. And the next thing Brooke knew, Serena was out of cell range and Brooke was alone in her apartment, without the wine and takeout, laughter and gossip, and finding herself unable to breathe.

And now, she can't find her pill bottle anywhere—maybe it fell out and rolled under one of the bunks—and she knows she'll never find it in the dark. She stuffs her belongings back into the pack and flops back onto her bunk. She forces herself to breathe, in and out, slowly and calmly, until her heart stops racing.

She sighs and looks up, blinking her eyes as if she can clear her vision of the darkness. Then she turns her head toward Jane's empty sleeping bag. "What happened to you, Jane?" she whispers.

The sound of the rain on the tent echoes around her.

She will never fall asleep. She focuses on the sound of thunder in the distance, and on the rain, lightening up a bit, it seems, or perhaps that's just wishful thinking. Soon she is wandering through the ancient forest. The rain has stopped. The ground is dry. She smells the fragrant oils from the trees.

Then someone's screaming, obscured by the trees ahead, and Brooke is running toward the sound, shouting Jane's name. And when she gets there, she is face-to-face not with Jane but Margaret. Margaret shouts back at her: "Let go!"

Then Brooke is awake, breathing heavily as if she's still running, as if she actually had been running. The dream was so vivid she turns on her headlamp, checking to make sure hadn't actually left her tent—that she's still warm, dry, inside her sleeping bag. She breathes a sigh of relief. Just a dream.

She wonders how long she'd been asleep—hours, seconds? It's still raining. She hears the sound of feet on the wooden walkway, moving quickly. Then a woman's voice. Kerry? Then another: Bryan. More footsteps.

Something's happened. Maybe they've found Jane.

Heart thudding, Brooke scurries out of her sleeping bag and into her shoes, unzipping her tent and going out into the rain without her jacket. She feels the rain soak through her fleece top but ignores it as she follows the voices and the lights, which are coming from the direction of the toilets.

The first person she sees is Ian, on the ground just off the walkway, crouched over something. Kerry stands in the ferns next to him, and Bryan is behind her. When he looks up and sees her, he comes toward her, as if to stop her from moving forward, but it's too late.

Brooke sees a body on the ground, and she instantly recognizes Margaret's dark-green jacket, now mud-spattered and covered with dead leaves. In the unsteady light of the headlamps, she sees something else—a dark stain on the back of Margaret's head, spreading in her light brown hair.

CHAPTER 16

KERRY

Kerry stands on the walkway, aware of rainwater trickling down the back of her neck; of the jarring, random darts of light from various headlamps; of Ian's voice, saying his wife's name. She is wide awake to everything happening around her, but at the same time she feels herself shutting down, her mind strangely distant, as if she's watching all of this unfold on a television screen rather than right in front of her. The darkness is wrapping its cloaking arms tightly around her, as if to warn her that, this time, it may not let go.

What's worse is that she's growing comfortable in the safety of its embrace, of the freedom it offers from feeling anything at all.

"What happened?" Brooke asks.

Kerry forces herself back to the moment. "I think she fell and hit her head," she hears herself say, though in fact she has no idea what happened. It's clear that the way Margaret's body lies there, facedown with the wound on the back of her head, doesn't fit her feeble answer.

"Is she—" Brooke looks at her and stops, as if she already knows and doesn't want confirmation.

"I heard her scream."

Kerry turns around to see Charlotte standing among them. She hadn't even heard her approach.

Kerry had heard the scream, too. She knew instantly it wasn't a devil. She scrambled out of her sleeping bag and ran barefoot through the darkness, with the bobbing light of her headlamp, still in her hand, barely keeping her on the walkway.

Then she saw Ian, standing just off the walkway. Immediately she knew something was wrong—not only because he wasn't looking up into the trees, as usual, but looking down, and also because of the look on his face: an odd mix of shock, fear, disbelief. When Kerry pointed her torch down on what he was looking at, she felt the air leave her body.

Margaret's body. Motionless. Blood staining her light hair.

Ian didn't move.

Bryan came next, followed by Brooke—and now Charlotte. Malcolm is close behind, she can see. Their headlamps are flickering through the dark like stars.

Though experience told her what happened to Jane, a part of her still wishes she were wrong. But now, as Bryan looks up at her, the slight shake of his head indicates that there is no room for wondering with Margaret.

Kerry turns away and tries to gather her thoughts, to figure out what to do next. There was no part of her training that explained how to handle a death, protect a crime scene, detain a suspect, comfort the bereaved. People signed on for this adventure to escape from the world of crime and misery, not immerse themselves in it.

Then she reminds herself that there is no evidence of a crime. Perhaps Margaret *did* fall and hit her head; perhaps she is lying here like this only because she tried to get up and walk back to her tent, only to fall again. The walkways do get slick in the rain, and it's easy to miss a step in the weak, unsteady light of a headlamp.

Bryan straightens and stands close. "Did you get here first?" he says, his voice barely audible.

She shakes her head, then whispers back, "Ian." She looks at Ian now, trying to gauge his state of mind, remembering the row Bryan had mentioned, the times she'd found him lurking about in the woods. Had he been the cause of this, or had he tried to help, or had he arrived, like the rest of them, to the awful sight of Margaret lying in the rain?

"Did he say anything?"

"No." She's aware of Brooke's and Charlotte's eyes on her, and she looks down as Ian crouches near the body, cradling Margaret's head. A tender action, and Kerry hates herself for having to wonder whether it's out of grief or regret.

"We have to move her," Kerry says to Bryan.

"Police wouldn't like that."

"Well, the police aren't here, are they?" she hisses. "Do you want her to disappear like Jane did? We have to protect her from the devils. You know that."

He says nothing. The sound of a snapping branch emerges from the forest, and Bryan flashes his torch toward the noise. "That sounded bigger than a wallaby," he says. Then, abruptly, he darts into the woods.

"Bryan," she says sharply, but he's already gone. Great. He's chasing wallabies, leaving her with a dead body and panicked guests.

Malcolm has reached them now and is looking around, apparently not seeing Margaret. "What happened?" he asks.

"It's Margaret, darling," Charlotte says. She puts one hand to her mouth and with the other aims her torch at Ian's feet.

"Oh, God." Malcolm looks down at Margaret, and Kerry hears a sniffle from Charlotte. Malcolm puts a hand on Ian's shoulder. "Mate. What can I do?"

Ian stands and shrugs off Malcolm's hand as though it's an insect. Malcolm backs away, and Charlotte, crying more openly now, leans into him.

"Malcolm, please take Charlotte back to your tent," Kerry says. "There's nothing you can do for Margaret right now. And, Brooke, please walk with them." To Malcolm and Charlotte, she adds, "Make sure Brooke gets to her tent safely, all right?"

Malcolm nods and puts his arm around Charlotte's shoulders. Brooke looks at Kerry nervously, and Kerry says, "Go. I need you all back in your tents. Now."

After they are on their way, Kerry steps over to Ian. He is staring down at his wife. Except for that instant with Malcolm, he has been eerily calm. Kerry steels herself for an outburst of emotion—anguish, outrage—as she touches his arm and says, "Ian, I'm so very sorry."

He turns his dark eyes toward her but says nothing.

"When you got here," Kerry asks, hesitantly, "what happened?"

His eyes are dark, blank watercolors, swimming with unreadable emotions.

"Was she lying here, just like this?" Kerry asks.

"Yes."

"And you didn't see or hear anything?"

"No." That's when his eyes flare, a spur of defiance. "I heard you tell Brooke that she fell. Margaret is a mountain climber. She doesn't fall."

"I understand." Kerry feels a flicker of relief; he wouldn't insist it wasn't a fall if he'd been involved in any way—would he? "All I can promise is that we'll find out what happened. I'm going to call the ranger and the police, and by morning hopefully they'll be here and we'll get it sorted."

Ian looks down at Margaret's body. "And in the meantime?"

"I know this is awful," Kerry says, "but I'm going to ask you to return to your tent, too. Bryan and I will move her into Bryan's tent."

"Why?" He looks stricken.

"She can't stay here overnight," Kerry begins.

"I'll stay with her."

"No, Ian." Kerry feels tears threaten to break loose from her throat. "I'm sorry. You need to try to get some rest, and we need to—to do this. I promise we'll take good care of her."

She isn't sure what she'll do if Ian argues with her. She sees with relief that Bryan is emerging from the trees. Ian bends down to remove a silver necklace from around Margaret's neck, then steps back up onto the walkway. He looks at each of them in turn, then says, "We wouldn't even be here tonight if it wasn't for that missing American."

Kerry takes a breath. "Ian—" she begins.

"Margaret survived Mount Everest, and you try to tell me she ends up slipping on a wet walkway on Marbury Island? Not bloody likely. I don't know what's going on here, but I hold you responsible."

He turns and starts walking back toward his tent. Kerry is about to call after him when she feels Bryan's hand on her shoulder. "Don't be bothered," he says quietly. "He's upset. Let him go."

She nods. "What are you doing running after wallabies, any-way? I really could've used your help with Ian."

Bryan frowns. "I don't think that was a marsupial."

"What else could it be?" Then she remembers the warnings about the poacher. "You don't think—"

Bryan shrugs. "We can't be too careful. Not after tonight."

"Did you actually see anyone?"

He shakes his head. "No."

Kerry sighs. Whatever modicum of optimism she still had for this trip ending less than disastrously vanishes in almost a physi-cal rush, like a soul leaving a body. All she can hope for now is that things don't go from worse to dystopian.

She and Bryan painstakingly begin the process of carrying Margaret's body to his tent. Margaret is much heavier than Kerry expected, and while she knows it is, literally, dead weight, she also realizes that Margaret is pure muscle. And just then Kerry is cer-tain, with a sick feeling in her gut, that Ian is right. Margaret is not a woman who falls. Even if she had fallen, she would not have ended up like this.

They finally get Margaret into the tent, and they lay her gently on the floor on a sleeping bag. As Kerry uses the other sleeping bag to cover her, she has to look away from Margaret's eyes, half open, eyelashes wet with rainwater.

"You right?" Bryan asks, and Kerry nods, even though she isn't. She sees Bryan's things propped on one of the beds and says, "Why don't you move your stuff to my tent while I try calling Mark. I just need to get my jacket."

"Take mine," Bryan offers, handing her his rain jacket. "Save you some time."

"Thanks."

Mobile in hand, she leaves the shelter of trees and makes her way to the beach. Turning on her mobile, she sees that the battery is down to 11 percent, and she curses herself for not taking advantage of the generator when it was still working.

On the beach, the rain and wind intensify in the open air, sand and water firing from all directions. The mobile illuminates the thick raindrops as she dials.

"Mark? Mark? Can you hear me?"

"Just barely." His voice is muffled. She's woken him up, she realizes; she hadn't even registered that the clock on her mobile read one in the morning.

"Mark, I have bad news. We have another fatality."

"Sorry, Kerry? I can't hear you."

"Another fatality," she shouts. "A woman. She fell."

"Fell?"

"Well, that's what I'm going with so far. I don't know what happened." She walks a few paces down the beach, and the connection strengthens a bit.

"Jesus, Kerry," Mark says, sounding not only clearer but wide awake and alert. "What's going on down there?"

"I don't know. I'm worried. Bryan thought he heard someone in the woods right after we found her. Either she hit her head on the walkway or . . . it makes me think about that poacher you mentioned."

"Did Bryan see anyone?"

"No." She tries to shake the thought from her mind. "Even if there was someone poaching out here, why would he want to hurt us? It doesn't make sense."

"None of this makes sense."

"We need to talk to the police. Have they been able to dock yet?"

"Not even close," Mark says. "They tried today, but the winds were fierce. They can't try again until tomorrow—if the winds let up."

She feels her hope sinking. "Mark, I need them here now. We can't handle this sort of thing on our own."

"I know, Kerry, I know. But it's impossible. The last ferry to leave here broke four windows as it left the dock. And it's not much better on the mainland—downed trees, flooded roads, power outages. Believe it or not, you're safer out there."

"Are you kidding? Have you heard anything I've said?"

"Listen, take a deep breath for me, Kerry," Mark says. "I know how you feel out there, but the fact is accidents happen, and it sounds as though you've just been horribly, horribly unlucky on this trip. I'm sure that's all it is, bad luck. I know you don't want to hear this, but you just need to sit tight."

"What if these aren't accidents?" she says. "What if we have a killer in our midst?"

"You have capsicum spray, don't you?"

"No, of course not." She'd never thought of it—after all, why would she need pepper spray on an island with no animals bigger than roos?—but now she wonders why on earth she doesn't have it.

"Anything at all?"

"Swiss Army knife. That won't do me much good, will it?"

"She'll be right, Kerry. I promise I will get there as soon as possible. If not by land, then by ship. I've been trying to get in touch with Dan—the bloke who dropped you off? I'm hoping he might be able to use his boat to help get the police here."

"Right," she says, trying not to sound as worried as she feels. "Thanks, Mark. I'll be in touch."

She returns to camp, quiet now, with the only light coming from her own tent—Bryan, waiting for her. Not ready to face him yet, she goes first to the loos, now deserted. She shines her torch at the spot where Margaret had been. The ferns are flattened into a dark-green bed, a few leaves still stained red. But the rain is still falling, washing away whatever evidence there may still be regarding what happened—an accident, as Mark believes, or, perhaps, the perfect crime. One that gets washed away before the authorities can arrive.

She looks around for anything that might have been used as a weapon—a large tree branch or a rock—but nothing stands out amid the brush and leaves and devil scat. She can't help but look into the trees, where Bryan had disappeared earlier, and she wonders whether someone had been watching them—whether someone may be watching her even now.

Abruptly she turns and walks toward the dining tent. It seems like lifetimes ago they'd sat here, drunk and happy with the promise of adventure ahead. How quickly and horribly everything had turned.

She is surprised to find all the tent flaps down, the entrance zipped shut. She takes a quick peek inside and sees that it's dark, quiet, clean. Perhaps there is hope for Bryan after all.

As she heads back to her tent, she sees a torch flickering in the washroom—which must be Bryan, cleaning his teeth or washing up—and inside her tent she takes advantage of the privacy to change out of her damp clothing into leggings and a T-shirt. She hangs her pants and layers up to dry, knowing they'll only get a few degrees colder and perhaps even damper when it's time to put them on again.

A light bounces toward the tent, and moments later Bryan slides under the half-zipped flap. Standing less than a meter away from her, he strips down to his briefs, then flops onto his sleeping bag and exhales. "And then there were six," he says.

"It feels as though Margaret was right," she says. "It's becoming like *Survivor*."

He sits up again, leaning on one elbow, and looks at her in the dim light of his headlamp, which is next to him on the bunk. "What do you make of Ian?" he asks.

"I'm not sure. Did he seem upset to you?"

"Not enough, I reckon. Except to be mad at us. Could he be covering for something he did to her?"

"I hate to think it."

"I don't think she could have died falling onto the walkway. Even if she was at the top of the steps to the loo, that's only a three-meter fall. The gouge in her head was deep."

"Well, what's the alternative?"

"That's what we have to consider. Alternatives."

"I don't like the sound of that."

"I don't either." He's silent for a moment. "Something off about Ian. I don't know if I trust him."

She sits up then and faces him. "I saw him out prowling around the night Jane disappeared. He said he was bird-watching."

"In the fucking dark? That's more than a little strange."

"There's something else," she says. "Brooke told me Malcolm was having an affair with Jane."

"You sure?"

"I'm sure she told me that," Kerry says. "I'm not sure it's true."

"Maybe that's why he's in such a hurry to leave camp."

"We're not leaving."

"We can't stop him. And I think if he still wants to leave, I should go along. Not only to keep him on the trail but to keep an eye on him."

"Maybe he'll change his mind after this."

"Or maybe he'll be more eager to get away from here."

She lies back in her bunk with a sigh. "How did everything become such a bloody fucking mess?"

"It's not your fault," he says. "We'll get it sorted. Try to get some sleep."

"You, too."

Bryan turns off his headlamp, and the tent goes dark. She can hear his breathing grow steady and deeper. She lies awake for a while longer, worried about Malcolm leaving, and probably Charlotte, too. She knows they need to stay together as a group, but she also knows Bryan is right: if those two want to leave, there's not much she can do about it. Except one thing: if Malcolm and Charlotte head north tomorrow, Bryan won't be going with them. She will.

CHAPTER 17

BROOKE

When Brooke opens her eyes, it takes her a few seconds to remember where she is. She'd been dreaming about William, and for a few brief moments after waking up, she thought she was home, in their bed. Even if it hadn't really been *their* bed for a long time.

She lets herself think about their last conversation, the one in which she told him she was moving out. She'd expected—hoped—that he'd be stunned; instead, it was as if he'd been waiting for the news all along. While it confirmed she was doing the right thing, she was disappointed that he hadn't put up a fight. Or at least a small measure of protest.

But passionate arguments had never been William's style. His logical nature was among the things that had attracted her to him—along with his amazing intellect, his laser-like focus, his vast knowledge about so many things. All of which came with other things. His social awkwardness. The rarity of real eye contact. The intense and slightly robotic way he approaches almost everything in life, from cooking to sex. All the things that made her feel, for the first time in her life, that she wasn't onstage, that she could be herself around him.

She had to admit they'd been in trouble for a long time. She hadn't done anything to fix it for the simple reason that she didn't know what had broken. Now that she looked back, it seemed as if they'd always been a little bit broken. That maybe she'd chosen William so she could play another role—one that may have felt more real but that was still only another act.

She wishes she'd done more to save them, both before and after she left. Maybe it's the sudden loneliness she feels right now—on a remote island near what feels like the end of the world—but it's also the stab of remorse she's feeling over Jane, overflowing into everything else. The feeling she has never worked hard enough for her relationships, to salvage what matters.

Over the years—the past year especially—William became more challenged in his job and she less so in hers. She did enjoy her job, as she'd told Jane, but the admin work wasn't exactly challenging, especially once she'd learned how things worked backward and forward. She and William slowly became more and more distanced from each other, and while she could feel the space between them growing wider, she was uninspired—and, also, simply didn't know how—to close the gap.

Or maybe, now that she thinks about it, she was afraid. Afraid of cooking dinner for William only to be stood up by another late night at the office. Of initiating sex and being turned down. Planning a trip he wouldn't have time for. Maybe he felt the same way, or maybe he never even thought about it.

Brooke sighs and sits up in her bunk, noticing then that the rain is not as loud on the roof of the tent as it was when she went to sleep. She looks over at Jane's empty bunk, at her backpack. She thinks of Jane's parents, whom she hasn't seen in years—who would contact them? Brooke realizes she doesn't know any of Jane's friends, or whether she even has any friends. They'd had only one day to catch up on five years, and then she was gone.

It's still early, but Brooke can't stand being alone in the tent any longer, with the remnants of that dream, with Jane's things, with all that is lost. She gets dressed and goes to the dining tent, where she finds only Kerry, standing at the counter cutting up fruit.

"Morning," she says.

Kerry turns around. "Would you like some coffee?" She sounds as despondent as Brooke feels.

"Sure. Thanks."

"Fortunately, we still have fuel for the kettle," she says. "I'm trying to be grateful for the little things."

Brooke takes the mug Kerry hands her and lets it warm her hands. "We might have another thing to be grateful for—it looks like the rain is easing up a bit."

"Yes," Kerry says. "In fact, I remember the precise moment Bryan's snoring became louder than the rain. I just hope it lasts."

"This will make it easier for the police to—" Brooke is interrupted by a piercing, almost-human screech just outside the tent. Startled, she asks, "What was that?"

Kerry motions for Brooke to follow her outside. Out on the deck, the rain is little more than a mist. Kerry scans the trees, then points about halfway up a gigantic eucalyptus tree twenty yards away.

"There, see?" she says. "A yellow-tailed black cockatoo."

Brooke stares into the tree for several minutes, unable to see what Kerry is pointing at. Then a flutter of movement, wings emerging from the branches, the cockatoo coming into plain view. The bird looks not unlike an enormous crow, a deep rich black, with a round splotch of yellow feathers behind pink-rimmed eyes.

"He's calling to his mate," Kerry says as the bird bobs his head and emits another *ee-yow*. "You rarely see one without seeing the other."

Kerry's eyes are still aimed high among the branches, and she points again, toward a neighboring tree. Again, Brooke can't find the bird until she moves, dropping from the treetops into free fall, then expanding her glossy black wings as she swoops downward. Brooke glimpses the bright yellow tailfeathers just before the bird lands on a branch next to the other cockatoo.

"They love gum trees, which is why they love this island," Kerry says.

"Are they safe here? From predators, I mean?"

"Well, the only real danger for them is poachers, which didn't used to be a problem."

"Didn't used to? You're saying it is now?"

Kerry sighs. "The ranger thinks someone's been stealing eggs. They keep a close eye on the bird populations, and there's been a steep drop for the parrots in the last couple seasons. The cockatoos, green rosellas, swift parrots—these are rare birds already. And they nest in trees, so we know they're not being predated on by other animals."

"Why would anyone take their eggs?"

"There's a very active black market in parrots. They'll even take the chicks, smuggle them out of the country stuffed into luggage. It's horrible. I don't know how these people sleep at night."

"Don't they ever get caught?"

"Not nearly enough. One reason I was drawn to guiding on this island is that it's so remote that having tourists here actually helps protect the birds. As long as we're out and about, the poachers have to stay in the shadows. Of course we hope they decide not to come here at all."

Brooke suddenly remembers the day they landed: the footprints she saw on the beach, the figure disappearing into the forest. "Do you think there could be a poacher on the island right now?"

She sees a shadow cross Kerry's face before she answers. "I don't think so," she says, her eyes still on the trees, as if unwilling to meet Brooke's gaze.

"I saw someone. On the beach."

"When?"

"When we landed. Remember? At first I thought I was seeing things, and you and Bryan both said it was a wallaby. But what if it wasn't?"

Kerry goes silent.

"What are you thinking?" Brooke says. "Could he have something to do with Jane?"

"I honestly have no idea. But the idea of another person on this island, lurking around in the shadows . . ." She shakes her head.

"It's okay. We'll get through this." This feels to Brooke like the first honest thing she's said in a long time.

"Yeah, you're right. I'm sorry everything is such a mess."

"My life was a mess long before I got here," Brooke says. "And on top of it all, I'm off my meds for the first time in weeks. Accidentally."

Kerry gives her a sad smile. "Good on you," she says. "They'll do you no good in the long run anyhow."

The bird cries again, and Kerry looks up, searching.

"What happens to the birds when someone takes their eggs?"

Kerry shrugs. "I can't even imagine what they go through. Imagine someone stealing your baby right out from under you. But parrots mate for life, so they try again."

"That part's inspiring, at least," Brooke says. "I envy that. Mating for life, I mean."

"Me, too. I can't seem to manage it myself."

Brooke looks at her. "My marriage lasted only five years. What about you?"

"I wasn't married, but we were together five years, too. I had a lot of hope for us. For a lot of things."

The wistful note in Kerry's voice sounds like an echo coming from inside herself. "Like what?"

"The devils. I've spent most of my career trying to help them."

Involuntarily, Brooke shivers; at the mention of the devils, she sees only Jane's raggedy scarf, the ravaged phone, the rain-thinned blood. "You mean the animals that killed Jane?"

"They didn't kill her."

"But what they did—" Brooke stops. "It's so violent. I can't believe you have such fondness for them."

"I understand how you feel," Kerry says. "But they're only trying to survive. They're suffering from a highly contagious disease and heading very quickly toward extinction. Marbury Island was giving them a chance at new life."

"What do you mean, *was*? Because of what happened to Jane?"

Kerry nods. "Something's not quite right if they're that hungry. And the fact that they have done something to a human— that's another issue altogether, and nothing good can come of it.

But I haven't been working on this island long enough to know what's wrong, or how to fix it."

The cockatoos suddenly take flight with a chorus of loud caws, and Kerry turns back toward the tent. "Your coffee must be cold by now."

Inside, as Kerry pours her a fresh cup of coffee, Brooke can tell that the shadow that seems to surround Kerry has darkened. "Was it work that caused your breakup?"

Kerry puts the coffeepot down on the table and drops into a chair. "It's a bit more complicated than that, but in a way, yes. What about you?"

"A bit less complicated, actually," Brooke says, sitting down next to her. "I've been thinking about it a lot, and I just think, in the end, I married him for all the wrong reasons." She hesitates, not sure whether she wants to say this out loud. But maybe she needs to. "I didn't want to face giving up on my dream," she says finally, "and it was easier to pretend he was taking me away from all sorts of impending success than to admit I'd already failed. I did love him, but I was also looking for an excuse to run away."

Kerry gives her a rueful smile. "Failure," she says softly. "That's been such a theme in my life lately. Work, relationship, devils. This trip."

"You can't blame yourself for this trip," Brooke says. "What's happened isn't your fault at all."

"I'm not so sure about that."

Kerry's voice has grown even quieter, sinking into depths Brooke senses are lightless and impenetrable, and she feels a stab of panic, as if what began as commiseration over lost love is leading them both down a steep emotional spiral—and then what? She knows this feeling, this wanting to disappear from the world—she's seen it in Jane, after every breakup or missed role; she's seen it in herself, after she moved out—the wish to vanish so no one has to witness your unraveling.

"Well, if it's anyone's fault, I still think Malcolm has something to do with it," Brooke says, hoping this will help jolt Kerry back to the moment. Back to figuring out what happened to Jane.

"Because they were having an affair?"

"Because he and Margaret were also having an affair." Brooke tells her what she overheard.

Kerry seems to snap back to attention. "Are you sure?"

"There was no doubt about what I heard. And then Margaret confirmed it."

"How? When?"

"I saw her out in the woods, near where Jane—disappeared," Brooke says. "She freaked me out a little, maybe because we were all alone, in that spot. Anyway, I told her what I knew. To see if maybe she knew anything about what happened to Jane."

Kerry's eyes narrow. "What did she say?"

"She didn't believe me about Jane and Malcolm. But now I'm even more worried. I mean, what if Malcolm decided to silence Margaret as well as Jane?"

"Let's not jump to conclusions."

"There's no jumping required to reach that conclusion."

"It's just—" Kerry stops.

"What?" Brooke studies her for a moment. "What are you thinking?"

Kerry leans forward. "I'm telling you this, one woman to another, because I want to keep you safe. I saw Ian out in the woods the night Jane went missing."

"What? Why didn't you tell me?"

"I didn't think much about it—he said he was out birding. But now, with Margaret—it just makes me wonder, that's all."

"You think Ian found out about her and Malcolm?" Brooke feels her body flush with heat. What if he'd overheard her talking to Margaret? What if Brooke had been the one to inadvertently destroy their marriage—and possibly Margaret's life?

"I don't know," Kerry says. "Nothing makes sense. I'm just counting the seconds until investigators arrive."

"Well, I don't trust either one of them," Brooke says. She hears footsteps on the deck and turns to see Ian standing in the doorframe of the tent. She can't tell by his face how long he'd been there.

"Good morning, Ian," Kerry says, standing quickly. "Would you like coffee or tea?"

"Coffee." He winces, as if the word physically pains him.

Kerry hands him a steaming mug. "Is there anything else you need right now?"

"I need to get back to the mainland with my wife."

"Yes," Kerry says. "Right. I know. I hope to have news for you about that after breakfast."

Ian walks back outside and lowers himself into a glistening deck chair, facing away from Brooke and Kerry. He doesn't take even one sip of his coffee as he stares out into the gray morning, the misty rain coating his hair like dew.

Kerry returns to the counter and slices bread, and Brooke sits there with her cooling coffee, wondering what to do. Given what Kerry said, she doesn't know if Ian deserves words of comfort or whether he should be feared. Then she thinks of how none of the other guests had been sympathetic about Jane when she went missing. She's staring at the back of Ian's head, a jumble of emotions competing for space in her mind, when she's saved from her thoughts by Malcolm, who walks into the tent and slips off his pack, leaning it against the dining table.

Kerry turns around. "Malcolm, I know you're eager to go, but I hope you'll sit down with us before you decide anything."

Bryan walks in next, dressed for the weather and for hiking. "I'm taking anyone who wants to go. We leave after breakfast."

"We'll be in Saltwick before dark, right?" Malcolm says.

"It's twenty kilometers away," Kerry says.

"Not a problem."

Brooke looks from one of them to another, unbelieving. Malcolm and Bryan are really going to leave them behind, after all that's happened?

Another landing-day memory flashes in her mind: Malcolm checking his phone on the beach, just before Kerry told them all to put them in airplane mode. Has he been looking for an excuse to leave all along?

When Charlotte walks into the tent, Brooke is surprised to see that she's wearing sandals, leggings, and a loose sweater—instead of a backpack, she's carrying a book. She doesn't look at all ready for a day of hiking.

"You're not going?" Brooke asks her.

"No, darling, I've decided to wait." Charlotte sits down and helps herself to coffee. She doesn't look at her husband. "I've no need to get back to Sydney, since I can write anywhere, so if Malcolm wants to go trekking through the muck in the rain, he's more than welcome."

"It's not merely a trek," Malcolm says. "We'll be sending the authorities back straightaway. The sooner Bryan and I get to civilization, the sooner we all get to civilization."

Brooke looks at Malcolm and wonders what his plan is. To leave the island as quickly as he can, knowing most of the evidence has been washed away by the storm? She'd be more surprised by him leaving Charlotte behind if she didn't already know he was sleeping with not one but two women other than his wife. It's as if he doesn't believe in real-world consequences at all, as if the reality shows he produces have actually become his life.

Then she remembers Bryan's words: *anyone who wants to go.*

"I'm going with you," Brooke says, then turns and heads for her tent, hearing Kerry's voice call after her but unable to hear what she's saying. The wind has picked up again, whisking away Kerry's words, and Brooke realizes she's in for a cold, wet, nasty hike—but she has to go. She has to keep an eye on the man who could be responsible for what happened to Jane.

In her tent, she takes one last look around for her prescription bottle, but she can't see it anywhere, and she doesn't have time to do a more thorough search. She shoves everything into her pack so haphazardly that she has to sit on top of it to get the zipper shut. Then she sits on her bunk and looks at Jane's pack. It doesn't seem right to leave it here, but there's no way she can carry two. Maybe she can at least take some of Jane's things with her.

She grabs the pack and pulls it toward her, surprised to find it's lighter than she expected, given Jane's efforts to lift it. The first thing she notices is that the bottle of Jack Daniel's is gone. She looks around the tent, but in the dim light she can't see it. Maybe it rolled out into the ferns.

She sifts through the clothing, the toiletries, not sure what she's looking for. She was thinking she could take something Jane's family might want to have, something she herself might want to keep, but why would Jane have anything more than the necessities for this trip? It doesn't feel quite right to take one of Jane's shirts, or a pair of shorts; they aren't even the same size.

Just as she's about to end her rummaging and zip up the pack, her fingers brush against some sort of box. She grasps it and pulls it out.

A pregnancy test.

She thinks back two nights, to the Lifetime dramedy they'd recreated in the dining tent, to the unexpected turn Jane had taken. *And since I'm having your baby, she'll find out about us eventually.*

She'd never had the chance to ask Jane where that line came from, what it meant. All she knew was that Jane wanted to get back at Malcolm, in whatever way she could. *Hamlet* had been Jane's inspiration for their little drama—*the play's the thing*, she'd said. She'd taken aim at Malcolm, wanting to *catch the conscience of the King*. And then, it had all backfired so horribly.

Brooke thinks now of their college production of *Hamlet*, a triumph for them both, as they'd each gotten one of only two female roles in the play. Jane had played Ophelia, brilliant in her portrayal of the girl's descent into madness, and Brooke had won the role of Gertrude, the weak and disloyal widowed queen. How odd to think of them in these roles now, a decade later, especially under these circumstances: Jane losing her mind over love; Brooke helpless and falling all too easily into another man's bed.

And then she feels a burst of resolve. The least she can do for her friend now, Brooke tells herself, is to follow Malcolm and find out what happened.

When she returns to the dining tent, Bryan is the only one there, leaning over the soap-filled sink. Breakfast dishes are piled on the counter next to him. Brooke notices that he's barefoot and no longer wearing rain gear.

"I thought we were leaving soon?" Brooke asks.

Before Bryan can answer, Brooke hears someone enter the tent, and she turns to see Kerry, dressed in hiking gear, wearing her pack.

"You're taking us?"

Brooke is relieved when Kerry nods. In the aftermath of Jane's vanishing, her night with Bryan has morphed from a wild, erotic night to a shameful act of back-turning on her oldest friend. A reminder of how things might've been different if only she'd resisted.

Besides, she feels more comfortable with Kerry, who knows all that she does about Malcolm and doesn't have a bromance going on with him over reality television.

A few minutes later, Malcolm returns alone.

"Ready, guys?" Kerry asks.

As they head out of camp, with Kerry in the lead and Malcolm behind her, Brooke looks back briefly, wondering where Ian and Charlotte are. Wondering whether she'll ever be back to this place again. Whether she'll ever be able to say a proper goodbye to Jane.

She trips over a tree root and turns around again. Now's not the time to look backward, she tells herself, only forward. And as she braces her body against the increasing wind, she settles her eyes onto the center of Malcolm's back. She thinks again of *Hamlet*—"the devil hath power / T' assume a pleasing shape—" and wonders whether Jane had perhaps seen the devil in Malcolm all along.

CHAPTER 18

KERRY

With each step it feels as if they are emerging into light, and the faded glow of sun behind bruised clouds gives Kerry a false hope she doesn't dare embrace.

An hour ago, they left the sylvan confines of dense forest for a eucalypt overstory, which let in undulant daylight, and now they're under moving storm clouds, winding their way along the coast. The trail is flooded in spots, forcing them into high fescues, sending wallabies and roos sprinting through the bush. They've passed a half-dozen wombats in patches of grass or sipping water from newly formed ponds. To their left is the white-tipped ocean, the sound of waves crashing into shore intermingling with the wind, still strong but not as savage as before.

Malcolm, finally, is quiet. He tried, for the first hour, to quiz Kerry about what the plan would be once they reached town, how they would deal with the issue of Margaret's body, how to deal with Ian's loss. When she responded with *I don't know*s to every one of his queries, he seemed to grow nervous and began to talk about local news and Tasmanian history, as if desperate to keep some sort of conversation going, but she was in even less of a mood to play genial hostess, as though nothing were wrong.

Eventually he retreated into himself, and Kerry stepped up her pace to one that is now keeping them all breathing a bit too heavily to talk. Kerry remains in front, followed by Malcolm, with Brooke trailing behind.

In addition to worrying about all the questions Malcolm raised and many more, Kerry is trying to come to terms with the fact that her first guiding trip will also be her last. Her thoughts drift to what's next in her life, and all she sees is an empty dark place, like a forgotten cave.

And that's when she remembers the dream she had last night. A good dream. A beautiful dream.

It was so real at first. She was standing with everyone in the group—including Margaret and Jane—in a field, with the ocean far away. Dotting the field were wombats, mowing low the grass in their slow-motion waltz.

Then she saw the devil—a rare daylight sighting. Everyone was entranced, and Kerry knelt down and called out to him, entreating him to come to her, as she would a dog. And he did, as the others followed her lead and dropped to their knees, hands out as if to pet him.

But unlike a dog, who'd greet everyone and bask in their attention, the devil walked past all the outstretched hands and soft voices and right up to her, and when she reached out, he let her pet him, that silky black fur, wet black nose, that tiny whiskered face.

When she awoke the next morning, she felt for the first time as though her life's work had not been a mistake after all—that in some way, the devils had chosen her as much as she'd chosen them.

When they reach the top of a ridge overlooking Northshore Beach, Kerry stops. "Water break," she says, pulling out her own water bottle and waiting for Malcolm and Brooke to do the same. They need to stay hydrated; they need to keep moving. They are not yet halfway, and the trip is going to take much longer than usual with the storm-related detours.

She looks down on the white-sand beach, the green waves churning just beyond the shore. If this were a normal tour, she would descend the sandy berm and lead them along the powdered-sugar beach in a wide curve north. She would stop along the way to point out the bounty of seashells, letting them pick up whatever they wanted and then making sure they put everything back where they found it. She would scan the horizon for seals and dolphins, and if she were lucky she'd catch a glimpse and point them out. They would likely see a pair or two of musk ducks floating by on the water, pied oystercatchers nesting just above the shoreline. Best of all is what they would not see: other humans, other signs of humanity—no trash, no footprints, no speedboats. They would feel as though they'd stepped back into the nineteenth century.

Abruptly, Kerry returns her water bottle to its pocket and says, "Let's go." She veers right, onto the remnants of a footpath through a thick patch of marram grass. This shortcut, she hopes, will shave some time off their hike, getting them to the next camp within an hour and on pace to reach Saltwick before sunset.

It takes a few minutes for her to realize she doesn't hear footsteps behind her, and her pulse quickens as she stops to wait, listening intently. She can't hear the sound of them following and begins to wonder whether something happened. She is just taking her first steps back toward the ridge when she sees Malcolm come around a turn, with Brooke not far behind him.

She lets out a silent sigh of relief. Brooke has made her paranoid, she realizes—even if everything she believes about Malcolm were true, he wouldn't dare try anything. Would he?

It's just then that she realizes she hasn't called Mark to tell him she's on her way to town. "Let's take another quick water break," she says, then walks a few paces away. She turns on her mobile— no signal—and sighs audibly this time as she turns it off again and returns it to her pocket.

Brooke and Malcolm, both sitting on boulders, look exhausted. Malcolm's shirt is soaked with sweat, and Brooke's hand shakes a little as she takes another drink of water. Kerry hopes they'll make it to the next camp, where she should be able to get a signal and call Mark while they take a break.

"The next camp is not too far ahead," she says. "We'll stop for lunch there."

"Can't we sit here for a bit longer?" Brooke asks.

"I'd like to change my shirt," Malcolm says, easing off his pack.

"This isn't a good place to rest," Kerry says, noticing movement around his feet.

"Just give me a minute."

"I'd be glad to, but that colony of jack jumpers isn't going to." Kerry nods toward his feet, where the ants are now swarming. Just as Malcolm looks down and sees them, an ant climbs past his sock.

"Jesus!" He slaps frantically at his shin.

"It stings, I know."

"Why didn't you warn me?"

"I tried."

Brooke, who'd made a point of sitting a couple meters away from Malcolm, stands up, even though she isn't close to the jumpers.

Kerry watches Malcolm rub at the bite mark on his leg, waiting to make sure he doesn't have a reaction. Most of the time the stings are merely painful, but people have been known to go into anaphylactic shock. Fortunately, she can tell by Malcolm's hearty cursing that he's having no trouble breathing, and they set off again.

Whether it's the fear of more swarming ants or the promise of rest, Malcolm and Brooke keep up with her as Kerry leads them at a continued brisk pace toward camp. She keeps an ear on their footfalls behind her, crunching through the fallen euc leaves, and keeps her eyes ahead, through the drying mist in the air. She leaves no room for thoughts, nothing but the cool air against her skin and rainwater dripping from the branches and the still-soggy ground under her feet.

When they reach the campsite nearly an hour later, Kerry is relieved to see all of the tent flaps securely zipped closed. Then they reach the dining tent, and her stomach sinks. The main entrance is unzipped.

"Why don't you two have a seat here on the deck," Kerry says. The sun is still fighting to emerge from the clouds, but it's not too cold, and for once, it's not raining.

She pauses before ducking inside. She reaches in and feels for the light switch, relieved when the lights go on, if dimly; at least this battery still has a little juice in it. She ducks into the tent and takes the large emergency torch from the counter and looks around.

Somebody has raided the cooler—bottles of water appear to be missing—and the stash of energy bars and scroggin has also been depleted. The beer and wine are still inside the cooler, and the other food bin is still locked shut.

Whoever was here was apparently interested only in refueling before moving on. But to where? She moves around the room with the torch, looking for clues as to how recently this mystery person was here. It's impossible to tell whether someone was here days ago or minutes ago.

A hand comes down on her shoulder, and she jumps, spinning around as she suppresses a shriek.

Malcolm is standing behind her, a dark figure with the daylight behind him.

"What is it?"

"I just wanted to see if there's any extra water."

"Help me open the tent flaps for more light," she says, "and we'll see."

The two of them open the flaps, and as the room brightens she sees an empty beer bottle in the sink. If she had to guess, at least one of the guest tents has been slept in. But she doesn't have time to check.

Malcolm, at the cooler, takes out a tallie and a bottle of chardonnay. "Looks as though this is all the liquid you've got."

"The water from the tap is filtered rainwater," Kerry says. "It's fine for drinking."

Malcolm uses the end of his T-shirt to twist off the cap of the beer bottle. "This is probably safer," he says, "and besides, we've earned it."

She sighs. "Malcolm, we have at least ten more kilometers to go today. You can't afford to get dehydrated."

He ignores her and returns to the deck, where they open the paper lunch boxes Kerry had filled for them earlier with fruit, sandwiches, and energy bars. As Malcolm takes a long drink from the tallie, Brooke nibbles on an apple, facing slightly away from Malcolm. Kerry can see that she's sitting very still, hyperaware of his presence, his every movement.

Kerry leaves them and walks through the bush toward the water about fifty meters from camp. Above, the cirrus clouds taunt her with slivers of blue, and the clearing sky makes her wonder how things might have been different had the weather cooperated from the first day.

Her mobile begins ringing as soon as she turns it on, and she looks at it hopefully, thinking it's Mark. It's Bryan.

"Where are you?" he asks immediately.

"Camp two. Why?"

"I've got bad news."

"What is it?"

"I've lost Ian."

"What do you mean you've *lost Ian*?"

"He's headed your way—if he doesn't get twisted all around and end up back with us."

"But why? You were supposed to keep Ian and Charlotte there with you."

"Yeah, I know that, Kerry."

"So?" Kerry says. "What happened?"

She hears Bryan draw in a breath. "Charlotte started in on the wine almost as soon as you left," he says. "I think the stress is getting to her. She got pissed as a newt."

"What does this have to do with Ian?"

"She and Ian were talking, and suddenly she just spit the dummy," he says. "Taunting him. Saying she couldn't believe he didn't know."

"Know what?" Kerry asks, but she's beginning to have a terrible feeling about what comes next.

"About Malcolm and Margaret."

"Oh, no."

"You don't sound surprised," Bryan says. "Did you know about this?"

"Yes. No. I don't know. Brooke mentioned it, but I don't know what to believe anymore."

"Well, this would've been good for me to know about twenty minutes ago," says Bryan. "I could've prevented this whole thing from getting out of hand."

"So, what happened?"

"Ian's face turned a shade of red I've never seen before. Said he's going to find Malcolm and bust his hole. He took off before I could calm him down."

"Shit." Kerry looks up at the sky, as if to find an answer among the ineluctable clouds.

"I'm sorry," Bryan says, "but you could've told me. I might've cut Charlotte off and prevented her from getting totally blind, for one."

"Even if I'd believed Brooke, I didn't know Charlotte knew. Nothing you could've done."

"If you're at the second camp, you have a good head start, at least," Bryan says. "I'd get to town straightaway, so he doesn't have a chance to catch up with you."

"Does he have any water? Does he even know where he's going?" The last thing she needs is another missing guest.

"He took his pack, his damn camera. Don't worry about him. I'm more worried about what'll happen to Malcolm if he catches up with you."

It's hard to know what would be worse—letting Ian get lost on the island, or letting Ian catch up with them and try to mete out his revenge on Malcolm.

"There's something else you should know," Bryan says. "Charlotte said Malcolm wasn't with her the night Jane disappeared. She said she woke up from a dream and called out to him, but he wasn't there."

"What? Why would she say that? Why now?"

"It's the wine talking, I guess."

"Or anger. Probably both."

"So," he asks, "how're you getting on?"

"We're right." She remembers then that her battery is dying fast and she still hasn't called Mark. "Bryan, I better go. Call me if anything else comes up."

"You, too."

She ends the call and holds the mobile in her hands for a moment as she looks out over the ocean. A ray of sunlight hits the water, far in the distance, and lights it up like shimmering glass.

She looks down at her mobile again, dials Mark. The signal is strong, but there is no answer. "Mark, please call me," she tells his voicemail. "We've set out for Saltwick. Three of us, anyhow. Long story. Call me."

She turns off the mobile and goes back to camp, where Brooke is sitting on the wooden planks of the deck, feet stretched out in front of her, as far away from Malcolm as possible. Malcolm has sunk deep into a deck chair, and, apparently finished with his beer, is now drinking from the chardonnay bottle.

"Are you ready?" Kerry asks them. "Time to get moving."

Brooke jumps to her feet, but Malcolm heaves his backpack on with some difficulty. Kerry knows he's going to be dangerously dehydrated and that he'll slow them down, especially if the sun comes out and if it gets any warmer. But she doesn't care. She'll drag him into town if she has to.

Judging by Brooke's expression, she'll have help. Brooke alternates between avoiding looking at Malcolm altogether and shooting him withering looks. Maybe Kerry should be less worried about Ian and more concerned about Brooke.

They set out along the water, and Kerry tries to envision the scene Bryan described: quiet, composed Charlotte, drunkenly blathering to Ian about his dead wife's affair. It's hard to imagine her being so cruel—but then, Kerry remembers, trips like this create an entirely false sense of intimacy. You spend every waking hour with the same people, and you feel as though you know them. You don't.

Soon the trail curves inland again, and the coolness they lose in ocean breezes they gain in shade from the old-growth blue gums overhead. Kerry begins to gradually pick up her pace, but the slow boil of her increasing stride doesn't work as she'd hoped; the other two linger behind, and she has to slow down to let them catch up.

When they come into earshot, she notices they have been talking—though it sounds more like arguing. Oh, no, she thinks. She can't possibly deal with a row between them right now.

"What have I done, exactly?" Malcolm asks. "I don't understand where this animosity is coming from."

"Maybe because you lied to and betrayed my oldest friend?"

"That's what she told you, is it?"

"Don't tell me she made it up," Brooke says. "I know what kind of man you are. I heard it for myself, firsthand, when you were with Margaret in her tent."

"I don't see how any of this is your business."

"It's my business because Jane is gone and Margaret is dead. Don't you think that looks really bad for you?"

"I'm not going to dignify that with a response."

"You don't need to respond to me," Brooke says. "You can tell it to the police."

Kerry raises her arms to bring them to a halt. "Guys, please. I don't want to talk about, or hear about, any of this right now. It's not the time or place."

Brooke shakes her head and keeps walking, falling into step with Kerry as they continue on. Kerry steals a glance back at Malcolm, who is close behind, and feels torn. On one hand, she isn't sure she and Brooke should be turning their backs on him, if he's as dangerous as Brooke believes him to be. On the other hand, he doesn't seem at all bothered by Brooke's accusations. Is it because he's innocent? Or because he's a psychopath?

They walk in silence for the next two hours; the only words spoken are Kerry's when she stops them for short breaks for water and to step into the woods to use nature's loo. During the brief breaks, she examines their faces: Brooke's is clammy-looking, with rosy spots high on her cheeks; Malcolm's, with two days' worth of stubble catching the sweat that runs down, is red and furrowed. They'll both make it, she knows; physically, they look exhausted but otherwise okay. But emotionally—she wishes she knew. She feels herself shutting down—the only way she knows to cope—shoving all the fear and uncertainty deep down to the dark places from which she's recently emerged but which she somehow knew would one day come in handy—the black holes of her soul that still have an inexorable gravitational pull, where no light can enter, the steep horizon over which everything goes to disappear forever.

At last, up ahead, Kerry sees an ankle-high limestone rock marking the turn. This was the marker she missed last time. Back when she thought that previous trip was the worst possible guiding experience she could have.

They are finally getting close to town. She turns to say, "Almost there, guys," and gets silent, bone-tired stares in return.

After another thirty minutes, they emerge from the trail onto a gravel road with a sweeping view across manicured lawns and patches of trees all the way to the water. In the distance Kerry can see the pier, still empty. The waves are still riled and foamy, and the winds are high, but above them the clouds are moving quickly, revealing tentative patches of blue.

She stops and waits for Brooke and Malcolm.

"That it?" Malcolm asks.

"That's Saltwick."

She can tell by his expression that he doesn't quite believe her. She hadn't really prepared them; she hadn't done her usual talk, telling them about the history of the town and what it's like today. In fact, calling Saltwick a town is a stretch. There are no residents, other than a park ranger, and there are only a dozen old buildings and remnants of buildings from the convict and settlement era.

Seeing civilization again, even in such a small dose, tugs Kerry from the depths, the relief of knowing that she will soon be joined by others, people in uniform, people who might have slept more than six hours over the past two nights. She feels her mood lift and senses the other two are relieved as well.

"Most of the buildings housed convicts in those early years," she says, as they continue walking, to offer a distraction. She doesn't yet see anyone in town who can help them, and she's not ready to field their questions. "The others were built by an Italian entrepreneur who ran a few businesses here, before they went under during the financial crisis at the end of the nineteenth century."

"What sort of businesses?" Brooke asks, her eyes fixed on the varying shades of blue and green water in the bay.

"A bit of everything," Kerry says. "Mining. Cement. He basically failed at all of it, which turned out to be good in the end."

"Looks like a ghost town."

"The storm has cut off Marbury from the mainland for the last few days. Usually this time of year, we'd see visitors coming for the day on the ferry, and people camping. Mark, the park ranger, lives here five days a week, and there might be a few backpackers."

As she leads them down the road into town, they sidestep large gray geese crossing the road as they forage in the grass on either side. "Those are Cape Barren geese," Kerry says. "They're distinctive for the neon-green spot over their bills."

"And their legs," Brooke says, indicating their bright pink color. "Like flamingos."

"Remember when you asked me about the cockatoos?" Kerry says. "As I told you, their eggs are safe in the trees—but that's not the case with Cape Barren geese. They nest on the ground, and the devils often eat their eggs. They might have to be relocated."

"You mean the devils or the—" Brooke stops mid-sentence, and Kerry stops and looks at her.

"What's the matter?"

Brooke is staring at a point up ahead, where the town of Saltwick meets the woods. "Do you see her?"

Kerry follows her eyes, and then she notices a blonde woman with a small blue day pack at the edge of the woods. "That backpacker over there?"

"That's not a backpacker," Brooke says. "It's her. It's Jane."

"Jane? What are you talking about?" Kerry looks again, more closely. The woman is heading into the woods, her long blonde hair trailing out of a baseball hat. "Jane isn't blonde."

"That doesn't matter," Brooke says impatiently, as the woman disappears into the thicket of trees. "It's Jane. I'd know her anywhere."

She starts out toward the woman, but Kerry reaches out and grabs her arm. "Brooke, no. We've got to get to the ranger station."

"Go ahead without me." Brooke shakes loose Kerry's hand and frees herself from her backpack, letting it drop to the ground before she begins running toward the forest.

"Brooke, wait!"

Kerry shouts again, but it's too late: Brooke has reached the treeline, and before Kerry can utter another word, she slips inside and disappears.

She thinks of Bryan, of Ian. In only one day, they have lost two additional guests. She wonders if he's been in touch with Nigel; she didn't think to ask.

Then she turns to Malcolm. "Did that look like Jane to you?"

"I didn't see her."

She looks at him, unsure whether to believe him, but she can't tell one way or another. His eyes are bloodshot, and the smell of wine and beer is oozing out of his pores. "Come on, then," she says, and they continue to the park ranger station.

When she sees the building in front of her, her legs nearly buckle with relief. Soon she'll be sitting in Mark's office, with a working phone, with a cup of tea, with people to tell her what to do. Granted, she'll also have to talk to Nigel and the police, but she will no longer be completely alone in all of this. She needs to feel less alone, for once.

When she reaches the door, she pulls on the knob, which doesn't turn; the door doesn't give. She rattles it a few times before she looks up and sees a hand-scribbled sign tacked to the door: OUT FOR THE DAY, it reads, with Mark's mobile number scrawled below.

"Where is he?" Malcolm asks.

And then she remembers what he had said the last time they spoke—*I promise I will get there as soon as possible. If not by land, then by ship.* Could he have left for the first camp without calling her? Or maybe he tried.

She pulls out her mobile and sees that it's completely dead.

"What now?" Malcolm asks.

Kerry feels suddenly, overwhelmingly sapped, as if she can't possibly take another step. What now indeed? She and Bryan are without more than two-thirds of the group they began with, the dock is still apparently closed, they are cut off from civilization, and the town is empty and devoid of anyone who can help them.

But, she reminds herself, first things first. One step at a time. "We need to find a power outlet," she says, with more confidence than she feels, and she leads him to Saltwick House, the posh former residence of the Italian entrepreneur, now operating as a guesthouse, with full baths, large suites with comfortable beds, and a parlor, dining room, and expansive front porch. The

Marbury Island Track Co. has exclusive use of it all summer, as the final, luxurious destination of its guided walks.

As they approach, Kerry thinks of how different it was supposed to be. This is where the group was supposed to arrive not today but tomorrow, not in straggles but all together, happy and hungry and ready for hot showers, electricity, and another gourmet meal. Now, as she approaches with Malcolm huffing along miserably next to her, she sees it up ahead, a lovely red-brick building that would normally look so welcoming, now looking shady and forlorn under a tenebrous sky.

CHAPTER 19

BROOKE

It's Jane.

She's sure of it, despite the obvious differences. Despite the long blonde hair stuffed under a dark-green baseball cap. Despite the black hiking shoes and drab green shirt and too-large khaki pants, clothing Jane would never normally wear. Despite the fact that this woman appears nothing at all like Jane, Brooke is 100 percent positive that this woman is Jane.

But how could she explain this to Kerry? It's not the way Jane looks but the way she *is*. It's years of knowing someone almost better than you know yourself. It's like looking in the mirror; that's how familiar Jane is to her, even after so much time. Brooke knows her too well: her proud, straight-backed posture; the way she walks heel first, legs straight, hips swinging as if strolling down a catwalk. And, right before she disappeared into the trees, the slight toss of her hair—even if it was the wrong color, even if most of it was trapped underneath her cap—was pure Jane.

Brooke knew she couldn't waste time trying to convince Kerry, so without thinking she began to run toward the woods, toward where she saw Jane enter the forest. And it's not until she is under the canopy of trees, suddenly plunged into shadows, that Brooke thinks to wonder why Jane would be here in Saltwick. On her own. In disguise.

She pauses to listen for footsteps, for the sounds of a body walking through the bush, and even as she waits for a sign, she wonders whether Kerry might be right. Maybe Brooke is simply so distraught that she actually believes she saw her old friend in a total stranger. Maybe her mind is playing cruel tricks on her.

But when she sees a branch move a few yards ahead, as if someone has just pushed past it and let it snap back into position, she turns in that direction, moving as quickly as she can amid the ferns underfoot.

She is so focused on following whatever moved the branch that she doesn't pay attention to where she's going—she doesn't know how it happens, only that her body goes airborne for a few brief seconds before she lands facedown, plowing into dead leaves and sharp slivers of bark from fallen branches. The now-familiar smell of eucalyptus oil fills her nostrils as she tries to refill her empty lungs.

She sits up painfully, the large, exposed tree root that caused her fall extending snakelike in front of her. She allows herself a moment to take inventory of what body parts may be bent or broken, then remembers the jack jumpers, and the thought of swarming ants propels her to her feet. Her legs and arms are fine; her right ankle smarts, twisted enough to hurt but not enough to turn around.

She shakes the dirt and leaves out of her hair and peers through the trees, hoping for a glimpse of something, anything.

"Jane?" she calls out, softly, then again, louder. She listens. All she hears are the unknown songs of birds, high above.

She lets her shoulders sink down, feels the weight of her body pulling toward the ground, seeking respite there. She's so weary she doesn't know how she'll find her way back; she's so brain-addled she is literally seeing things that aren't there, and she wants so badly to believe in the story her eyes are telling her.

With a sigh, she turns to head back toward where she came from, to get back to town—but then realizes she's gotten herself turned around. She looks again for the tree root that tripped her up, and now she sees several; the whole forest is blanketed with exposed roots. She can no longer tell which one she'd stumbled over; she no longer knows which way is toward town and which way is deeper into the forest. She looks up, but the ceiling of trees is thick; she tries to discern a horizon, a brighter light coming from one direction or another, but everything looks exactly the same.

She begins walking. She'll either end up back in town, or she'll end up closer to Jane. Either way is fine. This time, she steps carefully over bushes and ferns, downed branches and emerging roots, keeping an eye out for signs of another pair of feet that may have been here just ahead of hers. She walks ten yards. Twenty. Fifty, and still no sign of Jane, or of a clearing leading back to Saltwick.

Then she hears something move near a thick bush ahead, and she quickens her pace until finds herself face-to-face with a wallaby, whose wide eyes and unblinking stare make him look as shocked to see her as she is to see him. As he whirls around and hops away, three more wallabies, all camouflaged in plain sight, join the exodus, filling the forest with the sounds of a mini-stampede.

It occurs to her that this proves she's moving in the wrong direction—the wallabies would not have been there if Jane had come through this way. She turns around and begins retracing her steps, slowly, ears tuned to every noise amid the crunching of leaves and bark under her feet.

"Jane? Are you out there?" Brooke feels as though she's talking more to herself than to Jane, but she continues. "I know it was you. I don't know what you're running from, but you're safe. Malcolm's not here. You can come out now."

She doesn't know whether she's said the right thing, whether Jane had seen Malcolm and he's what made her slip into the woods—or was it Brooke she was running from? Brooke isn't even sure whether Jane had seen any of them; her glance in their direction had been so fleeting.

And that's when she realizes she's talking to a ghost. She hears Kerry's voice echo in her head—*that backpacker over there?*—and understands she hasn't seen Jane after all. This woman she's chasing—it could be anyone, but it can't be Jane. Jane is gone.

Brooke feels her knees buckle, and abruptly she sits on the trunk of a fallen tree. Her mind has created this impossible hope, a last, futile attempt to deal with the grief. All along, Brooke has tried to believe every explanation other than the simple truth: that something awful happened to Jane, and she is dead.

"I just can't accept that you're gone," she says, surprised to hear herself talking out loud again—but it feels good, as if she is finally having the conversation she should've had with Jane on the first night of this trip. And so she continues. Why not? She's in the middle of the forest, with no one to hear her other than the wallabies.

"I'm sorry I let so much time pass. I didn't mean for that to happen. The truth is—I was ashamed of what my life had become. I know you thought I had such a perfect existence. On Facebook, it looked that way. It was what I wanted to believe myself. But there was nothing perfect about it. Especially about William and me. The pictures of us on Queen Anne, on the waterfront, at Pike Place Market—those were all taken our first month in Seattle. I spread them out because, after that, there was nothing else to share. Nothing worth sharing. But I couldn't admit that I'd made such a big mistake." She feels a laugh escape her throat. "I guess I was a much better actor than I thought. I wanted to give up acting so I could live a real life. But Facebook is the biggest stage of all. I cast myself in the role of a lifetime—the role of a happy person. I fooled us all, didn't I?"

She hears a scuffling to her right, a sound coming from behind a trio of gum trees. She doesn't bother rising to her feet—it'll be another wallaby, no doubt, or maybe a kangaroo; it sounds big. She waits in silence, her eyes now quite well adjusted to the dimness of the woods, and she straightens her back as she strains to hear the sounds, which seem to be moving away. The scuffles slow, then stop. Then they start again, a pattern that sounds all too familiar. The sound of feet. Human feet.

She stands so quickly that she snaps off a thin tree branch just above her shoulder. She looks down for footprints and sees the tread of a hiking boot heading into the bracken.

"Jane?" Reality gives way to hope again as Brooke springs in the same direction, taking care where she steps, pausing every now and then to follow the sounds, though she knows she could be following any number of creatures, and she has no idea where she is or where she's going.

Even as she moves forward, she senses that she's only running after false hope. She also notes that it's getting darker—not because the forest is getting more wooded but because the sunlight is fading from the sky. It'll be night before long. Yet she keeps moving, hoping that she'll end up somewhere, anywhere. She's so tired and hungry she doesn't even care. She just wants out of the woods.

As if to answer her thoughts, just ahead she can see light through the trees. She sprints forward, then emerges into a grassy meadow that slopes up a small hillside. Along the top are the remnants of crumbling red-brick buildings, lined up end to end like bombed-out row houses. The convict settlement.

And there's no sign of Jane, or the woman she thought was Jane.

Brooke stops and scans the horizon. Far to the right, she can see the gold-streaked water as the late afternoon sun breaks through the clouds. And to her left the forest continues up and over the hill.

If Jane, or whoever she is, returned to the forest, Brooke will never find her. But, if she continued up the hill to the settlement, perhaps Brooke could catch up. At this point she is determined to find this woman, to prove herself wrong, at the very least.

At the same time these thoughts go through her mind, her brain also tells her she's crazy. That she's chasing a mirage, a memory, a wish, nothing more.

She begins climbing toward the ruins.

When she gets there, she stops to take a breath as she looks around, hands on her knees. If she hadn't learned from Kerry about the settlements, she'd have thought these buildings were ancient storage units; there are no windows, just tiny brick rooms whose walls and ceilings nature has peeled away, bit by bit, so that most of the rooms are exposed to the elements, to views of the southern half of the island. Dotting the hill beyond are several wombats, noses to the ground as they nibble and forage.

After catching her breath, Brooke begins to walk around. She stops at the first cell and peeks over what's left of the front wall, then stifles a scream when a pair of kangaroos jump out, then hop rapidly down the hill. She watches them go, the burnt-ochre glow of the sun giving their fur a reddish tint.

She continues on to the next cell, her search feeling both foolish and hopeful at once, and she looks around the corner more cautiously this time. She nearly has to suppress another shriek—she can see, amid the broken bricks and patches of grass, an army backpack, its zipper a gaping mouth. She doesn't recognize it, but this doesn't mean it can't be Jane's.

She hurries over to the bag and, kneeling next to it, pulls it open wider and looks in. Inside are several white, opaque plastic containers, like Tupperware. She takes one of them out of the bag and peels back the lid.

Nestled within layers of shiny metallic bubble wrap are a half-dozen small eggs, much smaller than chicken eggs. They are pastel in color, almost like Easter eggs, and lightly speckled.

"Oh no," she hears herself murmur.

Heart thumping madly, she carefully seals the container and places it back in the pack, wondering what to do. She has no phone; she has no idea where she is. And she's just stumbled upon something extremely incriminating, if these eggs are what she fears they are. Parrot eggs, ready to be smuggled out of the country.

She hears someone behind her and turns, rising to her feet in the same motion.

A man stands in front of her, his clothing matching the backpack, sleeves rolled up to display rough hands. His eyes are in the shadow of a wide-brimmed hat, his jaw covered in dark stubble. She starts to back away from him.

"Where do you think you're going?" His accent sounds vaguely Australian, but it's different from Bryan's or Kerry's. Or maybe it's the menacing way in which he speaks.

She doesn't answer, her mind reeling as she remembers the figure disappearing from the beach when they landed on Marbury just a couple of days ago. She recognizes the dark hair, the dark brown and green clothing that blends into the landscape. Had he been among them all along?

"It's you," she says. "I saw you when we landed."

She glances down at his backpack, thinking wildly of Jane. Maybe she wasn't drunk or suicidal or injured by Malcolm. Maybe it was this man Jane encountered the night she disappeared, getting in the way of a poacher and his prey.

The man hasn't answered her. She takes another step back. He doesn't seem to be panicked by her presence. She takes a bigger step back, ready to turn and run, when she feels the heel of her hiking shoe hit something. A wall. When she feels the cool rough brick against her back, she knows she's trapped.

She looks up at the clouds, stained yellow with the dying sun, and feels her lungs constricting, as if she'd been dealt a physical blow, when she realizes that despite this crumbling cell being more than a century old, it has a new prisoner, one with very little hope of release.

Kerry and Bryan had told them a little bit about the prisons, about the hundreds of men, and some women, brought here as part of the decades-long exile of convicts out of London, back when Australia may as well have been the dark side of the moon—far away and mostly unknown. Their crimes were usually minor—petty theft, breaking and entering—and as Brooke looks up at the man in front of her, she thinks of the crime he is committing, one that Kerry said comes with a fine that is a mere fraction of what his goods are worth, one that usually goes undetected and unprosecuted.

"So this is why you hid from us," she says, nodding toward the backpack. She can think of nothing to do to save herself but to try to buy time. To hope that there's some chance Kerry followed her, or is out looking for her.

The man takes out a large hunting knife and begins to polish it using the tail of his shirt. Brooke feels her breath freeze in her throat and has to force herself to keep talking.

"You were at our camp, weren't you? Were you watching us?"

He doesn't answer but holds the knife up, as if to inspect it. As if he's getting ready to use it.

"What did you to do to her?" The question comes out of nowhere, but something about seeing that knife, the dexterity with which he handles it, makes her fear it's been used before, on something even more sinister than hunting or poaching.

He looks at her at last. "Who?"

"My friend Jane. She went missing our first night."

"I have no idea what happened to your friend."

"Did you kill Margaret, too?"

"I don't know what you're talking about."

"You must know, if you were hanging around our camp. I should've known. Ian kept hearing things and thought they were birds. Is that what happened to Jane? Did she run into you by mistake?"

"I'm just trying to make a living."

"By stealing babies from their mothers? Some living."

He gives her a savage look. "What about all of you, stealing this land from the locals to use as your playground? First the Europeans, now it's the bloody tourists and greens. You can't go anywhere without a bloody permit anymore. It's you people that are getting in the way."

The wet brick behind her back feels arctic, but she presses deeper into it as he takes a step toward her.

"Listen," she says, "I was just looking for my friend. I'm not a park ranger. If you let me go, I'll leave you alone."

"Is that right? Now you've seen my face, seen my rucksack? You're just going to be on your merry way?"

"Yes. I won't say anything. I promise."

A crackle in the bush outside the walls catches his attention— Brooke hears it, too—and as he glances over his shoulder, she lunges forward, shouting at the top of her lungs for help. He stops her with a fist in her stomach, knocking the wind out of her, silencing her, in one swift movement.

She looks up from the ground, his newly polished knife flashing in the dying light. He towers over her, his body blocking the sky, the glare of rage and desperation boring through her. He kneels down. "You really want to die, don't you?"

"No, no," she murmurs, still barely able to breathe. As he inches closer, she closes her eyes against his insidious gaze, against what she knows will come next.

ACT III

CHAPTER 20

JANE

When I heard the sound of my name, I was already deep enough into the woods to remain lost, but I kept going anyway. At first, I couldn't believe she recognized me—I'd taken such care to stay hidden, even in my own body. But then I let my guard down; I broke character. And of course Brooke—and probably only Brooke—would have seen that.

It must've been the way I was walking, or the way I turned my head, or the way I slunk into the woods when I saw those three standing there. I expected them to still be in camp, especially after they found Margaret.

Margaret wasn't supposed to happen. But then, as every actor knows, nothing ever does go exactly as planned onstage. We're trained to improvise, to ad-lib while remaining in character. No matter what happens—a flubbed line, a misplaced prop, a missed mark—if you play it right, the audience never needs to know—and 99 percent of the time, they're none the wiser. In the case of the drama at hand, I think this is true not only about me but about Margaret.

It's ironic that my best performance yet has been entirely offstage—off the traditional stage, at least. And it's a shame that no director, no cast and crew, will ever know how well I've weathered the storm, so to speak: the rain had not been in the plan, either, and it's been nightmarishly inconvenient. I've spent the last two days cold, wet, hungry. Waiting for things that have not yet happened—like a hint of sorrow from Malcolm. Dealing with things that should not have happened—like Margaret.

But the show must go on.

And now I wait in the wings, skirting around the far edges of the maze of cells in this former prison, waiting for my cue, for a sign that I can sneak out of here and onto a ferry without being detected.

That is the plan, anyway—or was. Now that Brooke's seen me, I'm not sure I can still make it out of here, unless I wait until they're all off the island, unless they decide Brooke's off her head and they don't spend any more time searching for me. But she may not be willing to leave without me.

Her loyalty is astounding. When I reached out to Brooke, invited her on this trip for a chance to reconnect, to make up for lost time and renew our friendship, I was half-expecting her to turn me down. I couldn't be sure she'd agree so readily—and little did I know she was full of surprises herself. How very alike we still are, though neither of us had known it.

That first day required mustering all my resources as an actor; I was so tempted to confide in her, to let her in on the plan. I was reciting lines I'd written long before, following a carefully plotted storyline with a few knotty twists to serve its overarching theme.

Revenge.

William would be proud.

Not Brooke's William.

William Shakespeare. I'd like to think he'd appreciate this homage. The play's the thing, eh, Billy Boy?

To serve my purpose, I had to keep Brooke in the dark; her reaction to my disappearance had to be real. And it was. I have to admit, I was touched by her anguish. It makes me all the more sad to think of those lost years, and to think it'll never be the same once she knows what I've done. I've had to weigh this risk, and it hasn't been easy, but if I know Brooke, there's a part of her that will feel more admiration than anger.

The plan was not to be dead forever—but I've done my share of improv and know how to roll with whatever comes my way. Now it seems that maybe I will have to be dead to her forever after all, and maybe it's for the best. As with Gertrude in the final act, it may already be too late; I have already drunk the poisoned wine.

I've had to draw upon strengths I didn't know I had. I thought it would be a relief to be offstage, to be hidden away in the woods, waiting. But that turned out to be the hardest part. On the first night, the unholy rain tempted me to call the whole thing off, to return to the dry warmth of my sleeping bag and have a normal vacation like the rest of the group thought they were having.

But I couldn't give in.

In an attempt to stay dry, I crawled into the base of a hollowed-out tree. When I felt little creatures ascending my legs, under the balloon of my too-big khakis, I didn't make a sound, didn't even turn on my flashlight. I simply squashed them, feeling their little corpses against my skin, and tucked the pants into my boots to prevent further assault. I drew upon another form of acting I'm well familiar with—the roles I play to deceive even myself. To pretend this discomfort is all worth it. To pretend I'm not afraid of the darkness and the horrors it can bring.

I honed this talent not long after Brooke left New York. Some actors take classes; others have their skills thrust upon them, sometimes subtly, sometimes violently. The better the actor, the more they are hoping to hide.

I used to run at night, sometimes after a show to release the exhilaration that comes after the curtain, the adrenaline that makes sleep impossible until you burn it off. Sometimes I'd run at night because Brooke was at the theater and there was no one at home, nothing else for me to do, no other way to work through the envy and restlessness. I had no money, and running was free, available to me any time of day. Or so I believed, until that one night.

After Brooke left the city, I ran more than usual: her absence added boredom and loneliness to the lack of work and lack of money that sent me jogging through the streets. One drizzly November night, I ran through Long Island City and up to Astoria. It was after midnight, hardly late by New York standards, but the streets were empty when I reached Astoria Boulevard and turned around. I passed the Noguchi Museum and headed through Hunters Point along the waterfront. That's when another jogger pulled up alongside me, matching my pace.

I glanced over and saw that it was a man, stocky and about my height, and he wore a blue hoodie that covered his face—not unusual for a cold, damp night, but I didn't like it. I slowed my pace, and he slowed his, and that's when I knew I was in trouble.

Before I could turn or stop or even scream, I was on the ground, my head exploding in pain as it hit the pavement, shoulders digging into concrete as I flailed and fought. My brain sparked lights in black and blue and red, my voice strangled by the heel of his hand at my throat. He was on top of me, his weight suffocating, and he was trying to pin my arms to the ground. I did not make it easy for him. He wore a balaclava that covered his face, and something about that sinister getup, the way his eyes looked so beady in the ambient light, set my blood on fire, fueled my wasted muscles just enough to knee him in the groin, freeing my hands to smash into the hard bones of his face.

It hurt, I could tell, and I was twice rewarded for this: first, with his fist to my face in a blow that nearly knocked me out, and second, with his giving up. I lay on the ground, shaking and panting, and by the time I dared move, I couldn't see him anywhere.

Adrenaline. That's what powers me onstage, and that's what powered me home that night, on my own trembling legs, looking over my shoulder every couple of minutes to make sure he didn't reappear in the inky dark, under the borough's low yellow lights.

And he didn't. Once back in my apartment, I stood in the dark, wrapped in a blanket, watching out the window for hours, looking, waiting. But no one was there.

I'd won. I'd beaten him. And this was how I convinced myself that I hadn't really been assaulted and nearly raped.

I'd won, and therefore I hadn't suffered. And even when I didn't believe it, I knew how to pretend.

The left side of my face turned purple, then green, then faded to a yellowish gray. The psycho roommate who'd replaced Brooke didn't even notice until it was in its green phase, and even then she barely blinked when I told her I'd tripped while jogging. *You shouldn't run at night*, she replied.

You're right, I said, and I let her believe it was all thanks to her profound wisdom that I no longer ran at night.

The problem was, after that, I was unable to do much of anything at night. I won the role of Norma Desmond in an afternoon audition and made it through daytime rehearsals—but when it came time for the first tech rehearsal, scheduled for eight o'clock,

I couldn't leave the apartment. I called the director claiming food poisoning, and they used my understudy. I had every intention of being there the next night, but the same paralyzing fear immobilized me, and for the first time I couldn't act my way out of a situation. I couldn't pretend I wasn't afraid; I couldn't play the part of a normal woman.

I told the director I had a family emergency and had to quit the play. To my parents and sister in Kansas City—and, just a couple of days ago, to Brooke—I said the production had closed. The lie was so easy; not one of them asked a single question.

That was how I ended up on the cruise ship—not the gig I'd have wanted, performing second-rate plays for drunken passengers—but facing a combination of no income, an expiring lease, and an inability to find daylight-hours-only acting work in New York, I had no choice. Going home—admitting I couldn't make it—was not an option. Because if you saw my profile on Facebook, you'd see I was living the life I'd always wanted. I'd have to fall a lot farther before I'd take off that mask.

At first, I desperately missed the city. I found the relative quiet of the ship unsettling and lonely, and I couldn't sleep without the city's ambient sounds and lights, the sirens and neighboring voices telling me I wasn't fully alone.

But then, once I got over the stark unfamiliarity, I realized it was an environment in which I could finally feel safe. I began to relax amid the constant hum of the engine, under the bright deck lights, among always-open restaurants and casinos. On board, there was no such thing as night, even when it was dark. I had a cramped bunk on the lowest deck that I shared with three other actors, but I slept in the staterooms of single men more often than in my own bed.

By then, it had been nearly a year since that encounter in Hunters Point. Until the cruise, I wasn't sure I'd ever have sex again—I wasn't interested in anything the male species could offer me. I chose the first man carefully. He was older—around Malcolm's age—and traveling alone. He looked lonely, and when we started drinking together, he told me a sad story. A dead wife, an estranged son. He actually wanted companionship that week, even more than sex, and this was how I knew he was safe.

It got easier after that. I fucked older men and younger men, single men and married men. Did it help me take back what I lost that night? Who knows. But it helped me move on. It renewed my desire to get back to work, real work. I was acting all the time, but getting paid for so little of it. So I moved to LA, the perfect place to reinvent yourself, a place where it seems that every few months, people shed their old lives like a molting skin and emerge completely new. I emerged from my own cocoon no longer a stage actor but a commercial actress. I used my hard-won talents to sell pregnancy tests and dishwashing liquid, toothpaste and toilet paper. The drug ads were my favorites—at least they had a narrative—and that's how I met Malcolm. His agency has an LA office, and someone there saw me in a commercial for anti-anxiety meds, and for some reason when they brought it to his attention, he thought I'd be the perfect fit for a client in Sydney, a restauranteur who wanted to do a series of television spots. Whether they were interested in my anxious, pre-drug persona or my relaxed after, I didn't know, and the money wasn't much better than what I was making in LA. But I couldn't resist the free ticket to Australia, and I was already composing a Facebook status update in my head: *I'm now officially an international actor, on my way to Sydney for a new gig!*

Malcolm and I first met in a glass-paneled conference room in a high-rise building in downtown Sydney. He made me wait for almost twenty minutes, and I was standing at the window looking down at the Sydney Opera House when I first heard his voice. "The white whale," he said.

I turned around to face a fortysomething man whose suntanned face made his bright blue eyes sparkle. I almost said, *Please tell me you're not talking about my ass*, but at the last minute decided to go with a simple "Pardon?"

"The Opera House," he said, standing next to me and looking down on the building's billowing white sails. "When it was just an idea, little more than a sketch, they estimated it would cost seven million dollars to build. It ended up costing more than a hundred million. Took more than a decade to construct. The architect quit before the building was finished, and he never saw the completed structure."

"It looks like it turned out okay," I said.

"It's our most recognized landmark. Worth untold millions in advertising dollars."

"Is that why you flew me here from LA?" I couldn't resist getting my flirt on. "Because I'm worth untold millions in advertising dollars?"

He laughed and turned to look at me. "Something like that."

The job lasted two weeks, but from that moment on he kept making excuses to see me. He'd come to the set; he'd invite me to lunch. Then dinner, then nights in my hotel. It happened so seamlessly, and he was so singularly attentive that it would've been easy to forget he had a wife, a house in a suburban neighborhood I'd never heard of, two kids in college—except for the sneaking around. But that was the part I liked. Having him all to myself. I didn't have to share him because he wasn't even supposed to be with me. I knew it wouldn't last, and that was why I made the most of every moment. I let him consume me.

On my last day in Sydney, he came to the hotel to say goodbye, and we ended up spending the rest of the day in bed. I missed my flight, and he not only rebooked it for me but bought me another round-trip ticket for a month later.

"What's this for?" I asked when he presented it to me. I wasn't interested in becoming his mistress. "Do you have another gig lined up for me?"

"If you want one."

"Oh, right, I forgot—prostitution is legal here."

That's when he said it. "I'll leave my wife. If that's what it takes. I just want to be with you."

"I'll use this ticket," I said, "if you keep that promise."

And I did use the ticket—and the next one he bought me, and the next. He did get me a couple of bona fide gigs—both for pharmaceutical companies; for one, I was a psoriasis patient; for another, a young doctor—and these kept me there for weeks at a time and allowed him to expense the airfare. It didn't take long for me to figure out he had no intention of leaving his wife, and I pretended that I, too, had conveniently forgotten about his promise.

But then something changed. I was getting accustomed to the life he was giving me: business-class flights, luxurious hotel rooms, meals at the types of places you only see in movies and can hardly believe actually exist. I wanted that. I thought about Brooke's Facebook updates and how happy she was being married. I wanted that, too, perhaps even more than I wanted Malcolm himself.

With all of that longing swirling around in my head, we got into a fight. It began as an act, as I complained he hadn't begun the process of separating from his wife, that I felt like a whore, that I couldn't go on like this any longer—and then, as often happens, I became the character I was playing. It's something only another actor can fully understand, that there are these moments—when you know a character well enough and inhabit the role fully enough—in which you yourself completely disappear. You become that other person, even if that person doesn't exist.

And as I told Malcolm I wanted him, it became true. As I told him we were made for each other, this, too, became true. And as I told him I would wait for him, I knew I would.

Even now I think *love* is too strong a word; what I felt was more like a craving, a longing, something more physical than emotional. And when he kept putting me off, kept saying he needed more time, I finally used my own frequent flyer miles to fly back to surprise him. I went to his office, saying I just happened to be in town and thought I'd stop by. The craving I had for him was not unreciprocated, and we locked his office door and had sex on his desk. I remember being on top, looking out the floor-to-ceiling window—his office overlooked the harbor—and catching a glimpse of the Opera House. *Untold millions*, I thought, and that was when I came.

The plan hatched not twenty minutes later, when he stepped out and I got on his computer and saw his emails about a trip to an island called Marbury. With his wife.

I didn't construct my plan out of love or heartbreak, not as I sold it to Brooke. I made it because, when I saw the email, that night in Hunters Point flooded my body with memory. With everything I'd tamped down after that night, the fear and fury, the helpless anguish. I thought I'd freed myself of it all, only to realize it had been living inside my bones, and now it resurfaced with a force I couldn't contain. I wasn't going to let a man do that to me again. Not without paying the price.

On the night I disappeared from our camp on Marbury Island, I'd popped into the woods to hide my day pack in the crooked arm of a tree branch, and when I returned, Brooke was still at dinner. I was prepared to feign sleep when she got back to the tent, then to wait until she was asleep so I could sneak out again. This was one aspect of the plan that made me nervous; I remembered her as a light sleeper, and those tent zippers were noisy. Knowing Brooke, if she heard me get up, even if she assumed I was just getting up to pee, she might wait up until I was back again.

It turns out I didn't remember Brooke quite as well as I thought. I almost fell off my bunk when I heard her and Bryan's hushed voices and stifled laughter as they thumped across the walkway to his tent. As they stayed there, I was shocked and more than a little jealous. But it gave me the opportunity I needed.

I'd packed my day pack carefully. From what I'd read in preparation, I knew the devils would be out there, but I also knew that I'd need to motivate them properly to create the scene I wanted everyone else to see.

I'd arrived in Hobart three days early to prepare. The white lab coat I stole from the set of the pharmaceutical commercial came in handy when I walked into the blood bank at the Royal Hobart Hospital. My acting skills came in handy as I pretended I knew exactly what I was doing as I opened the refrigerator, pulled out a drawer, and took out a bag of B-positive, my blood type.

The day before the hike, I rented a car, and not far from Hobart, not long after midnight, I found what I needed on the A6. The dead wallaby was young, small, and, once tightly wrapped in thick plastic, fit into my day pack.

That night, as Brooke screwed Bryan in his tent—another added bonus: she would remember this with shame and regret when I went missing—I changed into my frumpy clothes and set off into the woods, to where I'd left the pack. I knew I had to stage the scene close enough to camp to be discovered, but not so close that anyone would hear me.

The rain helped. It helped keep everyone huddled in their tents as I snuck out of mine. It helped cover the sound of me destroying my iPhone with a rock, the sound of tearing as I punctured and tore my black shirt and green scarf. It helped muffle my own inadvertent cry as I ripped a handful of hair from my scalp and dropped it in the ferns. It helped muddy the scene of my demise just enough to make it look even more credible than I'd imagined.

I worried most about the wallaby—but as I huddled inside that tree trunk, listening to the devils, I knew that there would be little to nothing left, except traces of the pint of blood I'd spattered over everything, like a rabid Jackson Pollock, the forest floor my canvas.

I knew I didn't have to worry about the scene holding up under CSI-type scrutiny; I didn't have to convince a forensics team, only two inexperienced guides and their clueless guests. By the time the police arrived, I'd be gone.

But I couldn't leave too soon. I had to watch my unwitting audience react.

Brooke noticed first, of course. I heard her go to the toilets and call my name. I could hear in her voice that she was confused, nervous. I waited for the others to discover me missing. I waited to hear Malcolm's voice. I waited for him to call out to me, to join the search party. I was giddy with the thought of ignoring him, seeing him squirm, seeing him finally confess to Charlotte.

But it didn't happen.

When they all gathered for breakfast, I got as close to the dining tent as I could, to hear what was coming next. Not only would there be no search party, but Ian and Margaret wanted to keep going. And Malcolm said nothing. Nothing.

Then, finally, Kerry showed Brooke what I'd been hoping all of them would see—Malcolm most of all. Even though I'd hoped for a bigger audience, it was satisfying to know that everything had worked perfectly. Kerry, the one person I had to convince—I hadn't known our guide would be an expert on those wild little marsupials—bought the whole thing, told Brooke I'd been eaten by the devils. And what came next was even better.

Sometimes you prepare for a performance and you know it'll be solid. Sometimes, some combination of the right timing and the right cast and the right audience makes the play come alive in a way that even you and your director never expected. When Brooke told Kerry that I was having an affair with Malcolm, that he should be considered a suspect in my disappearance, I knew right then that I'd brought down the house.

And so I stayed another night. I'd planned to take off right away, to avoid being seen, to catch the ferry and go back to Hobart, to keep the play going for as long as possible, from a safe distance. But now I couldn't resist being there for the next act.

Then everything changed again.

Margaret.

First, I overheard her and Brooke. This was a plot twist I never saw coming, Brooke discovering Margaret was fucking Malcolm, though I suppose I shouldn't have been surprised.

I wanted to leave then, but it was getting dark, and I knew I'd have to endure one more night. That night was wetter than the first—or at least I was, with no change of clothes, no break in the rain. I was damp and clammy, teeth clattering together so hard I thought they might break. I couldn't warm up, and the energy bars I was subsisting on weren't doing much. *Fair is foul, and foul is fair*, I muttered to myself, like a madwoman.

As my body shook in the raw cold, I actually considered returning to my tent, bagging the whole plan. I could say I got turned around, I was attacked by an animal, it took me a whole day to find my way back. They'd believe me. No one knows just how good I am, except possibly Brooke, but she's the most gullible of all.

I was circling the camp, on the far edge near the toilets, where I planned to change again, to take off the frumpy clothes, make a dramatic return in nothing but underclothes, dressed in the role of victim. I was wondering how much I'd have to scratch up my body to make an attack seem believable when I heard something on the walkway. Margaret.

It wasn't in my plan for her to die. But then, nothing ever really goes according to the plan. Or, as the darkness deepened, and, with it, my mood, I came to believe that there was a greater plan at work and in that hellish night I half expected to see the three witches pass by me and nod.

When the hurly-burly's done, When the battle's lost and won.

In the end, what transpired was perhaps even better than any plan of mine, especially when it came to Malcolm's culpability.

But this also meant I had to move on, and fast. No waiting for morning, for daylight. I had to get out of camp and off the island.

I began my journey north stumbling in the darkness, until I got far enough away to use my flashlight and find a trail. Somehow I was able to follow it, and by early morning I arrived at camp two. I took all the water I could carry, plus a stash of energy bars and trail mix. I had a chance to dry out a bit and to don my wig and hat. I arrived in Saltwick ready to play a backpacker waiting for the ferry.

But the dock was closed. I took shelter in a nearby building, keeping an eye out, and when I saw a small boat arrive at the dock, I headed over. When I got there I heard a park ranger on his cell phone, talking about two dead bodies and the police, and I realized that while it didn't look like a police boat, it wasn't a public vessel. And then I saw the guy who'd brought us here—it was the same boat—and two uniformed police officers. I didn't know what exactly was going on, only that I had to disappear again.

I walked back through town, toward the forest, and as I did I realized something. Very few things can cause me to break character, but this stopped me cold.

I wasn't afraid.

I'd spent the night running through lightless woods in sputtering rain, and I hadn't even thought to be scared. My actions could be responsible for an innocent man being charged with a crime, and the thought didn't alarm me one bit. I was on the verge of being discovered and felt only confidence, knowing I could act my way through whatever came my way, just as I've gotten through everything else.

At first, I felt like my old self again, but then I knew it was different, this feeling, entirely new. I felt completely fearless.

I'd just reached the woods when I glanced over my shoulder and saw them—Brooke, Malcolm, Kerry. It gave me a jolt of adrenaline, and I ducked into the cover of the trees. Moments later I heard Brooke call my name.

Now, I stay low as I skulk among the crumbling bricks of the prison cells, listening. I hear voices, and one of them sounds like Brooke—but who is the other one? With the wind still high amid the uneven walls, it's hard to hear, but it's a man's voice, and I wonder if it's Malcolm. I want to find out. Yet at the same time, I know I'm too exposed here, that unless I can figure out where these voices are coming from I'm going to need to run back into the woods to avoid being discovered.

Then I hear a scream, a cry for help—it's Brooke, I'm sure of it now—and suddenly her voice is abruptly cut off. Something's happening. She's in trouble. I have to decide whether this is my cue, whether I stay in the wings or take the stage and remove my mask.

You're right again, Billy Boy—all the world's a stage. And this may indeed be the last scene of all.

ACT IV

CHAPTER 21

KERRY

Kerry pauses as they reach Saltwick House, looking up at the expansive front porch, its wicker chairs lining the wall, facing seaward. If this were a normal journey, she would leave them all on the porch to remove their hiking boots (no shoes are allowed inside) and to take a well-deserved rest. She'd go to the kitchen and return with lemonade and cookies. They would hydrate and rest and then, brimming with new energy, decide which hike they wanted to do for the afternoon.

Instead, she staggers up the front steps with Malcolm, utters a weary, "Stay here," kicks off her boots, and goes inside alone.

The main house has five bedrooms, and she passes them all as she walks down the long hallway, lined with black-and-white framed prints of the house over the past century, and she thinks of how empty the house will be tonight. There's also a separate cottage in the back they call the "honeymoon suite," and Kerry wonders for a moment who might've stayed there if they'd all arrived together. Ian and Margaret? Malcolm and Charlotte? Neither of them happy couples, but until Brooke told her their secrets, she wouldn't have guessed they were particularly unhappy either. Or perhaps they are what happiness looks like.

In the kitchen, she plugs in her phone. She checks the fridge, but because their schedule is off—one of the guides normally would've arrived here early and made the lemonade—there is nothing to drink, nothing ready to eat. She unlocks the pantry and takes a few energy bars out of one of the cupboards. Then she pours filtered water into a pitcher.

She returns to the porch, where she drops the energy bars on the table next to Malcolm and sets the pitcher down next to them. She hands him a glass. "I have to make a call," she says. "If you come inside, just be sure to take off your shoes first."

He nods, says nothing. As she turns to go back inside, she sees him take something out of his pack—the half-empty bottle of wine he'd brought with him from the second camp. He fills the water glass with wine, and she lets the screen door slam behind her.

In the kitchen, her phone has come back to life. She's missed several calls from both Bryan and Mark. She calls Mark first.

"Where are you?" she asks.

"Chasing after you, apparently. Dan managed to dock in Saltwick a couple hours ago, and he brought two police officers from Triabunna. We got to the landing near the first camp about an hour ago. Where are you?"

"Saltwick House."

"We're about to head back," Mark says. "With Bryan and Charlotte."

"What about Margaret?"

"We're leaving the officers here. There are two more on their way from Triabunna, and they should be there soon, now the winds have eased. Look, you have to keep everyone together."

Kerry thinks about simply agreeing with him, then decides to be honest. "I'm trying," she says. "Brooke ran off somewhere. But Malcolm is here."

"Good," Mark says. "He's the one we're concerned about."

"Why Malcolm?" she asks. "Did Bryan tell you?"

"That he was sleeping with both victims?" Mark says. "Yeah, he told me."

"So you think he's responsible."

"I just want you to keep him there. The officers should be there soon. I'll tell them to go straight to Saltwick House."

"I'm getting a little freaked out here, Mark."

"I'll be there within an hour," he says. "You'll be right. Just sit on the front porch, make conversation. Stay in plain sight."

She feels dread crawl through her stomach. "Am I not safe here, Mark?"

"I'm leaving now," is all he says. "Keep your mobile with you. Call if you need anything."

She looks down at her mobile, sees the screen go blank. Her battery is at only two percent; the only way she can keep her mobile with her is if she stays here, next to the power outlet.

She turns around and jumps when she sees Malcolm standing in the doorway. "Oh my God," she says. "You startled me."

He doesn't say anything, doesn't move. His eyes look dark. "How're you going?" she asks. "Have you had some water?"

"I heard you talking about me."

She tries to remember what she said, what he might've overheard, and stutters out, "Not you in particular, Malcolm. Just the situation."

He eyes her suspiciously. "Why do you feel unsafe with me?"

"I—I didn't mean it like that," she says. "You're misinterpreting the conversation."

"Am I?"

"Yes," she says. "I was talking about—about the weather."

He looks past her out the kitchen window. "The weather is better than it's been in days. Don't patronize me."

"I'm not," she says.

"They think I'm responsible," he says slowly. "For who? Jane? Margaret? Both of them?"

"I don't know. He didn't say."

"I would never hurt either of them."

"I never said that. No one did."

"But you're thinking it," he says. "Everyone's thinking it."

"That's not true." She glances down at her phone again. Three percent. She'll have to chance it. All she knows is that she wants to get out of this small kitchen and back onto the front porch. In plain sight. Where the police will see them both as soon as they arrive.

"Come on," she says. "Let's go sit on the porch. We might even get a peek at the sun."

"Is there anything else to drink?" he asks, nodding toward the pantry door behind her, where the key dangles in the deadbolt. "Anything to eat?"

The last thing he needs is more alcohol, but food would be a step in the right direction. She turns and pushes open the door. "There might be some crackers or something," she says. "You're welcome to—"

But before she can step aside to let him enter, he's right there, and the next thing she knows, she's inside the pantry, on her

knees, and he's on the other side of the door. She hears the sound
of the deadbolt locking into place.

"Malcolm!" She leaps to her feet and pounds on the door.
"Malcolm, what are you doing?"

"I need a moment," he says. "To think."

"For fuck's sake, Malcolm. Open this door. Now."

"I haven't done anything wrong."

"I believe you." Kerry finds the light switch and turns it on, so
at least she's no longer in the dark. "But locking me in a pantry
doesn't make you look particularly innocent. Go on, open up."

She hears him scuffling around the kitchen and realizes he's
drunk, probably dangerously dehydrated.

"I'm not perfect, I know that," he says. "I've made mistakes. I
have regrets. It's not easy, being in the business I'm in. Everyone
watching you. Everyone wanting something from you."

"I get that." She rests her head against the door. The room is
stuffy already, and she's finding it hard to breathe. "I'm in the
same business, Malcolm. We're here to please."

"But you can't please them, can you?" he says. "Not forever.
Not like they want. But they don't want to hear that. They want
you to be perfect, for everything to be perfect."

"I know. But it never is, is it?"

"No, it never is."

He goes silent then, and she listens for a few moments. She
hears nothing, not even the sound of him leaving. "Malcolm?" she
ventures.

"I'm sorry, Kerry," he says. "I really am. But I can't let them
come here and arrest me."

"Malcolm, no one's going to—"

Then she hears his footsteps, loud and lumbering and fading fast. The slam of the screen door.

She reaches for her phone, then remembers where it is. Plugged in on the kitchen counter.

She pounds on the door, even though she knows no one is there to hear it. She considers screaming at the top of her lungs but decides that's just another waste of energy. She gives the door a solid kick, then throws her body against it. It doesn't budge, and her shoulder bursts with pain. She remembers when Meg showed her this door—it's been reinforced, with a lock and a deadbolt, so that during the off-season no one can break in and steal the food and wine. She may as well be in one of the convict prison cells, back when they were solid and unescapable. She isn't going anywhere.

The bright light in the tiny space is making her head hurt, so she reaches over and flips the switch. As she does, she hears her phone ring, its vibrations against the kitchen counter. She yanks at the door again, to no avail.

She lets her body sink down to the floor, touching the tops of her knees, tender where she'd landed when Malcolm shoved her in here. He can't possibly be innocent—no man who shoves a woman into a dark closet and locks the door is doing it for any good reason. She's lucky he didn't do worse.

Or maybe he's not finished with her yet.

She closes her eyes, even though she's in complete darkness, and a bubble of emotion rises in her throat—tears, laughter, she doesn't know; it comes out of her mouth in a strange combination, a half-laugh, half-sob. That this is how it ends, after all she's been through. After giving her life to the devils, after nearly giving up on her own life altogether. She's tried to reinvent herself only to become the victim of a narcissistic madman.

Maybe she should've left this earth months ago, on her own terms. She thinks about that talk she had with Matt while she was at the hospital. *You have to find a way to separate yourself from the death*, he told her then. She was ready, back then, to try. Now, she wants to ask him: *Why? Isn't it all waiting for us in the end? Why prolong the agony?*

Sometimes she doesn't know how people do it, how they go about their lives without being overwhelmed by everything around them. She remembers one night when she and Paul had a date—it was after her release from the hospital but before all her days were tolerable—and he was dressed and ready to go, while she was unshowered, in bed, covers pulled up over most of her face.

"What is it?" he asked, and she could hear the frustration in his voice, the weariness.

"I wonder how my life would have turned out if I'd just pretended they didn't exist."

"Who?"

"The devils. All the animals. The roadkill we pass every day. I see a dead wombat, and I have to check her pouch for a joey because most people just drive off and leave them there to starve to death on the side of the highway."

"You're not responsible for what other people do," Paul began.

"And the wallabies that jump out at passing lights like moths," she continued, as if in a trance. "The carnage. We reseal our nation's roads every year with the blood of millions of wild animals."

Paul sighed. "You've got to stop taking everything so seriously."

She looked at him over the bedspread. "Is that how you do it? Pretend they don't exist?"

"No, of course not. But I have perspective. Which is something you desperately need."

"Maybe you need what I have," she said. "Maybe you and everyone else needs to take it all a bit more seriously and start saving lives."

"What do you want to do, Kerry?" he said, his voice raised and angry. "Do you want to let the roads go back to dirt and let the animals take back the island?"

"Yes, why not," she shot back. "It would be a better place if they could."

"You're not living in the real world anymore," he said, and now he sounded more sad than angry.

"No," she said, looking away. "It's you who's not."

He left then, and she didn't know where he went—to the club, probably, to hear the band they were supposed to hear together. She slept through the night and half of the next day, and she didn't even know when he'd come home.

Maybe he was right, she thinks now. Maybe she is attracted to unachievable goals, to people she cannot change, to animals she cannot save. She wonders if something as impossible as perspective is anything she has a chance at attaining in this lifetime.

She opens her eyes and, without turning the light on, stands up and runs her hands along the bottles in the wine rack. By touch, she picks out a red-wine bottle and unscrews the cap. She breathes in its scent, recognizes it as a pinot blend, and lowers herself to the floor again. She takes a sip, embracing the rich flavor of the wine, from grapes grown on Tasmanian soil, and realizes Paul isn't right at all. Life would be better if they could relinquish all this land, the whole entire state, back to the animals. They had been getting a pretty good start on Marbury until all this happened—until the species they've been trying to save destroyed a human body.

She sighs and takes another drink, more of a guzzle. She takes another, and another, until the alcohol floods through her body and helps numb her troubled mind.

CHAPTER 22

BROOKE

The last thing she sees before she shuts her eyes is the sharp edge of the knife, and she tenses in anticipation of what's next.

Then, the unexpected: a thud, the sound of wood splitting, followed by silence—an excruciating stillness fraught with a hair-raising anxiety, like the seconds between seeing lightning and hearing thunder. When she hears nothing more, she opens one eye, just in time to see the poacher falling toward her.

His face is twisted in pain, eyes and mouth locked open as he topples downward, and she tries to roll out of the way but isn't fast enough. He lands hard on the left side of her body, and she sees a trickle of blood dripping from behind his left ear as she scurries out from under him.

Gasping, she looks up to see Jane standing above them, the hair of her long blonde wig splayed around her shoulders. In her hands she holds a baseball bat–sized piece of splintered wood. Brooke turns toward the poacher on the ground and sees a sharp, narrow sliver of wood sticking out of the dark hair of his head.

She turns back to Jane in time to see her toss away the wood; it hits the side of a wall and bounces to rest. "It's true what they say." Jane pulls off the wig, releasing her familiar red hair. "Blondes do have more fun."

She drops the wig on the ground, near where her baseball cap lies in the dirt, and uses her foot to nudge the knife away from the man's body. Then she bends down and rummages through the man's backpack.

Brooke is staring at her, feeling as if she's watching a performance, as if she's not part of what just happened but merely observing it. Her body is shaking, and she is already sore from where the poacher hit her on his way down. At the same time, she can hardly believe she's alive. And she can hardly believe Jane is, too.

Jane pulls out a length of thin twine, then looks over at Brooke. "Well? Are you going to help me or what?"

Brooke breathes out, trying to steady herself, but her body feels paralyzed, locked up with the overflow of drama unfolding amid these dank prison cells. Unable to speak, she can only watch as Jane pushes the poacher's feet together and uses the twine to tie them tightly together at the ankles. "Normally, I like to be the one tied up," Jane says, "but you have to be willing to compromise."

She knots the twine and sits back on her heels. "Come on, don't just sit there," she says to Brooke. "See if there's any more rope in that bag. We need to do his hands, too, just to be safe."

In her shock, it helps to be given a task, and with trembling hands Brooke opens the pack, taking care not to disturb the eggs as she looks through the pockets. She doesn't find any more twine but holds up a small roll of duct tape. "Will this work?" Her voice is nothing more than a croak.

Jane smiles, and in that instant, Brooke sees Jane as she's always been: a consummate actress. Everything, to her, is a role—and Brooke wonders now, as Jane takes the tape from her and begins to wrap it around the man's wrists, whether anything—in Jane's life, in her own, and especially in their friendship—has ever been more than that.

Brooke rises painfully to her feet; her stomach aches where the man punched her; her shoulder and hip are sore from where he landed on her. She feels dirt on her face and the grit of it between her teeth.

"There," Jane says, standing up and brushing off her khakis, which are dirty beyond help. Where did she get these clothes, Brooke wonders. And the wig? How did all of this happen?

She remembers, then, the weight of Jane's pack, and the knowledge hits her like another punch in the gut: Jane planned this all along. Probably even before inviting Brooke on the trip.

Standing a few feet away from Jane, Brooke looks at her, knowing even as she does that she may only find the answers Jane wants her to find. But this is why the audience is as important as the cast, Brooke reminds herself. Because there are layers to every performance, and each role is only as shallow or as deep as the audience perceives it.

"So," she says slowly, "you're alive."

Jane laughs. "Of course I am. And, thanks to me, so are you."

Brooke's legs threaten to collapse under her, but she won't let herself sit down. "You let us all think you were dead," she says. "You let *me* think you were dead. Why?"

"I'm sorry, B." Jane shrugs. "What can I say? Malcolm *spurred my dull revenge.*"

"Will you stop quoting Shakespeare and listen to me?" Brooke feels anger eclipse her shock. "Do you have any idea what you've done?"

Jane steps a few paces away and picks up her day pack. From it she takes out a water bottle and holds it out to Brooke. "You look a little pale," she says. "Have some water."

Brooke shakes her head. Jane shrugs again and drinks some herself. "Look, it's not a big deal," she says. "I'm fine. No animals were harmed. Unfortunately, Malcolm wasn't harmed, either, but it was worth a try."

"Margaret is dead," Brooke says. "Did you know that?"

She watches Jane's face go blank as she lowers the water bottle. "What?" she says. "Dead? What happened?"

"No one knows." Brooke's mind is reeling. "I thought Malcolm did it. Because I thought he did something to you."

A groan rises up from the ground, and they both jump and turn toward the poacher. His leg is twitching, as if in a dream, and Brooke realizes he's on the verge of regaining consciousness. The thought clears her brain of its fog, and she thinks of the bird eggs in his pack. "We need to get out of here."

"What's the hurry?" Jane asks. "He's tied up."

Brooke gently lifts the poacher's pack. "We need to take these eggs somewhere safe," she says. "There's a ranger station in town. That's where Kerry was headed. She's probably still there. Let's go."

Jane stuffs the wig and cap into her pack and then slings it over a shoulder. "Look at you," she says. "A budding naturalist. We're quite a team, aren't we? Wrangling poachers. Saving endangered species."

"If we were a team you wouldn't have lied to me," Brooke says, starting down the wide trail toward town. "I still can't believe what you did," she says over her shoulder. "Have you lost your mind?"

Jane falls into step with her. "Maybe I have. I'm sorry, B. I
didn't mean to hurt you, of all people."

"Why did you run from me?" Brooke asks. "When we got into
town? I know you saw me."

"I wasn't sure it was you," Jane says. "I just saw three people
walking into town, and I hid. Keep in mind I've been out in the
woods for two days on my own."

"Keep in mind that was your choice," Brooke snaps.

Jane doesn't answer, and they walk in silence for a few minutes.
Then Brooke says, "You really thought you could get revenge on
Malcolm by faking your own death? How was that supposed to
work, exactly?"

"I just wanted to see him devastated," Jane says. "I was so certain he would fall to pieces the minute he knew I was gone. I
know he loves me. I know he wants to leave Charlotte."

"Why would he leave her for a dead woman?"

"I didn't plan to stay dead," Jane says.

Brooke listens as Jane tells her about the plan: the stolen
blood, the roadkill. Hiding in the woods waiting for Malcolm
to search for her. Heading north to Saltwick when that didn't
happen.

"So you planned to turn up when Malcolm mourned your
death, and he was supposed to be so happy he'd dump Charlotte
and propose on the spot?"

Jane sighs. "Look, I know it sounds crazy, but yes—something
like that. I just wanted a *reaction*. I wanted something from him
I wasn't getting." She turns her head to look at Brooke. "Come on,
B., you've been married a while. Don't tell me that Billy Boy never
did anything to make you crazy."

Brooke slows mid-step with awareness of how right Jane is, of how alike they still are. Of course she understands—it's what spurred her to leave William.

It began when she planned a stay-at-home date for the two of them. After months of distance seeping into their marriage, she felt they were entering a downward spiral they'd be unable to recover from. William always seemed to wear a look of grim resignation, as if every single event in life was something to get himself through, like a root canal or a tax audit. When she suggested he take some time off work, they'd had a fight about that, as much as it was possible to fight with William. He was so stoic, even in the middle of arguments. Brooke railed about how his job was affecting their relationship, how they were drifting apart, how they needed to get back on track or their marriage would be doomed. *I don't agree with that; I don't think that's true;* and *If you think so*, were his respective responses, delivered calmly even in the face of her shouts and tears. It was infuriating; he was infuriating. But at least he'd agreed to try date nights, and she began planning one every week.

The first was a happy hour in Belltown, to which he was an hour late. The next was dinner on Capitol Hill, after which he ended up returning to the office to work for a few more hours. After several weeks Brooke realized they weren't reconnecting in the way she'd hoped; for one, they never ended up in bed together. That was her inspiration to have a date night in; she would cook, and they'd be alone, and she would not, under any circumstances, let him return to the office.

But then he called from work to say he'd be late. When she asked how late, he said, "Don't wait for me."

Don't tell me Billy Boy never did anything to make you crazy.

Brooke felt the wineglass leave her hand and crash against the wall of the kitchen. She saw the pinot noir drip down and pool in the tiles like blood. The ringing phone—her neighbor, Marjorie—paused her momentary rage and stopped further damage, and after telling Marjorie that everything was fine, that she'd just dropped a plate, Brooke realized she could still salvage the evening, at least somewhat. She'd take dinner to his office. They could spend at least some time together, perhaps even shut his office door and fool around. She knew it was their only chance. Maybe, she thinks now, as she and Jane walk side by side, there's something desperately inevitable about last chances.

She'd quickly mixed the pasta and sauce and packed it along with salad, bread, and the tiramisu she'd bought for dessert. She gathered plates, silverware, wineglasses, a tablecloth, candles. She got in the car and sat through rush-hour traffic on the 520. On the other side of the bridge, she pulled into the parking lot at his office, heading for the corner where she knew he always parked. That's when she saw him exit the building and head toward his car.

She looked at the clock on the dashboard—less than an hour since they'd spoken. Maybe he was heading home to surprise *her*. She rolled down her window to call out to him—something like *great minds!*—but then she stopped. He looked defeated, weary, unapproachable. Instead, she waited for him to get into his car. She'd let him decompress after his long workday and simply follow him back home.

But he didn't go home. After crossing the bridge, he drove right past their exit on the freeway. Stunned, she could think of nothing to do but follow him as he drove toward downtown. He's having an affair, she realized, and she struggled to keep up with him as he turned up and down side streets—at first, she thought it was an attempt to ditch her, but then it became clear he didn't know she was behind him; he was looking for parking. Finally he turned onto Second Avenue and parked in front of a small bistro. She pulled into a no-parking zone half a block behind him and watched as he went inside.

She had to see for herself. She pulled the hood of her jacket up to hide her face and walked up to the bistro. From the sidewalk she could see into the large windows, and there was William at the bar. He had a beer in front of him and was talking to the bartender. He looked relaxed in a way she hadn't seen in a long time.

She walked down the block to where she had a good view of the front door, waiting for a glimpse of the next woman to walk in. The woman her husband was sleeping with.

As she watched, she saw two couples and a trio of girlfriends walk into the bistro, but not one single woman. After half an hour, she began to wonder whether there was another entrance she hadn't seen, and she returned to the front window.

William was still there, still at the bar, still alone. Now, a half-eaten burger was on a plate in front of him, and he was watching the Mariners game on the TV screen above the bar. She stared, unbelieving, for a long time, watching him share a laugh with the bartender, watching him finish his dinner, watching him order another beer.

And the entire time, she could not figure out whether this was better or worse than him having an affair.

Finally, she returned to her car, where she found a ticket on the windshield. She drove back to the apartment, threw away all the food, and called Serena, offering to sublet her apartment. She moved out the next day.

Now she catches Jane's eye. "Okay. Yes. I get it." She doesn't elaborate. "But you hurt a lot more of us than Malcolm, Jane. I thought you were dead. Kerry was out of her mind. And then Margaret—" She stops.

"What?" Jane says. Brooke can feel Jane's eyes on her. "You don't think that's my fault, do you?"

"I don't know," Brooke says helplessly. "It's just that everything went crazy after you—disappeared. Everyone was fighting, and then I heard Malcolm and Margaret—"

"Heard them?"

"Never mind." Brooke hadn't thought about the fact that Jane probably doesn't know about Malcolm and Margaret. "I mean, who knows what would've been different if you hadn't done what you did," she continues. "But you set off a course of events you can't undo."

Jane doesn't respond, and Brooke glances at her. Her face is flushed, from the heat perhaps, and she's staring straight ahead.

"So?" Brooke prompts her. "Why the disguise and everything, if you were just going to reappear in camp?"

"I wanted to be prepared for anything," Jane says. "You never know what the audience will be like, right?" She pauses and then says, "It looks pretty bad, me disappearing and then running off and leaving a dead woman behind. They're going to think I hurt Margaret."

"Why would they think that?" Brooke studies her, thinking of what a strange question that is, trying to read Jane's face.

She also remembers standing near Margaret's body, how Bryan heard something in the woods and took off after it. Was it a kangaroo, a wallaby? The poacher?

Jane?

"I don't exactly have an alibi, do I?" Jane says.

"Kerry thinks she slipped and fell."

Jane lets out a short laugh. "Wouldn't that be fitting. Mountain Woman conquers Everest, then slips on a walkway at summer camp."

They walk in silence for a while, and Brooke keeps her gaze ahead, trying not to stare at Jane, to try to peer beneath the mask. She thought she knew Jane—with whom she'd once shared an apartment, a dream, a life—and as an actor, character is one thing she should know, backward and forward. But she'd not imagined this.

Yet why hadn't she seen it? This wild plan was pure Jane, if Brooke really thought about it—and perhaps, if she had a little more imagination, she'd have figured it out. Or was she blind to Jane's madness because she herself was very much the same—leaving her husband without a word to anyone, traveling to the far reaches of the world without considering what came next?

"I found the pregnancy test." It's the only thing she can think of to say.

"Oh. That."

"Are you?"

"I thought I was," Jane says, "so I brought four tests. After the first three, I finally accepted I wasn't. I bought the fourth along thinking I'd find a way to scare him with it."

"Did you really wish you were pregnant?"

"I don't know," Jane says. "I guess part of me hoped it would be the thing to make him leave Charlotte."

"It would've been the thing to make you a single mother," Brooke says.

Jane looks at her. "Do you wish you and Billy Boy had had children? Do you think it would've kept you together?"

Brooke shakes her head. "I'm glad we didn't. And I'm glad you're not pregnant either. Haven't you learned anything from watching Lifetime?"

Jane laughs, a genuine laugh that reminds Brooke of the old Jane, the Jane who seemed more innocent than the one in front of her now. "Oh, I've missed you, B. All those weekends of Lifetime movie marathons. Those were the days."

"Those were the days," Brooke repeats.

"I've never had another friend like you," Jane says. "I hope you don't think I invited you along just for all this." She waves her hands in the air. "I really did want to start over. You and me."

"How exactly would we do that?"

"Well, you're single now, and so am I. Maybe you should consider a change. Move to LA. I've got a couch for you to sleep on for as long as you'd like."

"What would I do in LA?"

"Get onstage again," Jane says. "Get in front of a camera. You're so much better than you ever believed. Better than me, in fact."

"I doubt that. You had us all fooled."

"Are you going to be angry at me forever?"

"Maybe."

As they come to the crest of a hill, Brooke sees the lights from the small town of Saltwick stretched out before them—and she is relieved that, for the moment, she doesn't have to think about what Jane's done, or how she feels about it, or what she's going to do about Jane or William or the rest of her life. Right now, she only has to take care of these eggs and find someone to take care of that poacher.

"I think that's the ranger station," Brooke says, pointing. "That's where we're headed."

Jane stops walking. "You should go ahead without me."

"What do you mean?"

"I'm not sure I should make my appearance right now."

"Why not?"

"What if I get into trouble?"

Brooke looks at her. "*Now* you're worried about this? How did you think people would react?"

"Pseudocide is not a crime," Jane says. "I know that much."

"Pseudocide?"

"That's the term for feigning one's death," Jane says. "You know me, B., I prepare for every role. And it's not illegal, not by itself. It's not like I have a life insurance policy to cash in or anything."

Brooke shakes her head as she tries to follow Jane's line of reasoning.

"It's a great word, isn't it?" Jane continues. "*Pseudo*, from the Greek, of course, meaning *false, pretend*—added to *suicide*. Because that's where it all came from. A helpless feeling. I really did think about killing myself at first, to get back at Malcolm. But I didn't want to miss out on my own funeral."

"You sound like Sylvia Plath," Brooke says, "without the poetry."

"Ooh, I rather like that."

"Malcolm could've gone to jail for what you did," Brooke says. "He still might, because of Margaret."

Jane presses her lips together. "I can't say I'm surprised or disappointed about that," she says. "He deserves whatever's coming to him."

Brooke looks down at the town, bathed in the golden light of sunset. "I'm glad I never hated William that much," she says.

Jane laughs again, but this time it sounds sad. "Are you sure about that, B.? Maybe you just won't admit it."

Brooke tightens her grip on the pack she's holding. "I'm going to the ranger station. You can join me or not."

She begins walking and feels Jane behind her, then next to her. As they leave the woods behind, Brooke hears a shrieking cry, followed by a couple more.

"The devils," Jane says.

"That sound." Brooke shivers. She's not sure she'll ever get over the primal terror of hearing those ragged screams, which sound as if they're coming at her through the doorway out of hell. She begins walking faster, as if she can outpace the impending darkness, but the otherworldly cries surround them in the evening air.

"Don't worry, they're harmless," Jane says. "At first I thought they sounded scary, too, but then I grew to like it. It shows off their toughness."

"I can see why you'd like that."

They continue walking, and as they approach the ranger station, Brooke feels increasingly uneasy, and she's not sure why. Something is nagging at her. Maybe it's because even if Jane is safe, Margaret is not. Because something sinister did happen in their camp. Because whatever or whoever is responsible could still be out there.

And then, as the sun's last light begins to disappear, it hits her. She hears Jane's mocking words again—*Mountain Woman conquers Everest, then slips on a walkway*—and she realizes that she never told Jane where Margaret's body was found.

CHAPTER 23

KERRY

In the dream she's on the ferry, not the small one to Marbury Island but the large one from the mainland to Tasmania. She's running down a passageway, down one flight of stairs, then another, then skimming along the bulkheads in frantic search of something—what, she doesn't know. As she descends, deck by deck, the overhead sinks lower, the bulkheads close in on her, the lights dim. The ship heaves left, then right, and she's thrown to the floor. She ducks so she can squeeze through the next hatch, and all of a sudden it's unclear which direction is up or down. She crawls forward, only to find that the next hatch is sealed shut. She begins pounding it with her fists, the sound of flesh and bone on steel echoing through the narrow passageway. The banging grows louder and louder, until light blazes beyond her eyelids, and she opens her eyes to a whitish glare.

It takes her a moment to get her bearings, to discover that she's not trapped belowdecks on a ship but sprawled on the floor of the pantry at Saltwick House. She sees a figure silhouetted in the kitchen light streaming in and shrinks away until she hears a familiar voice say, "Kerry, what did I tell you about sleeping in the pantry?"

"Holy shit, Bryan." She feels groggy, hungover. "You scared me."

"That's all the thanks I get?"

She gets to her feet, feeling her head spin. "Sorry. How did you know I was in here?"

"Malcolm."

"You found him? Where is he?"

"At the moment, he's in his room with Charlotte." Bryan lowers his voice as she stumbles out of the pantry, blinking in the bright light of the kitchen. Outside, it's nearly dark.

"He cracked the shits when we pulled up to the pier," Bryan says. "He was sitting there like he was waiting for us to show up. He jumped into the boat, pissed as a newt, demanding we take both him and Charlotte to Triabunna."

"So Mark's here, too?"

Bryan nods. "And a copper, arrived at the same time we did. Mark's actually at the station. Copper is here waiting to have a word with Malcolm. Charlotte convinced him to let them come here so Malcolm could take a shower. He needs it." He looks at Kerry. "So do you, by the way."

She leans against the counter, putting a hand to her forehead. "Thanks."

"Well, well." He steps closer, peering into her face. "You've been drinking yourself, haven't you?"

"No."

"No?" He raises his eyebrows.

"Maybe a little. What else was I supposed to do while I was locked in that pantry?"

"Good on ya," he says. "I'd have done the same."

"I know *you* would have."

He disappears into the pantry and returns with the half-empty wine bottle from which she'd been drinking. "I say we finish this off, now that we're here."

"We're here, but this trip isn't over."

"Well, that's true," Bryan says. "Which reminds me."

"What?"

"Nigel will be here tomorrow."

"Shit."

"Don't get your knickers in a twist. I filled him in on everything. He understands."

"Understands what exactly?" Kerry says. "That I began the expedition with six guests and ended up at Saltwick with only one?"

"Well, if you put it that way . . ."

"How else would I put it?"

He takes a drink from the bottle and hands it to her. Her head is already pounding, but she is feeling far too sober for what she knows the next twenty-four hours will bring. She accepts the bottle and takes a long swallow.

"How's Charlotte?" she asks.

"Sobered up. Embarrassed. Feeling oddly loyal to Malcolm, under the circumstances."

"Maybe she blames Margaret more than Malcolm. Some women are like that." Kerry winces as she has another thought. "Could she have been involved in what happened to Margaret?"

He laughs. "You really are drunk," he says. "Tiny Charlotte versus Mountaineer Margaret? I doubt it."

"Well, I'm glad it's not our job to get it sorted."

He nods. "So where'd you lose Brooke?" he asks.

"She took off into the woods just as we got to town. She thought she saw Jane." She gives him the bottle and pours herself a glass of water.

He takes another drink. "Uh-oh. She going troppo?"

"Maybe. The woman was blonde and didn't look anything like Jane. I think Brooke is just a little—"

"Mad?"

"In denial," Kerry says. "She's never wanted to believe anything happened to her friend in the first place. And then she convinced herself that Malcolm killed her."

"You have to admit, she may have a point," Bryan says. "He did lock you in the pantry."

Kerry shrugs this off, but of course she's been thinking the same thing. "If he were that dangerous, wouldn't he have killed me?"

"Maybe he was planning to come back to do just that."

Kerry shakes her head, hoping it masks the sudden shudder that shoots through her. "You sound just like Brooke," she says, trying to sound casual. Meanwhile, she's hoping the police officer is keeping an eye on Malcolm's room. Does he know there's a window?

"Speaking of Brooke, where is she now?" Bryan asks.

"You didn't see her in town?"

"No."

"Shit," Kerry says. "I was hoping she'd find her way back."

"She can't have gone far. We'll find her."

"What about Ian? All by the time Nigel gets here?" She grabs her mobile off the counter. "I need some air."

Out on the porch, she breathes in the evening air, still feeling disoriented. It takes her a moment to notice that someone is sitting on the far end of the porch. She backs up, rattling the screen door, as he stands and takes a few steps toward her. He's very fit, dressed in a striped shirt and tie, and when she sees the police badge on the front of his belt, a handgun on his hip, she relaxes.

"Sorry to startle you." He has the early signs of a beard and looks to be in his mid-thirties. "I'm Detective Inspector David Conyers. You are?"

"Kerry Chapman."

He glances at his notepad. "You're the lead guide?"

"Past tense, at this point, but yeah."

Behind her, someone's pushing at the screen door. She turns and opens it for Bryan.

Then she looks at the detective. "I thought you'd be guarding Malcolm," she says.

"There's no need for that just yet," DI Conyers says. "But I was just getting ready to go speak with him. I'll need to speak with you, too."

"Of course."

He glances at his notepad again. "Is Brooke Sanders here?"

"Not presently."

"Kerry lost her in town," Bryan says.

Kerry resists the urge to elbow him in the ribs. "We do expect her to be here soon," she says. "Along with another guest, Ian Riley, who disappeared on Bryan's watch."

The detective looks from one of them to the other, not amused. Kerry's mobile rings, and she glances at the screen; it's Mark. "It's the park ranger," she says to the detective, and he nods. She sees Bryan leading him inside as she walks to the end of the porch to take the call.

"Mark. Finally."

"Hey, Kerry," he says. "Good news. Those two missing hikers of yours? They just showed up here at the station."

"Really?" She can't believe it. "Okay, don't let them go anywhere. I'll be right there." It's not a long walk to Saltwick House, but she doesn't want to take the chance that they'll get lost or disappear again.

She calls out to Bryan as she puts her hiking boots back on. His face appears at the screen just as she's tying the laces. "They're at the ranger station—Ian and Brooke. I'm off to bring them back here. See ya."

She leaps down the porch steps, and as she heads into town at a jog, she realizes just how much the past two days have taken out of her, or maybe it's only the past two hours. Her feet ache, her stomach roils with nausea, and her brain feels so muddled she wonders if she'll ever be able to think straight again.

She slows as she heads down the slope toward the center of town. When she reaches the ranger station, she sees Mark standing out front, waiting for her. Without thinking, she closes the meters between them at a run and throws her arms around his neck. She feels his arms around her back, holding her close, and she allows herself to rest there, feeling her body relax in a way it hasn't in days, possibly months, probably years. She lets her breathing slow until it matches his: easy, calm, normal.

Then she remembers she hasn't showered in nearly three days, and she probably reeks of wine. She pulls away, murmuring, "Sorry."

"Don't be sorry," he says. His fingers brush her hand, and she knows that he means it. "I'm so glad you're here."

"I still can't believe we made it."

"When I saw what happened at the first camp—" Mark shakes his head. "It was carnage. I don't know how you managed to cope with all that."

"Not very well, I'm afraid."

"No," he says, "you did all you could. You did everything right."

"Tell that to Nigel."

"I plan to."

She smiles at him, then sighs. "I suppose I should collect my guests and get them back to the house," she says.

He nods. "Before you go, there's something else," he begins.

Just then she sees the door open behind him, and she feels the first sense of relief she's felt in days. Even after that first trip, that close call with Meg's snakebite, she never imagined she'd end up feeling grateful simply for seeing her guests alive.

Brooke emerges first, looking tired under the yellowish outdoor light of the station. Behind her is another figure—tall, but Kerry sees immediately it's not Ian; it's a woman. A thought races through her mind—a woman, here with Mark—and she immediately regrets the koala hug she'd given him.

Then she sees the flame of red hair, and she stares, blinking, at what she can only believe is an apparition.

Jane's wearing filthy clothes a size too big for her, and her hair is untamed around her face. She looks exhausted, with dark circles under puffy eyes, and a day pack dangles from her slouched shoulder. Kerry looks from Jane to Brooke and back again. "What the fuck is going on?" she asks quietly.

"It's a long story," Brooke says. "But first, we have something to show you. There is a poacher out there. Or was. We found him."

"What?" Now Kerry looks at Mark.

"That's what I was about to tell you," he says. "He assaulted them at the old settlement, and they tied him up. I need to get over there straightaway." He holds up a pair of handcuffs. "From DI Conyers. I'll keep him here at the station until another officer can get over from Triabunna."

Brooke steps forward, holding out a rucksack. "These are the eggs that he stole. We were really careful with them. I hope they're okay."

Kerry takes the pack and looks at Mark, noticing that he has a flashlight and was outside waiting because he's ready to go. "Are you sure you want to do this alone? Why not wait for Conyers?"

"Poachers are my business, not his. For the moment, at least." He puts a hand on her shoulder. "She'll be right. You need to take care of those eggs. I'll be back soon."

She watches him disappear over the hill and into the darkness. The pack grows heavy in her tired arms, and she turns to Brooke and Jane. "He's right. I need to look at these eggs. You two need to get over to Saltwick House."

She sets the pack down gently and walks them to the road. "Follow this road for about two hundred meters, and you'll see the house on the left. There's a sign out front, and the porch lights are on." She looks at them. "Bryan's there. I'm going to call him to tell him you're on your way. If he doesn't see you in fifteen minutes, we're organizing a search party."

Brooke nods, and Jane wisely says nothing. She watches them walk along the gravel road for a few moments, and then turns away.

She calls Bryan, tells him to look out for Brooke and Jane, but she hangs up before he can ask any questions. She doesn't have any answers, anyway, especially to the most pressing question: Where is Ian?

The only small comfort she can take in him still being missing is that he knows how to handle himself in the woods, and he knows the route. It was clear he'd studied it obsessively before even embarking on the trip, and she can only hope that he hasn't injured himself, that he's choosing to stay away.

At least the skies are clearing, she tells herself, looking upward and seeing a smattering of stars across the deepening blue. Then, as she picks up the poacher's rucksack, she has another thought: What if Ian, too, had run into the poacher? It wouldn't be unusual, with Ian knowing where to find birds as well as any poacher would. And what if they'd crossed paths and he'd been assaulted, like Brooke and Jane, with no one around to come to his aid?

She feels her hope sink once again, and she tries to put these thoughts out of her mind as she enters the ranger station; there is nothing she can do about Ian right now, and she has to do whatever she can to protect these eggs.

The Saltwick ranger station is a three-room, single-story wood structure that, beyond its small reception area, houses two offices; a miniature galley for preparing tea, coffee, and lunch; and, at the back of the building, a workroom that Mark euphemistically calls their "research institute"—a windowless room with a large, sturdy workbench surrounded by cabinets and lockers. At one end of the room is a large chest freezer where they store deceased animals before sending them to the mainland for autopsies or research. Behind the station is a small private cottage, where the ranger on duty often stays overnight, usually during the busy season.

Kerry pulls a stool up to the workbench and carefully opens the pack. "Hello, babies," she says softly as she gently removes the first container. She sees how many there are—at least half a dozen—and can only hope they're packed well enough to save the chicks inside.

Not that this will matter to their parents. She thinks of this a lot—what happens when adult birds return to empty nests? Do they wonder what happened? Do they detect the scent of human hands? Do they mourn?

She takes out another container and thinks of the generation of orphans that will need to be raised at the sanctuary. She'll be there, of course, probably for every moment of these birds' lives, now that she's out of a job. She wishes there were a way to return these eggs to their nests, but that would be hopeless and foolish; the adult birds have probably given up on them by now. At least they've been saved, not sold on the black market. If they have to be in captivity, a sanctuary is far better than a pet store.

She opens one of the containers on the table and looks inside. The eggs are packed in bubble wrap, and while none of them are cracked, they need to be kept warm or the chicks inside won't make it. She places her fingertip on one of the eggs, and it feels slightly warm to the touch. She inspects the container and realizes that it's insulated, and that below the bubble wrap is a small hot-water bottle. It's barely warm.

Quickly closing the container, she does a rapid triage in her head. Boil water with the kettle to refill the hot-water bottles. Rewrap the eggs carefully, rotating the ones closest to the water bottle so that they'll get more heat this time around. Search for an incubator, on the off chance that somewhere—

She hears the front door open and breathes a sigh of relief. "Mark? That was fast. Hey, I'm looking for an incubator—any chance you've got one somewhere?"

There is no response, and suddenly she freezes, her hand on top of one of the containers. "Mark?"

She turns to face the hallway. She can see through the hall to the entrance area, where whoever just entered would be visible—or should be.

"Hello?"

She steps into the hall and peers into the first office. Empty. Then, slowly, she looks into the next one—also empty.

It must've been her imagination. She walks out to the reception area; no one is there. She checks the door, which is slightly ajar—but she can't remember whether she'd closed it properly herself or not. Maybe a backpacker saw the lights and opened the door, found no one inside, and left.

She's in the hallway on her way back to the workroom when she feels a sudden rush of air, then a hand tight around her arm, cold steel against her neck.

"I think you have something of mine." His voice is low, his breath hot in her ear.

Her heart beats wildly against her rib cage. Mark, she thinks desperately—what has this man done to Mark?

"I don't think so," she croaks out.

He shoves her roughly forward, into the workroom. "What do you call this?" he demands as he presses the blade into her neck. She feels a sharp sting.

"Those eggs do not belong to you."

"They bloody well do, after all I've gone through to get them. Now put them back in my rucksack."

276 MIDGE RAYMOND AND JOHN YUNKER

He's holding her arm so tightly she's losing sensation in her hand, and she tries to wriggle free. "I can't. I can't move my arm."

He releases her arm and in the same quick motion grabs her by the hair, yanking her ponytail hard enough to make her gasp. "That better?"

She feels the knife against her neck as she returns the first egg container to the rucksack. She moves very slowly, stalling for time, and he gives her hair a sharp pull. "Faster," he says.

"I'm being careful," she says. "These eggs are worth nothing if the chicks are dead. You should know that."

He presses the tip of the knife to a spot on her neck, and she feels the prick of it as it breaks the skin. "You won't be so fucking cheeky if I sink this in any further, will you?"

Without another word, she puts the other containers back into the pack. "Right, then," she says, taking a step back. "Take it. I won't say anything."

He pulls the knife away as he shoulders the rucksack, but he keeps a firm grip on her hair. "Bloody right I'm taking it. And I'm taking you, too."

He steers her by the hair back out into the hallway. "There's a boat at the dock. We're going to walk over there just like two naturalists out looking for birds. And then you'll point that boat to Triabunna, and I'll walk off on the other side. If you do as I tell you, you can sail on back. Easy, right?"

"Yeah. Easy."

At the door, he pats her pockets, finds her mobile. He takes it out and tosses it into the rubbish bin in the corner. Then he leans close. "If you scream, if you say even one word, before we get to Triabunna, I'm going to stick this deep into your throat and haul you overboard. Understood?"

She nods. She has a feeling he's going to do that anyway, and she knows then she can't leave the island with him. Not if she's going to have any chance of staying alive.

He opens the front door and looks around before pulling her behind him, this time by the arm, and once outside, he puts his arm around her, his hand clutching her shoulder in a vise grip as they walk toward the waterfront. From a distance, they might appear to be a couple, his arm around her in a warm embrace, no space between them. Any closer, and it would become obvious that this is because he is using his other hand to hold the blade over her windpipe.

She is walking slowly, trying again to stall for time, and he impatiently tugs her along. They pass the old commissary, then the cement silos, now deteriorating back into limestone and gravel. They reach the town's most modern structure, the steel pier that juts out into the darkness, where the formerly wild waters now appear asleep.

Suddenly she hears a familiar cry—a mangled, high-pitched animal sound coming from the bushes behind them. The man turns, pulling her body around with his.

"What the fuck was that?"

"Devil," she says.

"That's no devil."

"Maybe it's injured."

He pushes her hard, and she stumbles forward on the dock, toward Dan's boat. She feels another stab of fear when she wonders where Dan is. How would this man know the boat would be empty if he hadn't done something to Dan?

She's about to board the boat when he shoves her from behind, and she falls headfirst onto the deck, barely able to get her hands in front of her in time to break her fall. Wrists screaming, she raises her head in time to see him releasing the ropes.

Then he yanks her to her feet and leads her to the wheel. He takes off his pack and stows it in the same place they had put their own backpacks, three days ago, on their way to the first camp.

He waves the knife at her, and she starts up the engine. As it rumbles to life, the boat shudders underneath them, and she looks at the dark body of water ahead. She knows this is her last chance, and she feels as though she's going to faint from panic—and that's when she knows just what to do. She sets the throttle to neutral and lets herself crumple to the deck.

She hears him yelling, feels his feet pounding her body, but she doesn't move.

Then, a shout, a scuffle, and she looks up to see a mess of arms and legs, fists and faces, then a splash, and then another.

She rushes to the side of the boat, sees Bryan's blond head bobbing in the water. She pulls out a life vest and shouts his name. He hears her and turns, and she throws the vest as hard as she can. He catches it and slips one arm through it, still struggling with the other man, who's underwater.

The boat is drifting away from the dock, and, trying to keep her eyes on Bryan, she manages to steer it back, clumsily, ramming it into the rubber tires lining the pier and securing it as best she can with the rope.

She picks up the rucksack and puts it safely on the pier, then scans the water for Bryan. The clouds have parted enough to let a sliver of moonlight onto the water, but she can't see anything.

"Bryan!" When he doesn't answer, she shouts his name again. And again.

She hears a sound, but not from the water—it's coming from land. She scans the shoreline and sees the dark outline of a man pulling a body over rocks.

As she runs toward it, she sees another body, running toward her from the other direction—she recognizes with relief that it's Mark. By the time she gets to shore, he's helping Bryan drag the poacher's body up onto the sand. Mark pounds the man's chest until he spits out water and coughs himself back to life.

Kerry's breath is ragged, and her ribs hurt from where the poacher kicked her. She sinks down to the ground next to Bryan. "How—" She doesn't have the energy to finish the question.

"When I got to the prison cells, he was gone," Mark says. "Saw the twine and tape—looks like he managed to slice them off. He must've had a knife on him."

"He did," she says, touching her neck. She feels the spot where the blade scraped the delicate skin.

"I was on my way back to the station when I heard you yelling for Bryan." Mark looks at her, seeing the smudge of blood on her neck. He puts his hand on her chin, turning her face slightly to have a look. "You right?"

"Just a scratch," she says.

He inspects her neck until he seems satisfied that the injury is minor. Then he turns to Bryan. "Good on ya, mate. Crikey, I can't believe you both didn't drown out there."

"Good thing I'm a surfer," Bryan says.

"Let's get this bloke handcuffed, hey?"

Kerry stands back as Bryan hauls the poacher to his feet. Mark cuffs his hands behind his back.

"Where's Dan?" Kerry asks.

"Asleep in the cottage, I reckon," Mark says. "He was knackered, and after all he's done I couldn't let him sleep on the boat."

Mark double-checks the handcuffs and turns in the direction of the station.

"Do you want us to come with you?" Kerry says.

"Nah, he's not going anywhere," Mark says. "I'll be right. Just send DI Conyers over when you see him."

"Will do," she says, and turns to Bryan. "How'd you end up down here, anyway?"

"I called, but you didn't answer your mobile," he says. "I headed over just to make sure you were right, and when I saw two people headed toward the jetty, I put it together." He wrings water out of his shirt and smiles. "How'd you like my devil impersonation?"

"It was shit. But it worked." She reaches out and touches his arm, still dripping with seawater. "Thank you. For this I'll let it slide that you let Jane and Brooke out of your sight."

He laughs. "Hey, at least I left them in good hands. That detective has got a lot of questions. I don't think he'll be done by tonight."

They walk back to the pier together, where Bryan secures the boat, and Kerry picks up the poacher's rucksack. "I hope you're feeling paternal," she says. "We've got a lot of eggs to keep warm."

CHAPTER 24

BROOKE

The lights are on inside Saltwick House, but all is quiet. Brooke hears the murmur of voices behind one of the doors, and she finds her pack waiting for her in the hallway; someone must've brought it here for her. There are enough empty rooms for her and Jane to each have one, but when she walks into one of the rooms, Jane follows her inside and flops down on one of the twin beds.

"God, I can't wait to take a shower," Jane says, staring at the ceiling. Then she sits up. "I'll need to borrow some clothes."

Brooke begins to empty her backpack, looking for what's clean and what might fit Jane's tall frame. As she does, she remembers her medication, and when her pack is empty, she sighs. "I can't believe I managed to lose my pills."

Then something lands next to her on the carpet. The prescription bottle. She looks over at Jane. "You took them?"

"I told you. They're a crutch. And look how well you've done without them."

"I wouldn't say I'm doing well," Brooke says, but she has to admit to herself that she'd all but forgotten about them. And she'd survived. More than survived.

She remembers what Jane had said on the first day on Marbury. *That's what friends are for. To remind each other what's real and what's not.* She tosses the bottle back at Jane. "Keep them. I'm done."

Brooke finds Jane a clean pair of leggings and a T-shirt. There are two full bathrooms in the house, so they both go to shower without saying much more. As Brooke stands under the steady stream of hot water, she thinks of the last shower she took, two days ago, under the stormy sky on the southern part of Marbury Island. The trickle of water from the bucket above. Bryan's skin against hers. The steam rising from their bodies in the cool air.

She returns to the room to find Jane sitting cross-legged on one of the beds, her hair combed back. On the small table between the beds is a bottle of white wine and a plate of cheese, crackers, fruit, and olives.

"I raided the kitchen," Jane says. "I don't know where Bryan is and I'm guessing there's no schedule for dinner anymore."

Brooke sits down on the opposite bed and takes the full glass of wine Jane offers. Sitting across from each other like this reminds Brooke of the first night on Marbury, in their tent—which in turn reminds her of their college days. They spent so many late nights sitting like this, talking, smoking, drinking. Dreaming. It would've been impossible then to imagine they'd end up right here, right now, under these circumstances.

And what *are* these circumstances, anyway, Brooke wonders. She thinks of the chaos of her friendship with Jane, whether it's worth it. And yet she feels, despite everything, that she's stronger now than she's ever been.

Jane, too, seems to be in a reflective mood. She mentions a few of the college-town bars they used to frequent, the wild cast parties they went to after closing nights—after opening nights, too, and many others in between.

"I can tell you miss it, B.," she says. "That night we did the Lifetime skit, you were so good. You just went with it like you've been doing it all along."

Brooke remembers the opening night of her first college play, how nervous she was. She was certain she'd forget all her lines or throw up onstage, or both. But as it turned out, one of the actors in her first scene forgot his line, despite her offering him a second cue; he just froze. She ad-libbed her way out of it, not realizing until later how effortless it was, how natural it felt to improvise. She asks Jane—who was in the same play but backstage at the time—if she remembers, and Jane smiles.

"Of course I remember. You're at your most brilliant when your life is not so heavily scripted."

"Is that why you keep insisting on throwing me into chaos?"

"Maybe."

"Well, I could use a script right now," Brooke says. "I just don't know how to deal with all this."

"How about ad-libbing a bit?"

"I don't see how you can be so cavalier about this." The words erupt out of her before she can stop them. "I mean, my life may be a mess, but at least I grew up, Jane. At least I got married and have a real job and I'm not pretending to be an actor anymore. And I'm not flying across the planet seeking some sick revenge on a married man who doesn't give two shits about me."

Jane goes still, and Brooke waits, her heart banging against her ribs so loudly she feels certain Jane hears it. A moment passes, and Jane says, "You're right. You did grow up, and you left me behind. And that hurt, I admit it."

"So you wanted revenge not only on Malcolm but on me, too."

"No," Jane says quickly. "That's not why I invited you. But I thought the old you would've enjoyed it. I guess I was hoping you hadn't grown up so much after all."

Brooke shakes her head. "How did you even come up with such a fucked-up idea?"

Jane picks up the bottle and refills their glasses. She pops an olive into her mouth and looks at a point past Brooke's head. "Do you remember that off-campus house we rented on Sherman Street?"

"The one with no insulation and no heat?"

"And rats."

"Oh, yeah. I forgot. They bothered you much more than me."

"No shit," Jane says. "Remember that day I came home and found that rat in my room? He was the size of a guinea pig, walking around on the carpet sniffing my clothes."

"Your clothes being on the floor probably had something to do with why you had a rat in your room."

"Cute," Jane says. "Anyway, you were in class or something, and I didn't know what to do, so I trapped him under a bucket. Then I ran out of the house looking for someone to help me. I found this old guy two houses down out mowing his lawn. I begged him to come take the rat out for me, and he refused. He said we kept him up too many nights with our parties and we deserved to have rats."

Brooke can't help but laugh, remembering coming home and finding Jane on the front steps, waiting for her. "He was probably right."

"So do you remember what you did with the rat?"

"Yeah, I put him into a cardboard box and brought him outside."

"And you made me set him free."

"I don't remember that part."

"I was terrified," Jane says, "and that's why you made me do it. We always challenged each other, remember? We always made sure fear wouldn't stop us from anything."

"I guess we did."

"Anyway, he was just lying there, eyes open, breathing fast. When I opened the box, I thought he might leap out and bite me and give me rabies. But you said he looked like he might be sick, and you wanted to put him somewhere safe to let nature take its course."

Brooke remembers the tiny body, how soft his fur looked. She hadn't touched him when she shuffled him into the box, but when she looked down at him in what looked like a tiny coffin, she wanted to. She wanted to offer comfort somehow, but all they could do was let him go, or try to. After Jane opened the box, the rat didn't move, and they eventually left him in the box, under a bush, and went back inside. "I wish I knew what happened to him."

"I do know," Jane says. "I went out there, about twenty minutes later. I peeked inside the box—and the rat was gone. Vanished."

"What do you mean, somebody took him?"

"No, B. That little rat was *pretending* to be sick. He was acting so he could get himself out of my room. And that's when I realized that acting isn't just something you do in theatres or sound stages—it's about survival. It's about getting through your own damn life. I think maybe the most successful people in life are simply the best actors. Maybe that's all it takes, you know?"

"Maybe." But Brooke knows Jane is right. What she hadn't realized is how much she loves acting, how she should have embraced it rather than run from it. After all, it's the skill that got her through her early life—why not turn it around and use it for good, for joy, for fun for a change?

"And it's not just rats," Jane says. "There's this bird called a kill-deer. They nest on the ground, and they'll play like they're injured if you walk too close to their nests. Acting."

"How do you know that?"

"Ian told me."

"Oh. I don't remember that."

"We all act to survive, B."

"Well, I guess that makes you one fine actor," Brooke says.

"It makes both of us fine actors."

There is so much more she wants to say, so much more she wants to learn, but the wine has made her sleepy, and Jane can barely keep her eyes open. "To be continued," Brooke says, and they turn out the light.

With all that is still going through her mind, Brooke expects to have a fitful night, and she's surprised when sleep snatches her so quickly and doesn't release her again until sunlight streams through the window and across her face.

She sits up and looks out the window, seeing cloudless blue sky. It looks almost as if the past three days could've been a dream; the island looks like a different place entirely in this bright morning light. She looks over at the other bed and finds it empty.

She dresses and follows the sounds of Kerry's voice down the hall to the dining room. Seated around a long rectangular table are Malcolm and Charlotte, with Jane sitting across from Malcolm and Kerry at the closest seat to the kitchen. She sees Bryan through the doorway, moving around in the kitchen.

"Can we get you some breakfast?" Kerry asks.

"Just coffee for now. Thanks." Brooke sits next to Jane, and she can feel the tension filling the room. Malcolm stares down into a bowl of muesli, and Charlotte cups a coffee mug in two hands as she stares out the window overlooking the garden.

"Where's Ian?" Jane asks.

"Mark and Dan have been looking for him," Kerry says. Brooke sees her cast a quick, nervous glance toward Charlotte. "He—he took a different route to Saltwick yesterday. He can't be far. He knows where we are."

Brooke, too, looks over at Charlotte, who is staring at Jane with an odd expression on her face, a mix of curiosity and irritation.

"So, Jane," Charlotte says, "while we wait to be excused from this island, will you do us the favor of enlightening us on your adventure?"

"I wouldn't exactly call it an adventure," Jane says.

"Is *ruse* more appropriate?"

"I suppose if that's what you'd call nearly getting raped at knifepoint by some dickhead poacher, then sure, call it a ruse."

Brooke feels the coffee burn her throat as she swallows it too fast. She looks at Jane, who meets her eye and gives her a barely perceptible wink.

"Oh my God," Kerry says. "This was yesterday?"

"No, this was two days ago," Jane says, "after I was nearly eaten alive by those devils."

Kerry leans forward. "Did you see them? How many were there?"

"It sounded like a thousand of them," Jane says, "but I have no idea. I was pretty trashed that night, I'll admit, and I got lost on my way back from the bathroom." She looks down at the fruit on her breakfast plate. "It's really embarrassing, but I ended up passed out in the ferns. I don't know how long. But apparently there was some dead animal nearby, and the next thing I know I'm surrounded by Satan's little lapdogs, screaming and tearing about this carcass. I came to with one of them chewing on my shirt, and I ripped it off and ran. I lost my scarf, and my phone, but I was so terrified I had to get out of there. I didn't know where I was going, and by the time I calmed down enough to come back, I was completely lost."

"We found your scarf and shirt." Brooke feels everyone's eyes turning toward her, and she grows focused, her senses heightened. She remembers a director once reassuring her, after she'd had a particularly bad rehearsal, that she needn't worry—often people who are great in rehearsal don't perform as well with an audience, and vice versa. She feels as if, without Jane, she's been stuck in bad rehearsals these past five years—and now she can feel the stage lights again, as hot and bright on her face as the sun shining through the dining room window.

"They were totally destroyed," she continues. "The devils must've smelled you on them."

"And my phone?" Jane asks hopefully.

"I think it's still at the first camp. It was trashed."

"Still," Jane continues, "I wish I could've made it back. Because what happened instead—" She pauses and takes a drink of water, as if trying to steady herself.

Without thinking, Brooke puts a hand on Jane's arm, a motion unrehearsed but as natural as if she'd done it a hundred times before. She and Jane are once again behind the theater's fourth wall, just the two of them, separated from their audience by not only their roles but by their shared history. Whatever's between her and Jane, that inexorable pull, she's drawn right back into

Jane's magnetic field, as she'd been years ago, as she probably always will be. As perhaps she needs to be. She'll play along to the end.

Jane pats her hand, giving her a grateful smile. "I was lost, and soaked with rain, and covered in mud. I saw a flashlight in the distance, and I followed it—I was hoping I'd gotten turned around and I'd end up at the toilets or the showers in camp. But then this guy appeared, sort of out of nowhere, and he said he had a tent and some dry clothes for me. I forgot I had no shirt on, and I thought this was a safe place, you know—not like America, where people get murdered left and right. I thought he was a nice Aussie backpacker who was going to help me out. When we got to his tent, he played nice for a few minutes, got me some clothes and a towel. Left me alone to change. But before I could get fully dressed, he came back in, shoved me down, and put a knife to my head."

Brooke hears Kerry take in a breath. Charlotte is staring at Jane, wide-eyed; even Malcolm is watching her, looking concerned.

"We struggled but I couldn't fight him off, and then finally I kneed him in the balls. He collapsed, and I ran."

"Did he chase you?" Kerry asks.

"I don't know," Jane says. "If he did, I outran him. I didn't dare look back. I just kept running. Until my legs went numb and I couldn't see the trees through the rain. I found a hollowed-out tree, and I crawled in and spent the night there. The next day I kept walking, but I didn't know where I was going, and I was so afraid I'd be headed right back to this guy's campsite again. I think I got more lost because I kept turning and turning . . ." She trails off and takes another drink of water.

"That second night in the woods, I thought I was going to die," she says. "I was freezing and had nothing to eat, no water except what I could catch from the rain. Finally I found a road and saw a sign pointing toward Saltwick."

She looks around the table, meeting everyone's eyes as she does. Brooke watches them react—from Malcolm, surprise and a hint of admiration; Kerry, sympathy and concern; from Charlotte, something she doesn't quite recognize.

"I'm ashamed to admit this," Jane says, eyes downcast once again, "but when I got close to town, I went to the public campground. There were only a couple of tents, and they were empty. So, I went in and stole some clothes and some food and a day pack from one of the backpackers. I never should've done that. But I still had hardly any clothes, and I was starving."

"No one will blame you for that," Brooke says, soothingly.

"Of course not." Charlotte's small, dark eyes seem to search Jane's. "I'm so sorry, Jane. I had no idea you'd been through so much."

Jane raises her face and smiles at her. "That's okay. I'm alive, and that's all that matters."

"And, you saved me from the poacher," Brooke says.

"Will he go to prison?" Jane asks Kerry.

"I'll see to that." The voice comes from the doorway.

They all turn to see Detective Inspector Conyers standing there; they'd been so engrossed in Jane's story that no one heard him enter the building.

The detective looks at Jane. "I'd like to take your statement. Will you come with me to the ranger station?"

"Do I have to?"

"I'd like to get it recorded," he says. "It won't take too long."

"I'll come with you," Brooke says.

Jane stands. "It's okay," she says to Brooke. "I'll be fine."

From the porch, she watches Jane walk away with the detective, feeling dread gnaw at her stomach. When Jane had spun her tale, Brooke had been caught up in the moment, in the drama of it: all the world's a stage and nothing to lose. She hadn't thought of the consequences, of the fact that if Jane sticks with her story, she'll be committing perjury. And despite what Jane told her about pseudocide not being illegal, neither of them know Australian law well enough to know whether she hasn't done anything wrong along the way. Or maybe there's just something about being on a former convict settlement that is making her paranoid.

She is so lost in thought she doesn't realize Charlotte has joined her on the porch until she hears the screen door snap shut behind her.

"It'll be okay," Charlotte says, her voice soft and reassuring. "I sat in on Malcolm's interview, and the detective was very kind and professional. It's not like the television shows you see in America."

"I just feel bad for Jane," Brooke says, donning the mask once more. "She's been through so much."

"I know." Charlotte sighs, then looks at her watch. "It's still so early. Since she'll be there for a while, why don't we take a walk?"

"A walk? You forgot, I just hiked twenty kilometers to get here."

Charlotte smiles. "I did forget. But I'm thinking of something quite a bit less strenuous. There are some spectacular fossil cliffs just on the other side of town. It would be a shame not to see them while you're here."

"I should wait for Jane," Brooke says. "She'd want to see them, too."

"I think this will be our last chance. We're due to head back to Triabunna after lunch." Charlotte bends down and starts putting on her shoes. "I'd welcome a little company."

Brooke relents and finds her own shoes under one of the porch chairs. She doesn't really want to go, but sitting around here for hours waiting doesn't appeal either. And there are so many unanswered questions that perhaps Charlotte can answer, if Brooke dares to ask. About Malcolm. About Ian. Maybe even about Jane.

They follow the gravel road through town, past various historic structures: a museum, a dormitory for summer campers, a row of former settlers' homes. Among them all are animals: kangaroos and wallabies among the large bushes, wombats and Cape Barren geese foraging in the grasses.

It only takes a few minutes before they leave civilization behind for a wide, grassy field that tilts upward to the sky. The grass is so well manicured by the slow-moving wombats that Brooke feels as if they're strolling along a golf course—except for the stones strewn about the field, often covered with wombat scat: small, dark-brown squares that often appear on top of the rocks. They like to mark their territory by shitting as high up as they can, Kerry had told them.

Charlotte says nothing other than to comment on the weather, which is stunningly beautiful: blue skies with scattered clouds, a light breeze. "If only it had been this way the whole time," Charlotte says.

"I know," Brooke agrees. "I wonder if things might have been different."

"I've wondered the same thing," Charlotte says.

At the top of the hill, the land ends abruptly, giving way to an expanse of turquoise sea that sparkles in the sunlight. They stop at a sign that warns HAZARDOUS EDGE AHEAD. To their right, limestone cliffs curve for another mile upward to the sharp, jagged peak of the mountain.

Brooke raises her phone to take photos, stepping past the sign. She inches forward to peek over the edge and feels a wave of dizziness. The cliff drops at least two hundred feet straight down to where rock meets ocean.

"Let me take a photo of you." Charlotte is right next to her.

"Okay." Brooke steps away from the cliff and hands Charlotte her phone before she poses next to the sign.

Charlotte takes a photo, then waves her back toward the edge. "It'll be more dramatic if you stand over there," she says. "I'll try to get the sign in, too."

Brooke moves toward the cliff, stopping about three feet before the edge and turning around.

"Perfect!" Charlotte says. "So dramatic."

Something about having her back to the cliff makes her nervous, and she silently implores Charlotte to hurry up with the photo.

"Oops," Charlotte says. "I've switched it to video. Hang on a second." She squints down at the screen, reflecting bright sunlight. "So, will you two be heading back to America after this?" she asks.

"That's the plan," Brooke says. "I'm sorry we made such a mess of your trip."

"You have nothing to apologize for. You've been wonderful."

"With what happened to Jane and everything—maybe there was something I could've done. Anyway, I know she's sorry, too."

"You don't have to put words in her mouth, darling. If you were smart, you'd run as far away from her as you could." She finally looks up, holding out the phone in front of her. She wears an expression that matches the sharpness in her voice, as if she's newly alert, like an animal suddenly aware of its prey.

Brooke takes a step forward, away from the cliff.

"Not yet." Charlotte smiles and holds up the phone. "One more picture. *L'appel du vide*, remember? It's the vastness out there that makes this so picturesque. You have to be right on the edge to make the shot work."

Brooke stays still, but she's getting increasingly impatient, especially with Charlotte acting so strange. "Jane's not so bad," she says. "Not once you get to know her."

"I know her well enough to know what she's capable of." Charlotte's pleasant smile flatlines, and she lowers the phone and turns steely eyes on Brooke. "It's bad enough she fucked my husband, but to ruin our vacation—now, that's cruel."

Brooke feels her entire body flush, her face blazing under the sun. "I didn't know—how did you—"

"Don't defend yourself, darling. Or your so-called friend. A wife always knows. You should have learned that from your Lifeline dramas, or whatever they are. I know about Malcolm and Jane, about Malcolm and Margaret. But I must admit that Jane's disappearing act had me fooled. Any writer worth her salt has to admire her gift for a plot twist."

She takes a step toward Brooke, and Brooke edges a step sideways. Charlotte mirrors her movements, keeping Brooke on the cliff side of this little plateau.

"I'm sorry, Charlotte," Brooke says. "I didn't know about any of this until just the other day."

Charlotte let out a light, mirthless laugh. "Oh, darling, you can't think I'm that stupid."

"I swear I didn't." Brooke doesn't have to feign the pleading in her voice, the echo of fear. "And I didn't even know Jane planned to disappear."

"She wanted to hurt my husband," Charlotte says.

"Yes. She—well, she didn't know what she was doing."

"Of course she knew what she was doing, and I admire her initiative," Charlotte says. "It nearly worked out as she hoped. As I hoped."

"What do you mean?"

"If you think Jane wanted to hurt Malcolm, darling, you can imagine how I feel," Charlotte says. "I mean, twenty years of marriage and putting two children through uni, and this is how he treats his family? If only she'd stayed gone, he might be paying the consequences."

Brooke stares at her, momentarily forgetting she's standing so close to the edge of the cliff. "You *wanted* Malcolm to go to jail?"

"He still might," Charlotte muses. "There's Margaret to reckon with."

"What do you mean?"

"Margaret's death, darling," Charlotte says. "It's unfortunate, but it seemed natural that if Malcolm did away with one of his lovers, why not the other? Anything to keep his beloved wife from finding out."

Brooke stares at Charlotte, wondering if this small, good-natured woman is capable of what she's implying. "Did Margaret—"

"I thought it best," Charlotte says. "A man with his resources and connections might walk away from one murder, but from two? Not nearly as easy, is it?"

Brooke takes another step to the side, and Charlotte mirrors her again.

"That leaves me in a conundrum, you see," Charlotte says. "You're obviously loyal to Jane, even to the point of sharing her insanity. Which makes it all the more plausible that you'd leap to your own death after confessing your role in Margaret's."

"I had nothing—"

"That's not the point, dear," Charlotte interrupts, her voice quiet but her tone sharp. "I had nothing to do with Malcolm's unfortunate behavior, but that doesn't mean I'm not paying for it. Sometimes we have to suffer for the deeds of others."

"Charlotte." Brooke finds herself inching backward, and she's now not sure how close she is to the edge. But she can't look back; she can't take her eyes off Charlotte.

"Here," Charlotte says, holding out Brooke's phone. "I think it best that you take this with you. Maybe I'll just tell them you fell while you were taking a selfie. I can improvise just as well as you and Jane, you know."

Charlotte takes a step toward her, forcing Brooke backward, and though Charlotte is even smaller than she is, Brooke has no doubt about her strength. As the ground between them narrows, Brooke is now so close to the cliff's edge she feels the whip of the sea breeze rising behind her.

She has to try to run for it; it's her only chance. She lunges toward the right but slips on the dewy grass and loses her footing, landing hard on the slick grass. She hears herself scream as her body balances on the cliff's edge, legs over the yawning gap, arms and torso clinging to land.

But for how long? Charlotte is standing over her, and then she kneels down, taking Brooke's hands in hers. One upward motion, one quick lift with those sinewy arms, and she could shove Brooke right over the edge.

Charlotte puts Brooke's phone into one of her hands and wraps her fingers around it. "It's time to say goodbye, darling."

As Charlotte begins to raise her arms, suddenly she is knocked sideways, freeing Brooke from her grip, and before Brooke can even decipher what happened, she scrambles away from the edge. Once she's at a safe distance, she looks up.

A few feet away, sprawled on the ground, is Ian.

Just beyond him, Charlotte is scrambling to her feet.

"Ian, she's running away," Brooke says, and Ian leaps up. He easily chases her down, holding her tightly by the arm as Charlotte struggles and screams at him.

Brooke jumps up and runs over to them. "Ian, do you have your phone? Mine doesn't work here."

"It's in my pocket."

She pulls it out of his cargo pants and searches for the number of the ranger station. When the ranger answers, she tells him what happened, that they need the detective.

Charlotte has collapsed on the ground, and Ian kneels next to her. Both of them look shell-shocked, grief-stricken, distraught— and as Brooke looks at them, she thinks Jane is probably right, that in every relationship there's a point at which it's possible to drive someone to madness.

The three of them sit in silence, waiting as the sun beams down on them from overhead, until they see the ranger and the detective heading toward them up the hill.

CHAPTER 25

KERRY

Kerry stands on the dock with Ian as Mark and Bryan help escort Charlotte and the poacher onto Dan's boat with DI Conyers, who is taking them both, under arrest, to Triabunna. Malcolm boards with them, his face grim.

Dan will return for the rest of the group that afternoon. The ferry service has resumed and will drop off its first visitors within the hour. After the past few dark days, it won't be long until Saltwick and much of Marbury will be filled again with sunshine and activity, day-trippers on their rental bikes, backpackers heading out of town, sunbakers swimming and relaxing on the beaches.

Kerry and Ian head back toward Saltwick House in silence. She's still reeling from the news of Charlotte's confession: the murder of Margaret, the attempted murder of Brooke. All because of a philandering husband. It's amazing, really, how little it takes to make someone go completely mad. Infidelity was never one of her and Paul's issues, but Kerry can understand how, under enough pressure, a mind can turn against itself, turn reality inside out, dive deep into dark places from which it can't hope to escape.

She knows, even now, as she stands under a sunny sky in one of the most beautiful locations on Earth—where kangaroos and wombats graze without worry, where cockatoos and rosellas bicker and bark and put on colorful displays of flight—that her own darkness lurks so close under the surface of everything good, and that she'll need to work constantly to keep it at bay. But if she's learned anything on this journey, it's that she's not alone, that everyone has such unseen challenges, such invisible wounds.

As they pass a large boulder, a flame robin perched there watches them with black eyes above a vermillion chest. Kerry glances at Ian, feeling sad that he doesn't notice the bird, that he isn't even carrying his camera. He walks in the dazed procession of a man in shock. She's slowed down to keep pace with him. Jane and Brooke are off on their own, taking one last hike around the cliffs, and will meet them later for a farewell picnic. Kerry and Bryan decided to stick to the track's normal schedule, to try to infuse some normalcy into an otherwise mucked-up journey. Not to mention Kerry isn't sure when any of them last had a proper meal.

Ian hasn't said a word since he watched DI Conyers read Charlotte her rights. Kerry can't imagine how he can begin to process such news—not only the loss of his wife, but at the hands of one of their best friends. The adage *the truth will set you free* has never resonated with Kerry, and she wonders now whether Ian would fare better if he didn't know. For Kerry, knowing the truth about the devils sliding toward extinction does not feel like freedom; it feels like a heart-crushing burden—a call to stand up and fight for them, even knowing how impossible it all may be in the end.

They reach Saltwick House, and again without speaking they sit down on the porch. "Can I get you anything?" she asks after a while, and he shakes his head.

As much as she wants to know where he was from the time he left camp to when he showed up and saved Brooke's life, she doesn't ask. She knows he'll tell her when he's ready, and after another long silence, he begins to speak.

"At first I wanted to kill Malcolm," he says. "Not literally, of course. I just wanted to get my hands on him—I was so bloody angry. But by the time I got to Saltwick, I knew it was no good. It's not as if we had a perfect marriage, Margaret and I. If I hadn't given her reason to—" He stops for a long moment. "Well, there's no point in regrets now, is there?"

Kerry waits for him to continue.

"I had a lot to reckon with, and I wasn't ready to talk to anyone," Ian says. "So I just walked. When I saw that the weather was clearing a bit, I decided to hike to the top of Mount Marbury, since Margaret never got the chance. She had this stone made of Tibetan amber that she bought after summitting Everest—she wore it around her neck and never went anywhere without it, even here, on a hiking trip. I took it off her at the camp, and I left it up there at the top of the mountain, so a part of her would always be here."

He sighs and looks down. "I stood on a rock outcropping, and for a few minutes I seriously thought about joining her. I really did. We have no children. Nobody waiting at home for us. We had our differences, but we loved each other, in our own way. We had a nice life. I couldn't really imagine it without her. Despite everything, I still can't." He pauses, and his lips turn upward in a sad smile. "But I could hear her yelling at me. *You're not bloody done yet*, she said. Like she was right there, talking in my ear. Clear as day, in that tone that used to drive me mad. So I turned around and headed down the mountain. And that's when I saw it. It was so close I could have reached out and touched it."

"What?"

"The forty-spotted pardalote."

"You saw it!"

"I felt like the bird was a sign. It sounds odd, but I felt it was Margaret, communicating with me. Telling me she was sorry. Telling me to go on without her. I walked toward her, but she didn't fly away. When I got really close, she flitted off to a white gum and then stopped again. I followed her from tree to tree, and when I got down the mountain I heard a scream, and that's when I saw Brooke and Charlotte."

"It was a miracle you got there when you did."

"No," he says. "It was Margaret. I think she led me there, through that pardalote. She didn't want Charlotte to get away with murder."

Kerry looks at him and says nothing. As someone who believes animals have their own hearts and souls, and are far more intelligent than people will ever imagine, who is she to say they can't connect with humans on the level Ian is talking about?

She sees people approaching in the distance—Nigel, accompanied by Bryan. As they get closer, she sees that Nigel is not smiling, and she feels her stomach turn over.

"Ian, why don't you go inside and have a cuppa while I talk to these guys," Kerry says.

As Ian disappears into the house, she stands up to greet Nigel and Bryan. Nigel is the opposite of Bryan's tousled surfer-boy look; his hair is short and neat, and he wears hiking clothes that look straight from the catalogue. The one thing they have in common is suntanned skin; even with sunscreen and hats, it's impossible to entirely escape the sun in Tasmania.

"Hi, Nigel," Kerry says, hoping she doesn't sound as nervous as she feels. She just wants to get this over with. "I'm sorry I didn't communicate with you as frequently as I should have."

"You didn't communicate with me at all."

"I know. I understand. I plan to resign as soon as—"

"Let me finish, please," Nigel says. "I've been speaking with Bryan and two of the other guests, and they have had all good things to say about you, even under these circumstances."

"Really?"

Nigel nods. "I'd prefer it if you don't resign. I need both you and Bryan if we're going to salvage the season. If we're going to salvage the company. We're going to have to reschedule the next few groups and deal with the media, but we do plan to continue. And I need my best people to lead the hikes."

"When do you need me to start?"

"Pardon?"

"I thought I'd be out of a job," Kerry says, "so I've arranged to take the parrot eggs to the sanctuary on the mainland. I do want to come back to Marbury, though, so I'll just get the eggs settled in and assign them to volunteers. It'll only take a week or two."

"No worries," Nigel says. "We'll get it sorted. I think I'll team you up with Bryan again. You two seem to have a good rapport."

She looks at Bryan and sees him grinning at her. To her own surprise, she smiles back. Bloody bogan really did come through in the end—and, she reckons, so did she.

"Are you joining us for the picnic?" she asks Nigel.

"I'd love to."

"I'll get started on it straightaway," she says.

"Let me," Bryan says. "Go on, take a break for once."

"You sure?"

He nods, and she eagerly heads over to the ranger station to check on the eggs. But as she heads into town, she thinks of Ian's summit of Mount Marbury and decides to take a slight detour. She won't head up to the top of the mountain, but she wants to hike up a portion of the trail, where there's a field of wide, flat boulders—one of the few places on the island where rangers have reported seeing devils in the daytime.

She approaches slowly, not daring to hope she might see one. The odds are slim, but Ian's story about the pardalote allows her to hope for miracles—plus, with so many days of soaking rain, the devils will be ready to do a little sunbaking.

She scans the boulders, seeing nothing at first but dark-gray stone—and then she sees him, a good-sized devil, a healthy male, sprawled out in a patch of sun. A small laugh of pure joy escapes her at the sight: when devils sunbake, they lie spread-eagle on their bellies, back and front legs stretched out, so still and flat they could be taken for dead, but she knows better; this one is completely relaxed.

He raises his head at the sound of her laugh, his little claws on the ground in front of him. With his body spread out, she can see his markings: a white half-moon across his backside, white commas curving across each shoulder. His face is beautiful, perfect: the wet nose, the pink ears, the small black eyes, the canines poking out from his closed mouth like little vampire fangs. No sign of disease whatsoever. It's been so long since she's seen a healthy devil in the wild, she'd nearly forgotten just how magnificent they are.

He gazes at her, undisturbed by her presence, and she is flooded with relief that he has nothing to fear here, that Jane is alive and well, that the devils won't be blamed for what she thought happened.

She makes her way to the ranger station, where Mark is in his office on the phone. He gives her a wave as she continues on to the workroom. She gently checks on the eggs, refills the hot water bottles, makes sure they are all insulated and warm. There will be no way of knowing they're okay until they hatch, or until they don't. She's a little reluctant to leave the eggs with volunteers, but once they're safely in an incubator there's not much she can do but watch anyhow.

She's just finishing up with the last container when Mark comes in. "When are you headed to the mainland?" he asks.

"This afternoon. I'm going to Hobart with the group and then I'll take the eggs to the sanctuary."

"That's about an hour north of Hobart, hey?"

She nods. "I'll be there a week or two, then back here."

"I'm glad to hear it." A pause, then he says, "I usually get to Hobart for a few days when I have time off. Maybe we could get a drink or something?"

"Sure." She feels herself smiling, one of the few times she can think of when she hasn't had to think about it, to force it. "In fact, let's start now," she says. "Fancy joining us for our picnic?"

They walk together to the hillside overlooking the jetty. As they approach the hollowed-out cement factory building where Bryan has set up their lunch, Kerry is impressed by how lovely it looks: a large picnic blanket laden with sparkling wine, bread and salad, cheese and chocolates. Bryan is telling a story to Brooke, Jane, and Ian about wrangling his dinner away from a devil one night when he was camping in the north of Tasmania. Keeping the mood light, allowing them to forget for a few moments everything that happened in an attempt to allow them some pleasantness—maybe even a brief moment of happiness—during their last hour on the island.

For Brooke and Jane, she's not sure what happiness means, but the two of them always were hard for her to figure out, maybe because it's been so long since she's had a close girlfriend. Maybe loyalty between friends is easier than loyalty between lovers.

Then she looks at Ian, sitting alone, and she knows that even between friends loyalty only extends so far; his friendship with Malcolm is over. All those years, all that history, now finished.

Kerry pours herself and Mark a glass of sparkling wine. When Bryan finishes his story, she makes an awkward, abbreviated speech, thanking them for their patience and understanding, offering a moment of silence for "those who are not with us." She feels as though that's the best way to phrase it. The silence seems to last forever.

Then it's time to go. As Bryan packs up the picnic items, Kerry quietly touches her wineglass to Mark's. "A brief toast," she says. "To returning here in a few months' time with healthy parrots. If there's any chance we can release them, we'll do it here."

They descend the hill, and Dan helps them load the backpacks onto his boat. Bryan will be staying to clean up Saltwick House and to help Nigel put the other two camps in order, and after he says his goodbyes to the guests, he turns to Kerry and gives her a big hug.

She pretends to squirm away. "Get off me, you bloody pantsman," she says. But then she hugs him back. "Thanks," she says. "I'll see you for the next one."

"See ya," he says.

She hugs Mark, too, though with him she wishes she didn't have to let go quite so soon. He promises to call when he's in Hobart the following week.

She boards the boat, and Dan sounds the horn as they shove off from the pier. Kerry watches Mark and Bryan, who are standing on the dock as they go, and then she raises her eyes to the hills beyond, thinking of the devil sunbaking on the rock, imagining more of them there now, a dozen healthy devils sprawled out to soak in the sun.

ACT V

CHAPTER 26

JANE

Years ago, I read a story about a woman who went in for routine dental surgery and emerged with a French accent. Everyone thought she was faking it, trying to sound exotic, but as it turned out, it was a genuine neurological condition—it's called *foreign accent syndrome*, and it's caused by injuries to whatever part of the brain controls speech. How amazing, I thought at the time, to go in for a minor procedure and come out a different person.

I'm reminded of this now, as I'm about to leave this island—I came here as one person, and I'm leaving as another. The difference, of course, is I've been someone new nearly every day.

After the picnic, I hang back as the others make their way down to the dock, where the boat is waiting. On our hike earlier, Brooke and I watched as Charlotte and the poacher were taken aboard in cuffs, Malcolm trailing behind them. As the boat left the bay, I saw Malcolm look back, look up, as though searching for me up on one of the peaks. There was a moment when I felt us make eye contact, when I could feel him looking right at me.

Then we watched a ferry unload its passengers: spandex-clad bicyclists, day-trippers with their walking sticks and cameras. How pedestrian everything looked from that viewpoint, standing there with Brooke. How far removed from the previous days, when I was out in the woods alone, running with the devils through rain and thunder, primal and free.

It was a good run, this one-woman show.

But in all fairness, no actor stands alone, even when it's a one-actor production. I have several castmates to thank, unwitting and not.

I watch Brooke walk down the hill with Kerry—two of the unwitting. I could never have done this without them—without what Kerry saw in the woods and what she made Brooke believe, and without Brooke's help at Saltwick House as I re-spun my tale, getting me off the hook for anything they might've tried to accuse me of. While it's true that pseudocide isn't a crime, I'm pretty sure I was hindering investigations or some other such thing. But Brooke came through for me. She always does.

And Margaret—may she rest in peace—deserves a standing ovation. When I tried to sneak into the toilets and saw her lying there in the rain, I knew that whatever had happened to her, Malcolm would pay for her death, even if he wouldn't pay for mine. I confess it was a bit disappointing to learn that it was Charlotte who did the deed—but it will hurt Malcolm all the same. The media, the publicity—it could destroy his career, not only because his wife is a murderer, but now all of his affairs will come out. I've never been so naïve as to think I'm the only one. But the vacancy I was hoping for has appeared in the end; Charlotte will be gone. And he'll be left alone because men like him always are.

Though never for long.

The award for best actress goes to Charlotte—she went so much further than I ever dared. She seems to know what I know, that women need to take charge of their lives, of their destinies, no matter what that might mean. Shakespeare knew it, even four hundred years ago, when he created Lady Macbeth. A man in a woman's skin, some say. A modern woman, I say.

She was much like Charlotte and me—compelled to break free of conventions, of restrictions. She shunned any manner of silence and subservience. She was not afraid to get her hands dirty.

It's what we women do. We take care of the messes men create. Leave all the rest to us, eh, Billy Boy?

I continue down the hill, seeing that Ian has already boarded the boat.

Ian, who will never get the recognition he deserves. Ian, who was ready for divorce but not for death. Ian, who is the best non-trained actor I know.

It was Ian who comforted me after I discovered Malcolm's affair with Margaret. When I snooped through Malcolm's email that day and learned about the trip, I also saw his email to Margaret. While Malcolm and Ian were making plans for the trip, Malcolm and Margaret were making plans of their own. Their emails were anything but discreet.

I found Ian's number on Malcolm's computer and asked him to meet me in a pub in Rozelle. I broke the news to him there, but he didn't believe me; in fact, he got up and stormed out. Two days later, he called me back, and we met again. He'd found his own evidence on Margaret's phone. He also realized he'd already had the evidence—in their diminishing sex life, in their increasing arguments.

When we met again, we spoke of revenge.

We planned to hurt Malcolm, to punish him. We wrote and rewrote the script, taking every possible scenario into consideration; we wanted him to pay, however it might happen, however we might need to improvise. And Ian was so good in his role; I told him that before I disappeared, when I had the chance to steal a moment with him to talk. That's when he told me about the killdeer. Like us, he said, birds are masters of deception.

The only thing we didn't expect was Margaret.

Ian knew about the affair, but when Charlotte got drunk and told him about it, he didn't have to pretend he was hearing it for the first time: the humiliation, the helpless rage when he ran off to seek Malcolm was real. I didn't get a chance to talk to him alone until late last night, when we met in the garden at Saltwick House. I feared he'd blame me for her death. He doesn't. He blames the two of them—Margaret for cheating, Charlotte for killing her. But that doesn't mean he's not mourning.

He, too, is leaving here a different person, and his new role is going to be a tough one.

"Whatever you need, I'm here for you," I told him, and he knew exactly what I meant.

I'm still meandering down the hill when Kerry waves me over from the dock. I quicken my pace a bit. For so many years, I've yearned to be first—the first one in my class to snag a role on Broadway, the first to win a Tony, the first to star in a movie. But time has a way of minimizing firsts and leaving you with lasts.

So it seems fitting I'll be the last one on board. I've accepted that my career may not be what I dreamed of but that it can be something else, maybe something far more interesting. I'm still hoping Brooke will join me in Los Angeles; she doesn't have much else to go home to, and I could tell that she joined me in telling my adventure story with her whole heart—my sometime sister, back in the family. I'm quite certain our adventure will get leaked to the media, that my near-death encounter with the poacher will add years to his sentence, that those who care about animal rights and women's rights will relish the story. That Brooke and I can both use this to launch the next roles of our lives.

It may be fiction, yes, but who's going to believe a hardened wildlife smuggler over two traumatized female tourists?

The winds are calm today, which means a smooth journey ahead. As I approach the boat, I see Brooke waiting for me. As I promised her long ago, I gave her a front-row seat to my first major performance. When I step off the pier and down into the boat, I'm tempted to take a bow.

We stand together on the stern to watch Marbury Island disappear. Brooke says something about being glad the trip is over, and I murmur something like agreement. But as I watch the island shrink, I think of how much I want to return. How much I missed while I was backstage, how much I still want to see of this country. Most of all, I long to see a Tasmanian devil. I would like to see the animal who saved my life, who freed me from myself.

EPILOGUE

BROOKE
FIFTEEN MONTHS LATER

The letter reminds me of how long it has been since I last saw Jane. It was more than a year ago, in the cramped Hobart airport, with busloads of tourists swarming around us, and Jane had invited me, again, to live with her in LA. "It's never too late, B., to get discovered," she said. "Together, we're invincible."

She was right. Yet that's what concerned me.

Right then, I wanted to get away from her, from the chaos of the previous week, even if it meant returning to the chaos of a failed marriage. I told her that after I wrapped things up in Seattle, I would be free to join her.

And a part of me wanted it to be true. I felt as all actors do on closing night: relief and anxiety, joy and sadness. Closing night feels like a breakup. We mourn. We get drunk. We laugh and we cry. And then we break down the set and move on.

And that's always the hard part. To be honest, I had not even considered where I might live, what I might do, after leaving William for good.

As it turned out, leaving William wasn't as simple as I'd thought. While I'd been away, he'd begun breaking down the set of our married life, packing boxes and disassembling furniture.

When I went to see him at our apartment, I found my bound collection of Shakespeare in a box labeled with his initials, along with my signed first edition Anne Sexton and most of our wedding gifts. That's when I knew I'd be in for a fight.

William had the financial advantage, but not the emotional one. During my time in Tasmania, I felt as though I'd completed an evolution I'd begun a month earlier—perhaps even years earlier. Like the cicadas who spend years underground, waiting for just the right moment to emerge and embrace their new lives, my time had come. Just as Jane could bring out the worst in me, she also brought out the best. The most resolved part of me, the most self-confident—and the most stubborn. And I was in no mood to lose this fight.

And so weeks turned to months as William and I divided our belongings, our investments.

In the meantime, I connected with Jane again on Facebook. We messaged each other daily; I griped about my divorce, and she raved about her new acting gigs. Her new headshot smiled at me every time I visited her page, where I lived vicariously through her rejuvenated career. The TV commercial for dog food. The woman on the plane in an obscure Netflix movie. Small roles, sure, but she was paying her rent, having cocktails at hip LA bars—all while I was back to eating ramen and drinking box wine as my legal bills piled up.

And now, despite everything, I want to join her again. As if by proximity I can absorb her success, or at least her optimism.

Yet I still have my job, which is both underpaying and unsatisfying, except for my having joined the theater group, taking on small roles in short-run plays and staged readings. And though I want to continue acting, I'm not convinced, as Jane is, that LA is the place for me. Jane has the face and body and temperament for television and film—and what I'm learning is how much I love a live audience. I can't imagine how I might summon emotions while under the gaze of a camera lens, but for an audience—for real, breathing humans—I feel as though I'm made for it. The hush of silence as they wait for my next word. The chance to improvise. The exhilaration of living moment to moment.

I hadn't made up my mind by the time I noticed Jane's messages becoming fewer and further between, which I understood—she was busy with work, with getting on with her life. She still posted photos of nights out, of being on set, and I silently followed from the wings.

Given the constant anxiety of counting every billable moment I spend in correspondence with my attorney, I don't notice when a month goes by without hearing from Jane, and then another. It's not until nearly three months have passed and I haven't heard from her that I wonder: what now? Because with Jane, it's always something.

I should reach out to her—it's all too obvious. But something stops me. Instead of messaging her, instead of texting or calling like a normal friend, I find myself Googling her name to see if I can find it in the news. I'm not even sure what I'm looking for—celebrity gossip or obituaries—but I search obsessively. While a simple note or call would answer my question, instead I spend hours searching the internet for answers.

And to think that back in Tasmania, I'd thought Jane was the crazy one.

Maybe I'm not ready to be pulled back into her orbit—not yet. Maybe a part of me knows that I'll never find my own way if I can't do it without Jane. Without anyone, this time.

On the morning I enter my lawyer's office expecting a lecture about past-due invoices, she holds out a sheaf of papers: a settlement offer from William's lawyer.

"I think he met someone," she said.

I let out a sigh, feeling my entire body relax. I look through the papers—his offer is so generous he must be quite in love already—and sign at the dotted line.

Now I can not only pay my attorney's fees, but I'll also have plenty of money left over. To leave my job and start over. Somewhere.

When I return home, there's a letter waiting for me—postmarked Ashland, Oregon. I recognize the handwriting, as well as the location, a small, southern Oregon town famous for the Shakespearean repertory theater that brings world-class actors and directors from all over the globe.

I open the letter.

B.,

You're cordially summoned to the Royal Shakespeare Festival for a dramatic evening of Macbeth—*with yours truly playing one of the lead roles.*

Yes, you read that correctly—so get your divorced ass down here. I know you've been dying to know why I left LA, and now you'll see. — J.

I pull out a theater ticket and watch it flutter in my shaking hand. The date is for only a week away—typical Jane, assuming I'm divorced, assuming I'm available, assuming I will leap to any height to land back in her life.

It's no one's fault but mine that she makes these assumptions, and my first instinct is to shred the ticket along with her letter. But I'm far too tempted by her invitation.

I open my laptop and find Ashland on a map. From Seattle, it's an eight-hour drive south, located just north of the California state line. There's a small airport half an hour away, with direct flights from Seattle.

As I search images online, I discover a charming little town filled with shops and restaurants, galleries and wine bars, a university and a thriving theater company. Yet it's hard for me to picture Jane so far from the energy of city life—Ashland is on the edge of a national forest, in the shadow of the Cascades, with only twenty thousand residents. It's not New York. It's not LA.

I visit the theater's website and I find a blood-red logo for *Macbeth* on the home page. I'm about to click on it when I see a note at the very top of the page: IN REMEMBRANCE OF VICTORIA STRAMWELL. When I follow this link, I land on an obituary for a woman in her early thirties, Yale School of Drama–trained, who died tragically on a hike in the remote hills. Among the many roles she'd played over her five years with the Royal Shakespeare Festival, her most anticipated was to be Lady Macbeth in this season's production.

Instead, her understudy would be playing the role.

Oh, Jane. What have you done?

I look at the ticket again. If I were wise, I would tear it to pieces. I would delete my Facebook account. I would start my life over. Separate from Jane.

Yet images scroll through my mind—Jane and me, in the tent on Marbury Island, doing Lifetime; Jane and me, in college, doing Shakespeare; Jane and me, in Saltwick, doing what we needed to do to save our friendship, and ourselves.

Jane and I are each other's muses; we go together like the theater masks of ancient Greece. We are the sock and buskin, we are Thalia and Melpomene, and while neither of us is necessarily one or the other, we go together. We're a pair.

Folie à deux.

And I watch my hands move across the keypad, almost as though they're not under my own command, and on the screen, I find myself searching for flights from Seattle to a small airport just north of Ashland, Oregon.

AUTHORS' NOTE

Marbury/Devils Island is a fictional version of Maria Island/
Wukaluwikiwayna, a national park located off the east coast of
the Australian state of Tasmania. The town of Saltwick is a fictional version of Darlington, the island's small town.

Like our fictional island, Maria Island formerly housed a convict settlement, and several structures still remain. Other than
Darlington, which has ferry service from the mainland, much of
the island is remote, isolated, and requires permits to visit. The
island is uninhabited except for the presence of park rangers in
Darlington.

The conservation work for Tasmanian devils is ongoing and
not without its challenges. In 2012 and 2013, twenty-eight
healthy devils were released on Maria Island to protect them from
Devil Facial Tumor Disease (DFTD), a contagious facial cancer
that has affected up to 90 percent of their population. By 2016,
an estimated 100 devils were thriving on the island. This success
unfortunately decimated the little penguin and short-tailed
shearwater colonies on the island; however, the presence of devils
also reduced the population of brushtail possums, who had been
introduced to the island in the 1950s and who themselves were
also preying on seabirds. There's currently a population of sixty to

ninety devils on Maria Island, and healthy devils are being successfully relocated to disease-free areas of mainland Tasmania.

To learn more and to support wildlife rescue and conservation in Tasmania, visit the Bonorong Wildlife Sanctuary: https://www.bonorong.com.au.

ACKNOWLEDGMENTS

Thanks to the Australian tour company Maria Island Walk, which inspired the setting for this novel with its incredible four-day journey on Maria Island. Thanks to our fellow travelers—Karen, Jeremy, Janette, Matthew, Verena, and Wes—and to our amazing guides, Holly and Kat. Not only did they all survive the journey, they made it unforgettable in the best possible way. And special thanks to our Australian travel companions, who taught us so many Australian words and idioms.

Thanks to the Bonorong Wildlife Sanctuary in Tasmania for its critical rescue work and for helping to protect Australia's most endangered species. It was thanks to a tour here that we got to meet Tassie devils, whom previously we could only hear on the island in the middle of the night.

Thanks to Gail Fortune, for editorial insights that made this book better. Thanks to Theo, who inspired us to take this trip to Australia.

And a million thanks to Bob and Pat Gussin, Lee Randall, and Faith Matson, for bringing this book into the world.

BOOK CLUB
DISCUSSION QUESTIONS

1. Acting—onstage and in life—is a theme throughout the novel. In what ways do each of the characters pretend or perform, whether for themselves or for others? How does this affect the authenticity of their lives and their relationships?

2. Kerry's work with endangered species has affected her mental health. For a naturalist—or a climate scientist, or anyone working in an environmental field—what makes it possible to face difficult realities and still have hope?

3. Brooke and Jane share a codependent friendship—perhaps even, as Brooke notes, a *folie à deux* (shared madness). How does this both help and hinder each of them?

4. Kerry mentions that the healthy Tasmanian devils on Marbury Island sometimes eat the eggs of Cape Barren geese. To what extent is it acceptable to save one species at the expense of others?

5. Kerry and Brooke are both getting over failed relationships. In what ways does their journey on Marbury Island help them recover?

6. At times, Facebook is the only way Brooke and Jane stay in touch—and as Brooke notes, "Facebook is the biggest stage of all." How does social media distort the realities of people's lives and relationships?

7. On Marbury Island, the poaching of rare and endemic bird eggs is a concern. In what other parts of the world is poaching an issue, and who are the animals affected?

8. As the luxury "glamping" trip devolves into survivalism, how do the characters respond and how do their relationships evolve? Does the threat of death reflect positively or poorly on the characters as the novel progresses?

9. How does the loss of a cell phone signal raise the tension, not only in the novel, but in the lives of the characters? Though the characters believed they wanted to escape from civilization on this journey, how does it ultimately affect them to be entirely cut off?

10. The naming (and nicknaming) of animals can play a huge role in how humans perceive and relate to them. Would the Tasmanian devil, had it been known as, say, the Tasmanian rascal, have been so readily feared and discounted as a native pest? Even today, does the nickname help or hurt the protection of this endangered species?